IF YOU WERE MINE

MELANIE HARLOW

MH PUBLISHING

IF YOU WERE MINE

Cover Design: Letitia Hasser, Romantic Book Affairs

http://designs.romanticbookaffairs.com/

Cover Photography: Lauren Perry, Perrywinkle Photography

http://perrywinklephotography.com/

Editing: Tamara Mataya

http://tamaramataya.blogspot.com/

Publicity: Social Butterfly PR

http://www.socialbutterflypr.net/

For the women in my life...you are all pretty badass.

What makes the desert beautiful is that
somewhere it hides a well.

ANTOINE DE ST. EXUPERY

ONE

Claire

I DIDN'T INTEND to lie—it just slipped out.

I'm not even a good liar. Every time I tell a fib, my ears get cold and tingly and I have to rub them. I'm not even kidding. Growing up, when my mother would question my sister Giselle and me about who made the mess with the toothpaste or forgot to take out the dog or ate three cupcakes and left the wrappers on the counter, she always said I gave myself away immediately by grabbing my ears. (Giselle, of course, was a spectacular liar. She was a spectacular everything.)

So I was all set to answer truthfully. The words were right there on my lips. *No, actually, I couldn't find a date for your wedding. I'm coming alone.*

(Coming Alone: A Memoir of My Sex Life, by Claire French.)

"Because it's no big deal if you don't have a date. I just need to know for the head count." My friend Elyse, the bride-to-be, had cornered me by the copy machine in the office of the elementary school where we both taught. Her expression was something between sympathetic (I'm sorry you're still single as fuck) and gratified (thank God *I* found someone). "We'll have a singles table, and there will be plenty of people at it. Maybe you'll meet someone!"

Oh, God. The singles table.

I'd been relegated to the singles table enough times to know that it is nowhere I wanted to be on a Saturday night. Or any other night. Was there a more awkward place in the universe? I remembered the last wedding I'd attended solo. My table mates were an astonishing array of weird—one guy just wanted to tell me about the new sheets his mom recently put on his bed (Spiderman), another told me his safe word within five minutes (rutabaga), and a third bitched nonstop about how mad he was that his favorite character had just been killed on Game of Thrones ("Think about it: every scene you ever saw him in was a lie!"). Later, I'd caught the bouquet, and I'm not kidding when I tell you there was a collective sigh of relief among the crowd, and I actually heard someone, possibly my mother, say "Praise Jesus!"

I just couldn't.

"Actually, I *am* going to bring a date," I heard myself tell Elyse as I gathered my copies from the machine. My ears started to prickle and I clung to the stack of papers in my arms to avoid grabbing them.

"You are?"

I tried not to be offended at the shock in her tone. It's not like I *never* went on dates. It's just that most of them were complete duds. "Yes. I'll get that RSVP card to you right away. Sorry it's so late."

"That's OK. This is so great, Claire. I didn't realize you

were seeing anyone." She walked with me out of the office and down the hall. Her fourth grade classroom was directly across from the art room, where I taught. Elyse and I had been pretty good friends at one time, but in the two years since she'd been dating her fiancé we hadn't talked as much. I might be able to pull this off if she didn't ask too many questions.

"Well, you've been busy with the wedding, and it really hasn't been that long." I moved quickly—the sooner I could duck into my room, the better. Elyse was notoriously chatty, and she *loved* to gossip.

"Like how long?"

"Like a couple months."

"Wow! Good for you. How are things going?"

"Great!" I chirped too loudly. "Just great."

"Is he cute?"

"Gorgeous."

"What does he look like?"

"Uh, blond hair. Blue eyes. A little scruffy if he doesn't shave." Basically I'd just described my dream man, Ryan Gosling.

She lowered her voice. "Is he good in bed?"

"Fantastic." (Coming Alone would be full of stories about Ryan and me. We were dynamite together.) Reaching the doorway to the art room just as the bell rang, I breathed a sigh of relief. "Have a good one!" With a wave of my hand, I scooted inside and shut the door behind me.

Immediately I dropped the stack of flyers on the closest table and rubbed my chilly ears. It's not even like I was imagining that they were cold—they really were. I'd looked it up once, and the explanation was something about anxiety causing blood to drain from my face. That made sense to me, since lying *did* make me anxious. A lot of things made me anxious, though. I often wished I was more confident, but Giselle seemed to get all the mettle in the family. Maybe that's why she was in New York City, living her dream on Broadway and I was still here in the city where we'd grown up, living a mile away from our parents and teaching art at the same elementary school we'd attended.

"God, how can you stand it? Don't you ever want to get out of there?" my sister was fond of asking me.

Was it horrible that I didn't?

It's not that I didn't have dreams, too—they were just simpler. Quieter. Less flashy. I wanted a family of my own. I wanted to inspire kids to create and appreciate art in their lives, to find beauty in unexpected places. And I wanted, some day, to see my own works of art in a gallery or at a festival or even for sale in a gift shop. But I was still working up the nerve to submit anywhere. Soon, though. Maybe.

"God, we're so different," Giselle always said. She lived out loud, craved attention and was good at getting it, and was never happier than when she was center stage in full costume and makeup. In high school, I'd been content to paint the scenery and work on the stage crew, wearing black so the audience wouldn't see me and applauding Giselle from the darkened wings.

But I'd been happy there. Not everyone was cut out to be the star of the show.

While I readied supplies for the morning's classes, I thought again about the date situation—actually now I had more than a date situation, I had a *boyfriend* situation. Crap. Did I know anyone I could ask that fit the description I'd given Elyse?

If you did, you wouldn't be single, dumbass.

True. I frowned as I set out plastic containers of paint brushes on each table. Maybe I could pretend he'd gotten sick. I'd RSVP for two so Elyse wouldn't put me at the singles table, but I'd show up alone and say he had a migraine or something.

Yes, that was it! Perfect plan.

Or it would have been if Elyse had kept her big mouth shut. Countless times throughout the day, teachers and office staff came up to me and said how they'd heard I had a hot new boyfriend and they couldn't wait to meet him at the wedding. They also said things like *"Finally,* huh?" and "About time!"

On the drive home from work, I weighed the humiliation of showing up alone against the challenge of finding someone to play my boyfriend, and decided the humiliation might be worse. Seating arrangements aside, I was tired of being teased all the time about my single status. Did they think I didn't *want* to meet someone? Did they think it was easy to watch my friends fall in love and get engaged while my prospects went from bad to worse? Did they know how hard it was to look at myself and wonder what was wrong with me that I was thirty and had never been in love? Giselle was only one year older but had been in love—or so she claimed—like fifty times already, starting from age fourteen. She'd even been engaged once. (Very, very briefly.)

It wasn't like I hadn't tried to meet someone. I went on more first dates than anyone I knew. I let everyone from my mother to my hairstylist to my yoga instructor set me up, and I'd tried all the popular dating apps.

I'd met some OK guys. But I'd never felt that *thing*— that pulse-quickening, breath-taking, Hallmark-Channel *thing*. I knew it existed because I'd read about it in books and seen it in movies and even witnessed it in real life. Not with Giselle, of course. She was fickle as they come, and changed her mind about men as easily as she changed costumes. But my two closest friends, Jaime and Margot, were madly in love with their boyfriends, and Margot was already engaged. I saw what they had, and I didn't want to settle for anything less. I believed in soul mates, and I wanted my own.

But where the fuck was he, already?

"I'M GIVING UP," I told Jaime that night at our weekly Wednesday Girls Night Out. It was just the two of us since Margot had moved up to her fiancé's farm two hours north and only made it back to Detroit once or twice a month. "I'm going to die an old maid."

She rolled her eyes. "Don't be ridiculous. If I can fall in love, anyone can. And look at Margot—engaged to a farmer, for fuck's sake! These things happen when you least expect them."

I nodded glumly. It was true that love had struck my two besties when they'd least expected it, but I didn't have Jaime's fiery personality or Margot's elegant style. I felt like there were things about them that drew people in, traits I didn't possess. They had that extra something, just like my sister did. I wasn't insecure about my looks, but I did sometimes feel a bit bland compared to them.

Jaime was a sultry, curvy dark-haired bombshell, and Margot had that lithe, blond Grace Kelly beauty—I had a couple curves, my mother's gray-green eyes, and thick healthy hair, but nothing about me was extraordinary. If we were ice cream flavors, Jaime would be something fun like Birthday Cake, Margot would be something classic like Pralines and Cream, and I'd be boring old vanilla bean.

Nice and dependable, but blah. The safe thing you order when they're out of your favorite.

"Is this about Elyse's wedding?" Jaime asked accusingly, pulling her hair into a low ponytail.

Sighing, I propped an elbow on the bar and my forehead in my hands. "Kind of."

"Still can't find a date?"

"No. And Elyse cornered me about it today at work. I was just about to tell her I was coming alone when she mentioned the singles table."

Jaime made a disgusted noise. "The singles table. I hope Margot doesn't do that to anyone. God, weddings are the worst."

I picked up my glass of cabernet and took a drink. Margot was getting married just before Valentine's Day, yet another holiday to dread. "At least at Margot's wedding, I'll be at the head table. And I won't need a date, since I'm a bridesmaid."

"I don't see why you have to go to this other wedding at all. You're not even that close to Elyse anymore."

I winced. "I know, but I'd feel bad. I have to go. And now it's even worse because I told her I was bringing my boyfriend."

Jaime choked on her martini and set the glass down on the bar so roughly it sloshed over the rim. "Your *what?*"

"My boyfriend. You know, the one who looks like Ryan Gosling and fucks like a rock star."

"Excuse me?" She looked around, like she was waiting for the hidden cameraman to pop out. "What did I miss?"

I sighed and shook my head. "This is so dumb. I couldn't bear the thought of the singles table, so I made up a boyfriend."

Jaime burst out laughing.

"It's not funny." I gulped more wine. "What am I going to do?"

"Can't you just make up a reason why he couldn't be there?"

"That was my next plan, but Elyse told everyone about him and now I feel like I have to show up with someone or they'll all know I lied." Defeated, I slouched on my barstool. "Does Quinn know any hot, single guys with blond hair and blue eyes?"

"Hmm. I don't think so. I'd have introduced you to him already."

"Actually, I don't even care if he's single. I'm desperate. It's just for one night, and I swear I won't touch him. I don't even care if he's straight. Your brother have any cute gay friends I can borrow?"

"Wow, you are getting desperate." Jaime started to giggle. "Want to borrow Quinn? He's got blondish hair and blue eyes."

I gasped. "Jaime, that's genius!" For a second, all my problems were solved—and then I remembered why it wouldn't work. "Oh, wait. Elyse met Quinn at my birthday dinner a couple years ago. Right when you first started dating, remember?"

"Oh yeah, the dinner that he invited himself to and pretended we were a couple." Jaime laughed at the memory. "I wanted to kill him that night."

"I know." To the rest of us at the table it had been so obvious how good Quinn and Jaime could be together and how nuts he was about her, but she'd fought him every step of the way. Then there was Margot, who'd met her fiancé, Jack, when she was hired to do some marketing work for his farm—they couldn't stand each other at first, but fell head over heels within a week. I was happy for all involved, I really was, but I had to wonder what I was doing wrong that I couldn't find love when it seemed to fall from the sky for everyone close to me. I signaled the bartender for another glass of wine. "Why does this have to be so difficult? Am I trying too hard? Am I too picky? Is it my hair?"

"Your *hair*?"

Nervously, I gathered my long, dirty blond curls over one shoulder. I'd recently gone back to my natural color. "Yeah, does it wash me out? Do I look too pale? Too blah?"

She rolled her eyes. "Now you're just being crazy. It's not your hair. And I love you blond. Reminds me of when we were kids."

My second glass of wine arrived and I took a big sip. "God, why can't you just *rent* a boyfriend for a night like you can rent a movie?"

Jaime grinned over the rim of her martini glass. "Boyfriend On Demand?"

"Exactly!" I snapped my fingers. "You could just scroll through, pick the one that looks good, and he's all yours for twenty-four hours. I'd even pay more for HD."

"Huge Dick?"

I laughed. "Yeah."

"Actually, I think you *can* rent a boyfriend. I read about it somewhere—it's really popular in Japan."

"Are you serious?" I sat up taller. "Do they have it here?"

She shrugged. "Maybe. But I don't know how safe it is."

"What's it called? Do you remember?"

"No." Jaime shrank back and looked at me like I was crazy. "You can't seriously be considering *hiring* a strange man to be your date, Claire. You're not that desperate."

"I guess I'm not," I said.

But my ears were tingling.

TWO

Claire

TWO DAYS LATER, I still didn't have a date, and I decided to google it. (I'd like to mention that this was after drinking almost an entire bottle of wine while watching back-to-back holiday romances on the Hallmark Channel. I cannot be held responsible for my behavior after such an evening.) While the credits were still rolling on the second movie, I poured the last of the bottle into my glass and opened my laptop. I typed "rent a date" into the search box, took a sip for courage, and clicked.

I was immediately bombarded with tits and ass pics. Realizing my mistake, I specified I was looking for *male* companionship, hoped my eyeballs wouldn't be assaulted with dick pics, and clicked again.

A bunch of sites came up, and the top result was called Hotties4Hire.com. After glancing over my shoulder as if I was scared of being caught (which was ridiculous, since I lived alone) and a big gulp of chianti, I opened the link.

Need a date for a special occasion but don't have time to find one?

Tired of all the questions about why you're still single?

Want a platonic companion for a limited time who will pretend to adore you?

Look no further.

Hire a hottie has a man for you!

I perked right up. It was like the site was made for me! The guys looked attractive and not too serial-killery, and there were plenty of testimonials from satisfied customers.

"Hotties for Hire was exactly what I needed to get through the company Christmas party! Ron was a true gentleman, and so hot!"

"I can't say enough good things about Shemar! He was polite, attractive, and completely attentive all night!"

"Everyone was jealous of my Hottie at the wedding, and my ex almost fell over! I felt amazing all night long!"

The site was run by women, and they had Hotties in twenty-two states, Michigan included. THIS IS NOT A DATING SITE, they claimed. "If you're looking for a committed relationship or sex, this site is not for you, but if all you need is a fantastic evening with someone safe, friendly, and best of all, HOT, then we can help!"

Yes! Help me, Hotties!

Five minutes later, I'd paid my $29.95 to have access to Hottie profiles in my area and frantically searched for one that looked like Ryan Gosling. It didn't take me long to realize that the guys they used on the home page weren't entirely representative of the actual stock, but I didn't see anybody that looked like they just got out of the state penitentiary, either. Finally, I saw someone I thought might work—he had sandy hair, light eyes, a solid eight on a scale of one to ten, and his name was Fred.

According to his profile, Fred was a pilot and enjoyed traveling, meeting new people, and classic cars. He was six feet tall, thirty-one years old, and had never been married. He had two dozen five-chili-pepper ratings, and the comments were all positive. "So much fun!" said Lisa in Orlando. "An absolute doll," gushed Jasmine in Phoenix. "Charming and sweet!" exclaimed Shelly in Buffalo. "And an awesome dancer!"

Orlando, Phoenix, and Buffalo? Wow, he really got around. Was that because he was a pilot? Where was home? Not that I needed to care. All I needed to worry about was that he showed up on time and pretended to like me, which I hoped wouldn't be that hard of a job, as long as he was a better actor than I was.

For a hundred dollars an hour, he'd better be.

I took another gulp of wine and sent him a message via the site. *Hello Fred, my name is Claire, and I'm looking for a date for a co-worker's wedding the night of Friday, December 21st. Are you available? If so, would it be possible to meet for coffee first just to get to know each other a bit? Discuss the situation?*

Right before I sent it, I had a little panic attack. This was totally insane, wasn't it? *Renting* a man just to save face? What if he strangled me and stuffed my body in the trunk of his vintage Camaro or something?

Then I remembered the time I sat at the singles table and the guy next to me recited 369 digits of pi before asking me if I'd like to read his erotic Pokémon fanfic.

Click.

Thank you! Fred will get back to you soon!

I closed my laptop and sat there for a moment, trying to decide if I felt creepy and desperate or modern and edgy. There was nothing wrong with this, was there? After all, I was a woman of the new millennium! We weren't bound by old-fashioned rules about dating like our mothers and grandmothers! And this wasn't really dating, anyway. It was just...online shopping. For a human.

Oh, God.

I felt a little queasy. But desperate times called for desperate measures, and a few hundred bucks would be a bargain if it shut everybody up and bought me a seat at a better table. Plus I'd spend an evening with a handsome date whose job it was to flatter me all night long. No one would ever know that I was paying him. At the end of the night, we'd go our separate ways, I'd tell everyone at work a breakup story that sounded plausible and definitely not my fault (Fred, you bastard), and that would be that.

What could go wrong?

AT THREE O'CLOCK in the morning, I awoke in a panic.

What the hell had I done? Now that the wine buzz had worn off, regret attacked me from all sides. I jumped out of bed and bolted for the stairs, but my pajama pants were too long and my heel slipped, and I ended up bumping down the entire flight on my butt.

At the bottom of the steps, I scrambled to my feet, hitched up my pants and ran for the couch. Frantically I opened my laptop and clicked on the browser. *Damn you, chianti and Hallmark Channel!* Was there a way to retrieve my message? Had he seen it yet? What would I do if he'd replied?

My heart pumped hard as the Hotties for Hire site loaded. I was still logged in and saw right away that I had a message from Fred.

Hey Claire, I am available on that date. Sure, we can meet for coffee ahead of time. I actually do that with every date I book. I just ask for a $100 nonrefundable deposit at that meeting, which will be applied to your balance, whatever that turns out to be. Let me know, thanks!

My hands shook as I tried to come up with a reply that didn't make me sound pathetic.

Hi Fred, it looks like my boyfriend will be in town that weekend after all, so

No, that was ridiculous. Now I was making up a *second* fake boyfriend so that my original fake boyfriend wouldn't think I was a loser? What on earth?

I tried again.

Hey Fred, turns out I can't make it to the wedding. Sorry for the

No, that was stupid, too. What could have happened in the few hours since I'd messaged him that would prevent me from being able to attend?

I chewed the tip of one finger. Should I go through with it? I looked at his picture and read his message again. He was cute. And he sounded nice.

I can just meet him for coffee. What's the harm in that? If it's a disaster, I won't book the date. I'd lose my hundred bucks, but at least I wouldn't be stuck with him all night. And a coffee shop was a public place, so there'd be no strangling or dismembering or anything. Just a quick introduction and a brief chat about how things would go the night of the date. If we got along OK, I'd book him.

I sat up taller and typed a response.

Hey Fred, thanks for the reply. Could you meet me downtown at 5:00 pm on Wednesday the 19th? Great Lakes Coffee makes awesome lattes.

I took a breath and clicked send. Then I went back up to bed, rubbing my sore butt and wishing Boy-Meets-Girl wasn't so complicated. Why couldn't life be more like a storybook, where fairy godmothers granted wishes or handsome princes needed saving from shipwrecks or stable boys turned out to be the one?

FRED HAD REPLIED that my suggested time and location for coffee worked for him, so after school on the 19th, I ran home, took my hair down from its messy bun, noticed I'd gotten paint on my shirt, hurried upstairs to change it, rushed back to the bathroom, re-applied my makeup, and scolded myself a million times for being so flustered.

He was just a guy, right? And this wasn't a date; it was a business transaction. I didn't have to meet his approval—*he* had to meet *mine*! But my stomach jittered nonstop on the drive downtown.

I parked in a lot off Woodward and took deep breaths of icy cold air as I made my way up the snowy street. Right before I pushed open the heavy glass door of Great Lakes Coffee, I took a second to look through it, hoping to spot where Fred was sitting. Nothing worse than walking into a crowded place and trying to find someone while everyone stares at you. It always made me feel like I'd forgotten to put pants on or something.

But the place was busy, and I wasn't able to stand out there for long because people were behind me, rushing to get out of the cold. I held the door open for them, and once I was in, I stepped aside to remove my gloves and surreptitiously glance around. I didn't see anyone who looked like Fred sitting on the stools at the counter, nor seated at any of the tables close to me. *Hmm, maybe he's running late, too. Or maybe he's at a table in the back.*

Hoping to appear relaxed, casual, and not at all desperate, I strolled toward the counter to order, allowing two people to go ahead of me in line since I wasn't in a hurry. Desperate people hurried. After I ordered my lavender latte, I stood aside and waited, scanning the place again. Still no Fred. What would I do if he didn't show?

When my coffee was ready, I spotted two empty stools at the end of the counter and figured I'd grab them, just in case he made it. Unfortunately, the couple who'd come in behind me had the same idea I did, and we moved for them at the exact same time. "Oh, go ahead," I told them, backing off. "My...person isn't here yet anyway."

One more look around the shop. No Fred. My entire body drooped. Feeling dejected, I took my latte to a table at the back that had a couple open seats. I slipped out of my puffy white winter coat and hung it on the back of my chair, then I sat down and stared at the empty space across the table, feeling more than a little sorry for myself since it looked like I might be stood up by a date I was willing to *pay* for.

Maybe I was doomed—the stars were never going to align for me. Perhaps I was born under a black cloud.

After all, storybooks have curses, too.

THREE

Theo

I KNEW three things about Claire French within minutes of watching her walk through the coffee shop door.

One: She was a rule-follower. She didn't go in the out door, up the down staircase, or beyond the No Trespassing sign. She didn't jaywalk, speed, or cheat. She never parked in handicapped spots, always said yes when someone asked for a favor, and didn't cut people off on the freeway. A genuinely good person. I also got the feeling she saw mostly good in others, too. I liked that, although it probably meant she trusted too easily. Forgave too soon. Got taken advantage of.

Two: She was a girlie girl. A romantic. Everything about her was soft and lovely and feminine, from her fuzzy pink sweater to her long, wavy hair to her puffy white coat and little knit hat. Her voice was warm and honey-sweet, even to strangers. I couldn't smell her—and I wouldn't—but I knew that if I did, it would be like when I was a kid and my grandmother used to make these treats out of marshmallows dipped in melted butter and rolled in cinnamon and sugar, then sealed up in crescent rolls. While those things were in the oven, the entire house smelled like you could eat it, like in a fairy tale.

I didn't believe in fairy tales anymore, but I'd bet my life she did.

Three: She had no idea how beautiful she was.

Women like her never do.

FOUR

Claire

I PULLED off my hat and fluffed my hair, figuring I'd give him at least the amount of time it took to drink my latte. But before I could take my first sip, a guy in a black leather jacket set a coffee cup down on the table and sat opposite me.

I looked over at him, feeling slightly awkward since I'd have to tell him he couldn't sit there. He was handsome, with warm brown eyes and short dark hair, but he wasn't Fred. "I'm sorry, I'm waiting for someone," I said. "But I can move."

To my surprise, he smiled confidently. "Claire, right? I'm Fred."

I screwed up my face. "You can't be. Fred has blond hair and blue eyes. I saw his picture."

He laughed, almost condescendingly. "I don't use my real picture, Claire. People are crazy."

What? This made no sense. "I don't understand. How

can you advertise yourself with someone else's photo? Don't women get mad when you show up?"

He shrugged, his grin turning a little cocky. "Haven't had any complaints so far."

Actually, he *was* more attractive than the photo he'd used online—more rugged and masculine, with his scruffy jaw, big shoulders, and brawny chest. Meeting the real Fred was kind of like ordering the chicken piccata and being brought the Porterhouse, which hadn't even been on the menu.

But that wasn't the point.

(And I'd described someone completely different to Elyse.)

"So, what, you use a fake photo to lure potential clients and then you set up the coffee meeting to check them out first?" I asked indignantly.

"Wouldn't you?" He shrugged out of his jacket. "It's a scary world out there."

I crossed my arms, sitting up tall. "No! That's a scam. I don't like scammers."

"No, it isn't. I don't take any money from them. I don't even talk to them, I just leave."

Frowning, I said, "That doesn't seem right to me. These people are willing to pay you to hang out with them and probably feel bad enough about themselves already, and you just walk out without even giving them a chance?"

He shrugged. "Look, if it makes you feel any better, I've only walked off a job once, and that was because I thought I recognized the woman. I prefer to keep my personal and professional identities separate. That's fair, isn't it?"

Professional identity? He was a rent-a-date! I shook my head in disbelief. "Is your name even Fred?"

"Does it matter?"

"Yes," I snapped. "How am I supposed to know what to call you?"

He grinned as he leaned toward me and lowered his voice. "Call me anything you want. You're the boss."

Was he flirting with me or making fun of me? I cleared my throat and pressed my knees tighter together. "I'd like to call you by your actual name, please. Bad enough I have to pay someone to play my fake boyfriend. I'd like *something* to be real, at least."

He held his eyes steady on mine for a moment. I felt like he was sizing me up, trying to decide if he could trust me, so I stared right back without blinking. If anyone at this table was trustworthy, it was me.

"Theo," he said quietly, his eyes dropping to my lips for the merest fraction of a second. "My name is Theo."

There. Was that so hard? I smiled at him before picking up my latte."Well, it's nice to meet you, Theo."

"What, you're just going to believe me? You're much too trusting, Claire. I bet people take advantage of you."

I set the cup back down on the saucer with an angry clank. "Is your name Theo or not?"

"Shhh, it is, it is," he said, laughing. Then he glanced over his shoulder like he was in the fucking CIA. "But I don't give that out to just anyone. You should feel special."

Good grief. Could I take an entire night of this guy? I picked up my latte again, wishing it had something stronger than caffeine in it. This was not going the way I'd hoped. "I don't feel special. I feel ridiculous."

"Why?"

"*Why?*" I gaped at him over the cup I held with both hands. "What kind of person has to pay someone to take her on a date? It's humiliating."

"Think of it as a business transaction," Theo suggested,

lifting his muscular shoulders. He wore a dark brown Henley that reminded me of Dexter Morgan from the series about the serial killer.

Not an association I wanted to have at the moment.

"That doesn't make it any better," I said. "Dating is supposed to be about romance, not business."

"So why couldn't you get a date?" He picked up his cup, which looked like it held plain black coffee, and studied me critically as he took a sip.

I sat up taller, feeling my cheeks burn. "Stop looking at me like that."

"Like what?"

"Like you're trying to figure out what's wrong with me."

"Oh, I already know what's wrong with you." His tone was matter-of-fact. "I'm just curious what *you* think is wrong."

My jaw dropped. I was half-tempted to toss the remainder of my latte in his face, but some stupid part of me was like, *What if he does know what's wrong with me?* "And?" I demanded peevishly, angry with both of us.

"You're scared."

"Scared?" It came out louder than intended.

"Shhh. It's nothing to get mad about, Claire." He was frustratingly calm. "I just mean that you seem like the kind of person who's very careful not to take too many risks in life."

He was right. It infuriated me. "What! You've known me for two minutes! How can I seem like anything to you?"

His expression was smug. "I have very good instincts. I can tell a lot about a person very quickly."

"That's ridiculous. And I'm not scared."

"Yes, you are."

"OK, Mr. Psychic. I'll play your little game." I set down

my cup and leaned my elbows on the table. "If your instincts are so good, tell me exactly what I'm afraid of."

"I'm not entirely sure," he admitted, squinting at me. "I'd have to get to know you better."

"Ha!" I shot him an imperious look.

"But if I had to guess, I'd say you were afraid of rejection."

Well...wasn't everybody? While I was trying to decide how to defend myself, he went on.

"I bet you're a hopeless romantic, and you want the kind of love you read about in books or see in the movies. You want someone perfect. But you think someone perfect won't fall for *you*, for whatever reason, so you don't really give anyone a chance. You don't really put yourself out there."

"That's not true," I blustered. "I put myself out there all the time. I go on a million terrible dates because I can't say no to people."

"That's because you don't want anyone to dislike you," he pointed out. "Being nice is your thing. You hold the door for people, you let people cut in line, you give up your seat for others..." He glanced over toward the counter.

He was here. He watched me. "I'm polite," I said through clenched teeth. How many times had someone told me I was too nice? It was the compliment I got most often, and lately I was beginning to think it might not actually be a compliment.

"I agree, you're polite, but it's more than that. Why don't you think you deserve nice things, Claire French?" His light brown eyes danced over the rim of his cup as he took another sip.

I opened my mouth to answer the question, then slammed it shut again. What was he, some kind of psychotherapist? I *did* think I deserved nice things! Wasn't that why I was holding out for someone decent and good and right for me? It wasn't my fault it was taking so long! "Is this mental and emotional abuse part of the regular hottie package?" I fumed. "Or do I have to pay extra for it?"

He smiled. "I'm not trying to make you feel bad, Claire. I'm trying to help you. Give you some advice."

I crossed my arms over my chest again. "Who are *you* to give me romantic advice? What kind of guy rents himself out on dates with strangers?"

"The kind of guy who moves around a lot, can have fun in any situation, and loves meeting new people."

"Why *do* you move around so much? I saw on your profile you've had dates in like three or four different cities over the last year."

"I'm a drifter. I get bored easily."

That couldn't be his whole story. I cocked a brow. "Got a wife and kids stashed somewhere?"

"Nope."

"Where's your family?"

"No family."

"Where's home?"

"The open road. The endless sky. I'm not tied to any person, place, or thing." He said it with pride.

"That's sad."

He laughed. "No, it isn't. I prefer it this way. Some people want the happy ending, all wrapped up in a nice neat bow, and others are content to let the story go on forever—that's me. You're looking for a destination; I like the journey. I don't want it to end."

When he put it like that, it was hard to argue with him. Still, I felt like there was more to his story than what he was telling me. "Where did you grow up?"

"Enough with the questions. I'm glad you're so fascinated by me, but—"

"I'm not *fascinated*," I said hotly, "I'm just curious." But he did sort of intrigue me. Not only because he was so good-looking, but because he was so different from me. So confident, so laid-back. Content just to go where life led him, pretend to be someone new every place he went. But was that fun? Or was it lonely? And he was brave, too. Flying a plane? Taking responsibility for getting thousands of pounds of metal into the air and keeping it there? With people's lives hanging in the balance? Good grief! I was terrified of flying. Petrified. I was dying to go to Europe and visit the Louvre and the Prado and the Uffizi Gallery, but I'd never done it because I was too scared to get on the plane that would take me there.

"So let's talk about this wedding." Theo leaned forward, elbows on the table. For the first time, I noticed how full his lips were. How long his lashes.

Something fluttered in my stomach, and I put a hand over it. "It's a co-worker's."

"And how long have we been dating?"

I bit my lip. "A couple months, I guess?"

He nodded. "Where did we meet?"

"I thought about that. Maybe the art supply store? I teach art at an elementary school during the week," I explained, "and the wedding is a co-worker's, so we can't say we met there."

"You're a teacher." He said it like he was impressed. "Can I call you Miss French?"

"No."

He sighed. "You're no fun. So, art supply store. Am I an artist? What's my occupation?"

"I don't know. What about your real one? Aren't you a pilot?"

He cocked his head, narrowing his eyes as if he had to think about whether he was or not. "I wouldn't really call that an occupation. It's more of a hobby."

I stared at him. "I don't understand. What do you do for a living besides hire yourself out on dates all over the country?"

"How do you know I do anything?" He leaned back in his chair and put his hands behind his head, a cocky grin on his face. "Maybe I'm independently wealthy."

"Maybe you're a serial killer."

"I promise I am not a serial killer."

"Good."

"Just a lady-killer. Kidding, kidding," he said when I gave him a dirty look. "For fuck's sake, you gotta lighten up a little bit, Claire. Don't take everything so seriously."

"I'm sorry, but this is a big deal to me, and I'm worried. I'm going to be lying to co-workers and friends all night, and I'm a terrible actress."

"Don't worry, I'm probably good enough for both of us."

"You're not helping." I put my face in my hands. "God, this is never going to work."

"Why do it at all?" he asked. "Why not just go alone?"

I peeked through my fingers at him. "Ever sat at the singles table at a wedding?"

"Can't say that I have."

Slouching in my chair, I dropped my hands to my lap. "Trust me when I say that it's a fate worse than death. But I have no good prospects at the moment, and I'm tired of all the single jokes."

He shrugged, leaning forward again. "OK, so we're gonna go together and have a great fucking time and show them all how not-single you are. You've got a pilot who's crazy about you."

"Fine. And where do you live?"

"How about Royal Oak?"

"OK." Taking a deep breath, I crossed my fingers. "I hope this works."

"Trust me, it will work. You just have to relax." He reached over and touched me lightly on the top of my hand.

Our eyes met, and an unexpected little rush of heat swept up my arm. "I'll try."

I felt heat in my cheeks, and dropped my head. *Blushing like a twelve-year-old because a cute boy touched your hand. Nice.* I reached for my purse on the chair next to me. "Should I..." I swallowed and lowered my voice. "Should I pay you now? I brought cash."

"Sure. When I get home, I'll book the date officially and send you the contract to fill out and sign electronically." He grabbed his jacket and slipped his arms into the sleeves.

"What's in the contract?"

"My rate, the details about when and where, the Platonic Promise."

"Platonic Promise?" I handed over five twenty-dollar bills folded in half and he tucked them inside his coat pocket.

"The part of the contract where we both acknowledge that there will be absolutely no sexual contact whatsoever."

"Oh! Right," I said, feeling my face warm even more. "Of course."

"If you think you might have a problem with that, Claire, I can't book the date. "

Flustered, I flapped my hands. "No, no! Of course there won't be a problem with that. I—"

He burst out laughing and grabbed my wrist. "Jesus, I'm kidding."

"Oh." I laughed at myself a little, shaking my head. "Sorry. I'm just really tense about this."

"I can tell." He squeezed my wrist before dropping it, and I noticed how big and strong his hand was.

"It's gonna be fun," he said, standing up. "I promise."

Wow, he's really tall. Long legs. Wonder if he has a nice butt. "If I say I believe you, will you think I'm too trusting?"

His eyes went crinkly at the corners when he smiled. "In this case, you can believe me. I will show you a *very* good time."

Something about the way he said it made my thighs clench.

I tried not to think about that.

FIVE

Theo

CLAIRE SAID she didn't need to be walked to her car, that she was meeting friends for dinner at Union Street, so I bid her goodbye with a handshake and told her I'd see her soon. It always felt a little uncomfortable taking money from someone just for meeting me, but I'd made my peace with it. Women were much more likely to book the date if they'd already made a deposit, and I needed the income. Jobs had been scarce lately, Josie's house payment was due on the fifteenth, my fucking brother was still gone, and the girls had been sick lately. Medicine wasn't cheap.

Had I known I'd be supporting my brother's wife and kids one day, I might have tried harder to get a college degree and not fucked up my life so much. Every time I thought about the scholarship I'd gotten and pissed away by being young and stupid, I wanted to punch myself. Yes, school was hard, and keeping up my grades enough to stay on the team had been tough, but I should have stuck it out.

But I was a MacLeod. Leaving was our specialty.

My mother had left us before I was even out of diapers. My older brother Aaron had been nine at the time, and he once told me he'd seen a note from her that said *Tell the boys I love them.*

"Do you think she did?" I'd asked him when I was maybe six.

His answer had surprised me. "Yeah. I do."

"But...she left."

"Yeah. She did."

"Does Dad love us?"

He'd frowned. "Maybe. I don't know."

Our father was an alcoholic, in and out of jail throughout my childhood, and I'd learned that I much preferred it when he was in, since his releases always meant bumps and bruises I had to explain at school. Still, Aaron had taken the worst of it. He'd never let our dad lay a finger on me if he was around. When the asshole finally left for good, I was eight and Aaron was sixteen. We moved from Kansas City up to Detroit, which is where I finally had some semblance of a normal childhood. We'd lived with our grandmother, who'd actually cared for us. I'd attended a good school, I'd had friends, I'd played sports. I'd even gotten a football scholarship to a college in upstate New York. Aaron had finished high school and gotten a job at a construction company. On the outside, things looked OK.

But we were damaged in ways you couldn't see.

I wasn't proud of it. I wished I were different sometimes. But what was the point of that? If something is in your DNA, it's as much a part of who you are as your skin tone or hair color. It determines whether you'll be impulsive or sensible, daring or careful, emotional or rational. You can try to be someone else, but that's a losing fight. Better to accept what life handed you and roll with it. In my case, sometimes I wished rolling with it hadn't included several DUI's and twelve months served for grand theft auto, ruining any chance of getting FAA-certified, but hey. To a bunch of drunk twenty-two-year-olds, stealing that truck from the Eager Beaver Saloon parking lot seemed like a good time on a random Saturday night. And who needed a normal life, anyway?

I'd meant what I'd said to Claire—I liked not being tied to anyone or anyplace or anything. Was it lonely sometimes? Sure. But it made life so much easier. And no matter where I went, there were dishonest people who needed my services and were willing to pay a decent price for them as long as I disappeared afterward. (Insurance fraud doesn't have quite the same ring to it as "grand theft auto," and it's unlikely anyone will ever create a video game where the hero steals things at the owner's request, but you can't have everything.)

The money I made wasn't amazing, but it was enough to live on and help my sister-in-law and nieces out when my brother took off on her. They were here in Detroit, so this was the only town where I turned down con jobs, because it was a town I had to return to somewhat regularly. You don't shit where you eat.

It was also the only place I kept an apartment. While I was here, I always tried to book as many escort gigs as I could, because at least it was honest money, even if it was slightly weird sometimes. And it made my life a little less lonely. But I never broke the rules of the contract, because I couldn't risk being reported to the company. I depended on this income. It was risky enough using a fake profile, but I couldn't use the real one, of course, because a criminal record was not befitting of a Hottie.

To avoid attracting the attention of the IRS, I also did some occasional jobs for the carpentry business I'd started way back when, but most of the jobs were made up so I could launder the fraud money. It wasn't that I didn't like the work, and I'd been good at it, but you couldn't build up a reputation or clientele when you moved around as much as I did.

I walked up Woodward toward the lot where I'd parked, shoving my hands in my pockets to keep them warm. It wasn't usually this cold here in December, but it had to be less than twenty degrees right now, and a few solid inches of snow were already on the ground. I passed Union Street on my left, and it looked cozy and inviting inside. For a moment, I let myself think about what it would be like to take Claire on a real date someplace like that. To get to know her because I wanted to, not because I needed to. To feel like she wanted to be with me for *me*, not for who I was pretending to be. To share something real with her. *To keep her warm on a night like this.*

But that was ridiculous. Girls like Claire didn't go for guys like me, and even if she did, I'd only fuck it up.

I knew who I was.

A screwup. An ex-con. A "security risk."

It was better this way.

SIX

Claire

AFTER THEO LEFT, I texted Jaime and Margot to see if they were at Union Street yet. Margot had come to town for a wedding dress fitting this afternoon and was staying to have dinner with us. I couldn't wait to see her—it had been weeks.

Jaime replied that they were both there, so I zipped up my coat, tugged on my gloves, and hurried out the door into the blustery cold. I walked quickly, snow drifting down around me and crunching underneath my boots. Up ahead, I thought I saw Theo from behind and moved even faster. Sure enough, I recognized the black jacket, and I sped up to a near run so I could get a better look at his ass, nearly slipping on the snowy sidewalk.

It was worth it.

His jacket was just short enough in back to give me a nice view, and as an artist, I appreciated the fine lines of the human form. As a woman who hadn't had sex in a couple years and who'd never had the kind of sex she read about in books (the Hallmark Channel was a bit of a letdown when it came to sex), I nearly groaned aloud at the thought of grabbing on to a solid, round ass like Theo's. His entire body was so thick and muscular—he filled out that Henley like sand fills a punching bag. For a moment I imagined what it would be like to feel his weight on me. My stomach flipped.

As he passed Union Street, he slowed and looked inside, and I had the weirdest compulsion to run up and ask him to join us. But that was silly—it was Girls Night Out, and anyway, he wasn't my type. Tall, dark, and handsome was fine, but Theo was the kind of guy who thought he knew everything, and furthermore, he was going to enlighten you on it, whether you asked him to or not. I liked his smile, but not his smirk.

Maybe I envied his devil-may-care approach to life a little, but it wasn't for me. I wanted someone more traditional. Someone more settled, more *grounded*. Someone who wanted what I did—to fall in love, tie the knot, and put down roots. Lemonade on the porch swing in the summer. Snowman on the lawn during winter. Theo didn't seem like a lemonade and snowman kind of guy.

But if my future husband had an ass like his, I would not complain.

Not one little bit.

"SO?" As soon as the server brought our drinks, Jaime bounced in her seat. "I'm dying! Tell us how it went with Fred!"

Fred. It almost made me laugh. "It went...fine, I guess."

"And you found him online?" Margot's high forehead was creased with worry. "Are we sure this is safe?"

"I *think* it is." I shrugged. "I mean, the website appears legit, and he has good reviews."

"Good reviews, that's hilarious," Jaime said, picking up her martini glass. "You can review men just like a book or a movie." She took a little sip. "But there's no sex, right?"

"Right." I giggled. "There's a Platonic Promise in the contract that says there will be no sexual contact whatsoever."

"Is he hot?" Margot asked.

"He is, actually," I answered, crossing my legs, "although he looks nothing like the profile picture he used. It's not even him. And his name isn't Fred."

They both stared at me.

"Claire, this sounds weird," Margot said. "Did he tell you his real name?"

"Yes, it's Theo."

"Theo what?"

I tilted my head. "You know what? He didn't give me a last name."

My friends glanced at each other. "What does he look like?" Jaime asked.

"Tall. Muscular. Brown hair, light brown eyes. Scruff. Big hands." *Nice ass.*

She laughed. "You noticed his hands?"

My cheeks warmed. "I'm an artist. I notice people's hands a lot."

"But what's he *like*?" Margot pressed. "Does he seem decent? Is he a gentleman?"

"He's nice enough. A little arrogant, like you can tell he thinks he's God's gift to women, but also seems like he could be fun on a date. And he's what I got, so..." I shrugged. "He'll have to do."

"Maybe it will be fun." Margot tried hard to sound hopeful. I could tell she wasn't sold on the whole idea, but she probably felt too sorry for me to say so.

"And at least you know you won't have to worry about him pawing you all night, since he's not allowed to touch you," Jaime added.

"Right," I said with relief, although secretly I thought it might be nice to have a guy like Theo want to paw me. "I hate those dates. But he doesn't seem like that type of guy anyway. He led me to believe *he's* usually on the end of the potential pawing."

Jaime groaned. "Ugh, he's one of *those.*"

"Just make sure you meet in a public place and don't get into a car with him," Margot warned. "You have to be careful."

I picked up my Cosmo and took a much-needed drink. "I'm always careful."

"Yes, but you're also very trusting," she said. "Too trusting sometimes."

I sighed. "That's what he said."

"Theo said that?" Margot asked. "How would he know?"

"Was he judging you for hiring him?" Jaime demanded.

I shook my head. "No, it wasn't that. And he might have just been teasing me. Because he also said he knows why I don't have a boyfriend."

"What the fuck?" Jaime sat up taller in her chair. "I'd have punched him."

"What on earth did he say?" Margot asked.

"Oh, something about my being scared to meet the perfect person because I don't think I'll measure up," I said, trying to play it off like it was nonsense. "He said I was afraid of rejection, so I don't really give anyone a chance." I rolled my eyes. "Ridiculous, right?"

Neither of them answered quickly enough.

"Isn't it?" I asked, panic invading my tone.

They looked at each other and then at me. "Well, it's ridiculous that he *said* that to you," Margot began, "but I'm not sure he's completely off."

"What?" I looked at Jaime. "What do you think?"

She looked nervous, which was rare for her. "I definitely agree he's a dick for saying that to you, but I might want to hire him as a marketing strategist, because it seems like he's really good at reading people in a short amount of time."

"Seriously?" I looked back and forth between them. "You guys think he's right? I haven't fallen in love yet because I'm *scared*?"

"I don't think that's the *only* reason you haven't found someone," Margot said gently. "But I do think there's some truth in what he said about you being afraid of rejection, so maybe you don't give yourself a *chance* to fall in love. Like maybe you talk yourself out of it."

"On purpose? Why on earth would I do that?" This was unbelievable!

Jaime shrugged. "It might not be on purpose. Sometimes I think our subconscious works against us or something. Your brain is like, *Yes, I want to find someone so I'm going to go on this date*, and your heart goes, *But wait, this is scary and I could get hurt*. So you look for things wrong with the person, reasons why they're not the right one. We've all done it."

I inhaled and exhaled slowly, trying to stay calm.

"I think it goes beyond dating, too," Jaime went on. "You're brilliantly talented, and for as long as I've known you, your dream has been to sell your artwork, or at least display it somewhere, but you haven't done that yet, either."

"I'm going to," I said defensively. "Jeez, you guys."

An awkward silence hung among us, which was rare.

Margot touched my hand, her blue eyes full of concern. "I'm sorry if we hurt your feelings. We didn't mean to."

"I'm sorry, too," Jaime said. "I shouldn't have said that. I'm an asshole."

I took a shaky breath. "I'm OK. It's just not terribly pleasant to hear that your friends—and a complete stranger, which means it's probably obvious to everyone but me— think I'm sabotaging all my dreams because I'm a coward."

"You're not a coward," Jaime said fiercely. "You're just careful. But you're also beautiful and wonderful and gifted and we just want everyone to know it. Be brave! Put yourself out there!"

"I hear what you're saying. I just don't know how to do that." I frowned. "I wish I was more like my sister."

Jaime rolled her eyes. "I said brave, not egomaniacal."

I managed a small smile. "I'll try."

"You sure you're OK?" Margot asked.

"Yes. Look, it's not really anything I didn't know—I've been a Nervous Nellie all my life. There's a reason I don't get on airplanes, horses, or motorcycles. I'm not a thrill-seeker. And normally I'm fine with it. I'm probably oversensitive right now because I feel like I'm surrounded by happy couples, and I'm the misfit. The odd one out."

"You're not." Jaime was adamant.

"Of course you're not," Margot added.

I was, but it wasn't their fault and I didn't want them to feel guilty about being happy and in love. "Let's talk about something else." I turned to Margot and put on a smile. "Tell me what's new with the wedding."

While she filled Jaime and I in on how all the final details were shaping up, I found myself getting swept up in the romantic excitement. Although they'd considered getting married up at the farm, in the end Margot had caved to her mother's insistence that she get married at Fort Street Presbyterian, where five previous generations of Thurber women had tied the knot. She'd chosen a ballroom at the Westin Book Cadillac Hotel downtown for the reception. "Wait until you see the centerpieces. They're gorgeous," she gushed. "And the invitations came out beautifully."

With Margot's sophisticated taste—and unlimited budget—I had no doubt the whole affair would be exquisite from start to finish.

Jaime and I were throwing her a surprise shower next month. It was a challenge since Margot liked to micromanage every little thing, but we'd gotten her to set aside the date by telling her we wanted a spa day and "booking" a bunch of fake appointments. In reality, we were throwing her a champagne brunch, which included all different kinds of scones—a little inside joke about the time Margot had lost her cool at a party and hurled a bunch of scones at her ex-boyfriend.

It made me laugh every time I thought about it. She was normally the calmest, classiest woman in any room. Bad behavior was completely out of character for her. But if she hadn't thrown those scones, she wouldn't have had to leave town. And if she hadn't left town, she wouldn't have met Jack at the farm.

Maybe that's what they meant by being brave—doing something different. Something surprising and out of character. Something that invigorated me, forced me off the usual path, opened my eyes to new possibilities.

But what?

MY MOTHER HAD CALLED while we were having dinner, and I called her back on my way home, wondering what Christmas tune her ring tone was today. Holidays were like catnip to my mother, especially Christmas, so she was always in a good mood in December. Nothing made her happier than getting ready for the holidays, and she still carried on all the traditions of my childhood, even though Giselle and I were grown and out of the house. She still hung our stockings, moved the Elf on the Shelf around, and put out cookies for Santa. I swear if you cut her open, she'd probably bleed tinsel.

"Hi, honey!"

"Hi, Mom."

"How was dinner with the girls?"

"Great." I caught her up with Margot's wedding plans, and she sighed.

"How fun to plan a wedding! Muffy must be in heaven," she said wistfully.

Muffy was Margot's mother. "Message received, Mom."

"I'm not rushing you, honey. I just think it would be a fun thing to do, plan a wedding."

"Well, maybe Giselle will announce another engagement soon. One that actually sticks."

"Is she seeing someone new?" my mother asked, her voice full of hope.

"Not that I know of." I'd talked to my sister last week and she'd told me about a threesome she'd just had, but I didn't think my mom wanted to hear about that. "Anyway, did you call earlier?"

"Yes, I was just planning Christmas Eve dinner and I

wonder if you'd make Grandma Flossie's chocolate pudding."

"Sure." That pudding was a pain, but if I suggested making something easier, my mom would probably have a stroke. Christmas wasn't Christmas without Grandma Flossie's pudding! "What's Giselle bringing?" I asked, although I knew the answer.

"Well, she's flying in that morning, so she can't really make anything. And she's such a disaster in the kitchen, I'm not sure I'd ask her to prepare a dish, anyway."

"Right." I tried not to resent all the chores Giselle had always gotten out of doing because she feigned incompetence so well. Being a good actress was *really* useful in life, not just on stage.

"OK, dear. Talk soon." She made her customary two-air-kiss noise and ended the call, and I tossed my phone on the passenger seat, feeling vaguely annoyed with myself for not telling my mother I wanted to make a pie instead of the pudding, or that it bothered me that Giselle never had to help with family dinners.

And maybe my mother hadn't meant to dig at me with that wedding comment, although she was skilled at dropping hints and pretending to be innocent. But she also made no secret of the fact that she wanted grandchildren and thought she'd have them by now. One by one, all her friends were marrying off their sons and daughters and becoming grandmothers. It had become somewhat of a competitive sport among them.

Since Giselle always claimed she didn't want kids, that left me as the only player in my mother's lineup. *Sorry about your bad luck, Mom.*

That night I lay awake in bed, trying to think of possible ways to be more adventuresome, break out of my shell. For inspiration, I pictured Margot throwing those scones, and it hit me—the lipstick.

Margot always wore bold red lipstick. Maybe it wasn't the *reason* she was so confident, but it didn't hurt. When I thought about it some more, I realized Giselle often wore bright red lip color too. Hell, even Taylor Swift started dating more interesting men when she adopted crimson lips.

That's what I needed! Stage makeup! Something to make me feel like I fit the part of the confident, successful woman I wanted to be.

I brought my fingertips to my mouth and tried to picture myself with a candy apple pout like Giselle affected in all her selfies. It would definitely be something different for me. Since I had really full lips and generally didn't like to call attention to them, I usually stuck to neutrals, soft beiges and pinks with names like Sweetie and Blush. But now I needed something more daring, something with a name like Brash or Brazen or Badass.

I laughed to myself...this could be fun.

SEVEN

Theo

BALANCING two bags of groceries on each arm, I trudged through the snow up the front walk at my brother and sister-in-law's small, one-story house. *I'll shovel while I'm here. And she needs salt for the driveway, too.*

On the front porch, I set the bags on my right arm down and knocked on the door. Inside I could hear someone crying and someone else shrieking, "He's here!" A moment later two little girls appeared in the front room window over to my right. They stood between the curtain and the glass, which was smudged with handprints, waving excitedly at me. "Hi, Uncle Theo!" shouted Ava, who was six. Her little sister Hailey grinned and jumped up and down like I was Santa Claus at their doorstep. It made my heart squeeze— would Josie be able to give the girls a good Christmas? I'd make sure of it.

Damn you, Aaron. Get clean and get the fuck home. My brother was an alcoholic like our dad had been, and even though he'd been on the wagon during the early years of his marriage, sobriety went out the window when he'd been laid off two years ago. He'd been on an almost constant bender since, and he hated himself for it, but he felt like he couldn't change.

He wasn't violent like our father was, and the only person he ever got mad at was himself, but when I tried to explain to him that he caused his family harm when he took off, he refused to listen. *They're better off without me*, he'd say. *I'm no good for them.* He'd been gone for nearly two months this time, and even though he stuck an occasional envelope of cash through the mail slot, it wasn't much. Josie worked the night shift as a waitress, but damn near her entire paycheck went to the sitter. And she was exhausted all the time.

I loved my brother, and I understood why he was the way he was, but I wanted to fucking punch him in the face until he realized what an idiot he was to throw all this away. Maybe this house wasn't much, and hell yes life was tough when you were out of work and had a wife and three kids, but dammit—it was *his* house, and *his* wife, and *his* kids. They adored him. He had things worth fighting for, worth staying for. And the crazy thing was, I knew he loved them. It wasn't like he didn't care. So it scared the living fuck out of me that he could abandon them like he did. Like our mother had left us. Maybe he *was* wired to be that way. Maybe we both were.

One more reason for me to go it alone in life.

The front door opened and my sister-in-law appeared with crying toddler Peyton on her hip. Josie looked awful— skin sallow, dark circles under her eyes, thin dark hair escaping the ponytail on the top of her head.

Claire's thick, honey-colored waves popped into my

head. I wondered if they were as soft as they'd looked yesterday. *Jesus, will you stop thinking about her? You've already jerked off to her twice and it hasn't even been twenty-four hours since you met. What's with you?*

"Hi," Josie said wearily. "Come on in."

I scooped up the bags at my feet and went inside. The house was basically a box, with a front room and kitchen on one side, two bedrooms and a bathroom on the other. I noticed they didn't have a Christmas tree as I headed for the kitchen.

"What's wrong with Peyton?" I asked, setting the bags on the cluttered table. Broken crayons and tattered coloring books littered its surface, and I made a mental note to get them some new ones.

"It's her ears." Josie sounded as tired as she looked. "The doctor said the antibiotics should kick in soon, but in the meantime I'm out of Tylenol."

"I'll go get you some." I pulled milk and apples and cheese from one bag. "Just let me get the stuff that needs to be refrigerated put away."

"You do too much already," Josie said, peeking in the bags. "I can't believe all this food. Let me pay you back."

"Not a chance."

Ava and Hailey scooted into the room and threw themselves at my legs, wrapping their little arms around me. I shut the fridge, leaned down, and scooped them up, setting one on each arm. "Hey! How's Snow White and Cinderella?" I asked, planting a kiss on their foreheads. "Are we going to have another tea party?"

"Yes!" Ava shouted. "But I want to be Sleeping Beauty this time."

"Deal." I looked at Hailey, noticing she wore a fuzzy

pink sweater sort of like Claire had worn yesterday. "You gonna make me eat the poison apple again?"

She giggled. "Yes!"

I heaved an exaggerated sigh as I set them down. "Fine. I'm gonna run an errand for your mom real quick, but when I get back, we'll play. OK?" They nodded and hopped back up onto chairs at the kitchen table to resume coloring.

"Have you heard from him?" Josie asked me over the sound of Peyton's weeping. The hope in her voice made my throat get tight. No matter what he did, she loved him and wouldn't hear of splitting up. She had family in Ohio, an aunt and some cousins, and I sometimes suggested she take the kids and go there so she'd have more support, but she refused to leave. I didn't get it.

"No." I focused on putting groceries away, biting back the angry words I wanted to say. Josie didn't need to hear me cuss out my brother. It wouldn't feel good and wouldn't help. "I take it you haven't either?"

"Not in a couple weeks. Just that envelope last Tuesday, but it wasn't much. I hope he's OK."

I shut the fridge and straightened up, turning to her. "He should be here, Josie. Taking care of his family. Making sure *you're* OK."

"He'll come back," she said, and I could tell she believed it. "He always does."

"Have you given any more thought to Ohio?"

"No." Her mouth was a stubborn line.

"But—"

"*No*. When you love someone, you don't leave."

"*He* did."

Her eyes defied me. "He's never been taught that lesson."

"Aren't you angry with him?"

"Of course I am." She kissed the top of Peyton's head. "But he's suffering, Theo. I know he is. And he's too ashamed to come home."

"He should be ashamed." I was angry and wanted to shout, but I said it quietly so the two older girls wouldn't hear. "This is not the kind of father he wanted to be."

"This isn't him," Josie insisted. "This person who takes over when he drinks. It isn't him."

It was and it wasn't. I knew what she meant—the Aaron she loved was strong and brave and hard-working. Proud and ferociously protective of his girls. But inside him were demons he couldn't ignore. He tried to quiet them with booze, but it only made them louder. It was why I'd quit drinking six years ago. "He needs to get sober and stay that way if he comes back."

"He'll come back." Tears filled her eyes. "He's got to."

Something about the way she said it made my hair stand on end. I dropped my eyes to her stomach. "You're pregnant."

"Shhh." She threw a worried glance over her shoulder at Ava and Hailey. "I haven't told the girls yet."

"Does Aaron know?"

She nodded tearfully. "I told him last time he called. I shouldn't have. I think I made things worse."

My hands balled into fists. It killed me that she thought this was her fault. "You didn't. When are you due?"

"Early July, I think? It must have happened last time he was home, which was September." A tear dripped down her cheek. "We had those few good weeks."

Damn you, Aaron. "Have you been to the doctor?"

"Not yet."

"Make an appointment."

"But I can't aff—"

"Make. An appointment. I'll cover the cost. And turn the heat up, it's too cold in here for the kids." My tone left no room for argument.

Pressing my lips into a grim line, I brushed Peyton's matted blond hair from her face before heading for the front door. "I'm going to get the Tylenol and some salt for the driveway. Be right back."

AFTER I RETURNED from the drug store, I gave the kids their new crayons and coloring books and shoveled the driveway, the front walk, and the sidewalk, angrily scraping the metal shovel along the cement. I was so mad at my brother. *So fucking mad.* And why was Josie so blindly loyal to him? Even if he did come home, if he didn't get sober, he'd only take off again. That was the cycle, and she knew it. The past kept on repeating itself. Wouldn't she wake up every morning and think, *Is this the day he leaves us?* Didn't she want something better for her children? I did, and they weren't even mine!

Love was a fucked-up thing.

EIGHT

Claire

AUDACIOUS.

As soon as I saw that name printed on the bottom of the lipstick tube, I knew it was the one.

It was Thursday, and I'd stopped at the drugstore after work to purchase a tube of crimson courage. (Surely Margot would have frowned upon purchasing cosmetics at Rite Aid, but I didn't have her bank account. I needed the discount version of badass.)

When I got home, I noticed Theo had sent me a message via the Hire a Hottie website.

Hey Claire, just wondering if you'd like me to pick you up before the wedding or if you'd be more comfortable meeting me there. I'm good either way.

I thought it over and decided I would be fine with him picking me up. It wasn't like he was a complete stranger—

we'd met and messaged back and forth a little. Plus, it would be weird having to explain to people why we'd driven separately. But just in case Theo really was a serial killer, I called Jaime and told her he was picking me up. "So if you never hear from me again, it's because I was too embarrassed to show up at a wedding without a date."

"You have to check in with me all night long and let me know when you get home," she said. "And for the record, I think this is a bad idea."

"Duly noted. Hey, what do you think I should wear?" I asked, staring at my closet.

"*Not* the Wedding Dress," she said, referring to the loose-fitting black dress I wore to weddings so often it had a nickname.

"Why not?"

"It's boring."

"It's comfortable," I countered, reaching into my closet to pull it out.

"It's not sexy."

Jaime and Margot were always trying to convince me to dress a little sexier, or at least more stylishly, but I was never sure I could pull it off. "I don't need to look sexy, I just have to look not-single."

She sighed loudly.

"Never mind, I'll figure it out," I said as I stuck it back in the closet.

"Are you nervous?"

"Yes. I mean, Theo's nice enough, and maybe we'll have a good time, but I'm a little worried about the whole fooling people into thinking he's my boyfriend thing. I'm not the actress in the family. I've never done anything like this before."

Jaime laughed. "I know. I was thinking earlier that in

the twenty years I've known you, I think this is the craziest thing you've ever done."

That actually made me smile.

FRIDAY ARRIVED, and I still didn't know what to wear.

After school that day, I stood in front of my closet again and debated trying to look a little sexy, but bold lips *and* a bold outfit seemed like too much, and I was nervous enough without adding to it with an uncomfortably tight or low-cut dress. One thing at a time—the lips would be my statement tonight.

I decided to ignore Jaime's advice and wear the Wedding Dress. Maybe it was a little plain, but it looked good on me. I slipped the soft, loose dress over my head, and since it was cold outside, paired it with black tights and low-heeled booties. Cute, right? Pleased with my choices, I applied the red lipstick and assessed myself in the mirror. "On a scale of one to ten, you are at least an eight and a half," I told myself. "You might not be a bombshell, but you are definitely a bullet, possibly even a small grenade."

Blowing myself a little air kiss in the glass, I bounced down the stairs and out the door.

I ATTENDED the six P.M. ceremony by myself, since I couldn't afford to rent Theo for more than a few hours. After it was over, at *least* five people asked my where my mystery man was, their expressions ranging from curious to skeptical. "He couldn't get off work early enough to make the ceremony," I said, delighted with how easily the lie rolled off my tongue. The lipstick was working! My ears barely even tingled. "He'll be at the reception, though."

Back at home, I had only about fifteen minutes before Theo was scheduled to pick me up, and I spent it staring at myself in the bathroom mirror, applying another coat of Audacious, and practicing Giselle's selfie pout. After a few tries, I thought I had it down.

When the doorbell rang, butterflies took flight in my belly, which annoyed me. This wasn't a date—it was a business transaction, just like Theo said.

But just in case the second coat of blaring red lipstick was too much, I blotted some off.

He rang the bell again, and I tossed the kiss-marked tissue in the trash can. "Coming, coming!" I yelled as I rushed to the door. Then I pulled it open, and my jaw dropped.

Theo looked gorgeous. *Gorgeous.* My heart beat a little faster as I took him in, head to heel. He wore a dark suit with a white shirt and deep red tie. His dark hair was neatly combed, his scruff groomed, his shoes polished. And he was so *tall*—the top of my head barely reached his chin, even with shoes on. *I'd have to stand on tiptoe to kiss him.*

As soon as I thought it, I shoved the image out of my head. *He's not going to kiss you, dummy.*

"Come on in," I said, stepping back so he could get out of the cold. He wasn't even wearing a coat. "I'm just about ready."

"OK. No rush. I'm a few minutes early, anyway." He entered the living room and looked around as I shut the door. "This is nice."

"Thanks. It needs work, but I love it."

"What's this style of architecture called again?"

"It's a Craftsman-style bungalow. At least, that's what the agent called it when she was trying to sell me on the place."

"How long have you lived here?" He admired my Christmas tree in the front window before peering into the dining room. I still didn't have a table and chairs in there.

"Just a few months. I bought it over the summer, and I'm refurbishing it, one room at a time. But it's just me doing the work, so it's a slow process."

Theo moved toward the fireplace and studied the painting above it, a watercolor I'd done of cherry trees in bloom near my family's cabin up north. That squirmy, nervous feeling I always had when people looked at my artwork wormed its way into my stomach, and I halfway hoped he wouldn't notice my signature at the bottom. But he did.

"Did you paint this?" he asked.

I couldn't tell from his voice if he thought it was good or not. "Yes."

"It's beautiful."

The nervous feeling eased up, and a little pride warmed my insides. "Thanks."

He glanced around at the walls and on the built-in shelves, which held photographs of family and friends along with smaller paintings, sketches, and projects I'd done. "You did all these?"

"Yes."

"What's this?" He picked up a piece I'd recently finished, an old hardcover copy of a book of fairy tales, the pages of which I'd carved into an ornate tower like Rapunzel might have lived in and painted with watercolors.

"I call it an altered book."

"Amazing." He set it down and picked up another one. "Do you always do fairy tales?"

"No, but I'm inspired by them a lot. The romance, the history, the symbolism. I like mythology and poetry too." Walking over to the shelves where he stood, I pulled out one of my favorites, a volume of Shakespeare's sonnets into which I'd carved and painted a heart.

He admired it for a moment. "How do you do it?"

"I sketch an idea and then try to figure out how to break it down into layers within the pages. When all of the technical stuff is worked out, I carve the design into the book with an Xacto knife. Once all the layers are done, I paint it with watercolors and then bind the sides." Sharing *how* I did something was much easier for me than sharing the actual work. I could talk all day long about the process, and even teach someone to do it, but when it came to putting my art out there to be judged...that was hard. It felt like putting *myself* out there to be judged. I put the book back on the shelf.

"Do you sell your art?" Theo leaned down to look closer at a sketch of my sister.

"No. I mean, not yet," I added quickly. "I'd like to, someday."

He straightened up and looked at me. "When's someday?"

"I don't know." I shrugged. "Soon, maybe."

"Why not already?"

"You have to submit your work to festivals and galleries and...I'm not sure I'm that accomplished yet." The squirmy feeling was back under his scrutiny. My friends and family said I was good, but what if they were just being nice?

"I'd say you're pretty fucking accomplished. What's holding you back?"

"Nothing," I lied. "I'm just waiting for the right time."

He nodded slowly, his eyes narrowing a little, which gave me the impression he saw right through me. I waited for him to get on me about being scared again, but instead he asked, "Is that what you're wearing?"

I glanced down at my black dress. "Yes. Why?"

He frowned. "It doesn't fit you."

"What do you mean? Yes, it does."

"No, it doesn't. It's all loose and baggy. You can't even see your shape."

"My shape?" I should have told him to buzz off, but instead I found myself going down the hall to look in the full-length mirror on the back of the guest room door. Why, I have no idea, since I knew exactly what this dress looked like on me. But I thought it fit fine.

Theo followed me. "Yeah. You have a nice shape, you should show it off. Be more confident."

"Actually, I was perfectly confident before you got here. You know, none of the women who reviewed you mentioned anything about getting an outfit critique." I glared at him over my shoulder.

"I'm just trying to help," he said, holding up his hands like he was innocent. "You mentioned before that you have trouble with guys. I'm giving you a guy's perspective here."

"I never said I had *trouble* with guys." In front of the mirror, I turned this way and that to see if he was right about the dress. Was it too big? I wanted to be comfy, not frumpy.

"You didn't? Huh. Well, I guess it was implied, then."

"You really think this looks bad on me?"

"It's not that it looks *bad*, exactly." He shrugged, moving behind me to look at my reflection in the glass. "It just does't do anything for you. And all that black..." He winced, shaking his head slightly.

"What?" I stuck my hands on my hips.

"I don't want to hurt your feelings," he hedged.

"Oh, really? Since when."

"It's just that you look like you're going to a funeral or something, not out to have a good time. Love the red lips, though."

I pressed them together. "Fine. I'll change."

"And maybe take your hair down, too," he called out as I marched down the hall. "You have great hair. It's one of your best features."

"Enough!" I yelled, stomping up the stairs.

"What? It was a compliment!"

I reached the top of the stairs and ripped off the dress, throwing it to the floor. What an asshole! And I was probably an even bigger asshole for listening to him! Muttering to myself, I flipped through dresses in my closet and yanked out a new one I'd purchased on impulse while I was Christmas shopping a couple weeks ago. It was actually one I'd considered wearing earlier but had decided against because it was so tight. Tossing the dress onto my bed, I slipped off my booties and peeled off the black tights. There was no door to my bedroom, since the entire upper story was simply one big space, and I kept an eye on the steps, half expecting Theo to come up here and start criticizing my underwear.

I traded the cute black panties I'd had on for nude shapewear—a slip without panties. I wasn't in the habit of going places sans underwear, but the dress was so fitted, a panty line would show. I'd have to watch how I sat tonight. "This is why dressing sexy is a pain in the ass," I muttered. "You can't be comfortable." I swapped my black bra for nude as well, then shimmied into the dress, a burgundy lace shift with three quarter sleeves and an asymmetrical hem. The neckline was high, but the hemline was short, and the fit left nothing about my "shape" to the imagination. Unfortunately, I couldn't zip it all the way up on my own.

Dammit. I'll have to ask Theo to do it.

Frowning, I yanked all the hairpins out of my updo and let the mass of wavy hair tumble loosely around my shoulders. I messed with it a little in the mirror on the back of my closet door, but I didn't have time to do much else. Leaving my legs bare, I stepped into beige high heels and checked my reflection. Good enough? I swiveled right and left, finding nothing amiss. In fact, I actually thought I looked pretty damn good. But I'd thought so before, too. *I bet Theo will be able to find something to criticize.*

Had I known he was going to make me feel worse about myself, I'd have chosen somebody else. I didn't need any help in that department. Scowling, I turned off my bedroom lights and made my way carefully down the steps.

Theo, who'd been looking at the painting over the fireplace again, turned to look at me and whistled. Was it horrible and anti-feminist that I liked it?

I tried to keep the frown on my face. "I need help with the zipper on this dress, please."

"Of course." His eyes were wide and glued to me as I reached the bottom of the stairs. "Wow. *You* are stunning."

Surprised, I blinked at him. I don't think I'd ever been called stunning before. Was this part of his act? "Thank you," I said, a little uncertainly.

Turning around, I moved my hair so it wouldn't get caught. When his hand touched my back, I felt a little tingle move up my spine. And was it me, or did he take an inordinately long time with the task, slowly moving the zipper to the top? The noise it made seemed to go on forever.

"Hold on, there's a little hook thing, too." He stepped closer to me—so close I felt his breath on the back of my neck as his fingers worked to get the tiny hook through the eye.

My heart beat wildly, and I had trouble swallowing. *For God's sake, Claire, he isn't unzipping your dress! He's doing it up! Get a grip!* But something about the way he was performing the favor felt...erotic to me.

"Sorry," he said. "My hands are too big. There! Got it."

"Thanks." I let my hair fall, but I couldn't face him yet, so I walked over to the closet. Tried to sound breezy and casual. "You better drop me off at the door, or my legs will freeze."

"Of course."

Willing my face to cool, I pulled out my wool dress coat and turned around. Theo was staring at my legs.

"What now?" I asked, steeling myself for another critique. "Heels not high enough? Wrong color? Legs too pale?"

"No," he said, his eyes traveling up to mine. "Everything about you is perfect."

"Oh. Thanks." I shoved one arm in my coat, embarrassed by the way I was blushing. *What's your problem? He probably says that to all his clients—it's part of the job, to make them feel gorgeous and desirable and wanted. You're not special.*

"Here. Let me help." Theo reached out and held the coat up as I slipped my other arm in.

"Thank you." My fingers shook as I buttoned it up, and I had to concentrate hard on pushing each button through its hole, like a five-year-old.

"I'm sorry if I hurt your feelings earlier. Sometimes I say stuff without thinking."

"It's fine. You're probably right about the dress." Facing him, I pulled my dress gloves from the pockets of my coat. "My friends don't like that dress either. Not sexy enough."

"Not sexy at *all*."

I shot him a dirty look, and he immediately looked contrite.

"Oops. Sorry."

Sighing, I tugged on the gloves. "Don't worry about it. The thing is, I don't think it's the dress that's not sexy. I think it's me."

"You think you're not sexy?"

Again, my cheeks burned. Why the hell had I said that? Closing my eyes, I held up one palm. "Look, just forget it. I'm not fishing for fake compliments tonight, OK? I know I'm paying you to lie to other people, but you don't have to lie to *me*."

He cocked his head. "So the critical stuff about yourself, you'll believe, but the compliments must be a lie?"

It was so dead on, I wasn't sure how to reply. But before I could think of what to say, he shook his head.

"Never mind. I promise not to lie to you tonight, Claire. Any compliment I give you is real." His tone was quiet and serious. No smile teased at his mouth. "You're beautiful and sexy. And I don't know what kind of dumbasses you date for real, but if they don't make you feel that way, then fuck them."

There went those damn butterflies again. "Thank you. Um, you look nice, too." Nice was an understatement, but I couldn't think straight. Was he just flattering me? Or did he honestly think that? How was I supposed to know what was part of the act and what wasn't?

Jesus, I need a glass of wine.

"Thank you." Theo took his keys from his pocket. "Ready to do this?"

I shrugged. "Ready as I'll ever be."

"Don't be nervous. It's gonna be great."

"Three hundred dollars great?" I challenged as we went out the front door. I'd contracted Theo for the three-hour minimum, with a clause stipulating that I could extend it if I wanted to.

"Three *million* dollars great," he said, offering his arm for me to hold onto as I navigated the icy front walk in heels. "In fact, you're going to have so much fun tonight, you'll think three hundred dollars was a bargain."

I laughed as he led me to a black Ford SUV that looked at least five or six years old but had been washed for the occasion. He opened the passenger door for me and closed it again once I was in. At least he had manners. The reviewers hadn't lied about that. And he was so tall and handsome—I couldn't wait to walk into that reception on his arm. Everyone would whisper about me, and this time, it would be the right kind of whispering. I wouldn't worry that they were laughing at me or pitying me—they'd envy me.

I glanced into the back seat, and something pink caught my eye on the floor. The reach was a bit of a struggle in my tight dress, but by the time Theo got into the car, I was holding up a half-dressed Barbie.

"Secret daughter?" I asked. "Or secret Barbie fetish?"

Theo's face went slightly purple. "Secret niece. Where was that?"

"In the back seat."

"Well, fuck."

"I thought you said you had no family."

He grimaced. "I'm sorry. I generally keep my private life very private. It isn't that I don't trust you."

I stared at the Barbie, wondering if every word that came out of his mouth was something more or something less than the truth. "How old is she?"

"The Barbie?"

I gave him a look. "The *niece*."

"Oh. I have three of them. They're six, five, and two."

"Three of them. Wow."

"My brother's kids."

I sighed. "OK, why not?" Tossing the Barbie into the back seat again, I buckled my seatbelt. "But if it turns out you have a weird Barbie thing, I want my money back."

He grinned as he started the car. "Deal."

I grinned back. I liked Theo, despite his ability to rile me up. As long as he kept his fashion, beauty, and dating advice to himself, I was sure I could have a good time with him.

In fact, I was beginning to feel a little sorry it was all just pretend.

NINE

Theo

"LET'S TALK FAVORITES," I said to Claire as we drove to the reception.

"Favorites?" She looked over at me. God, that little furrow in her brow was adorable. What color did you even call eyes like hers? Sage green? And her lips—how had I not noticed how full and luscious they were the other day? And speaking of luscious, that dress gave her body curves I hadn't even imagined...and I'd imagined her quite a bit in the last two days.

It was kind of stressing me out. I wasn't used to one specific woman taking up residence in my fantasies like that —especially not a woman I knew in real life. Generally, I rotated through a reliable spank-bank roster full of anonymous lingerie models or unattainable Hollywood celebrities or porn stars with names like Cherry Poppins and Ivana Bigcock. But for two straight days now (and I can work a lot of fantasizing into two days), even Ivana was morphing into Claire by the time I was done.

I kept telling myself it was because Claire was sort of a novelty. I didn't meet a lot of women like her—beautiful, smart, nice girls with college educations, close families, and high expectations for the future. I wasn't celibate or anything, but mostly I stuck to bad girls looking for a good time. The few times I'd actually tried dating had been a disaster. No one could fuck up a good thing like I could.

And I *never* hooked up with clients. They were usually older women fresh off a breakup or divorce. Nice enough, and always happy with the attention I paid them, but I'd never been attracted to one before. And none of them had ever tempted me to break the Platonic Promise—Claire was a different story. Her hair, her mouth, her body in that dress, those legs...I glanced down at them and my dick started to perk up.

Serves you right, asshole. You made her put that dress on. Why the hell didn't you let her wear the sack?

Damn it, I should have. But I'd wanted to help her, too. It was obvious she suffered from a lack of confidence, and she was never going to get what she wanted in life if she sat on the sidelines all the time. She needed to put herself in the game. I was just trying to coach her a little.

But fuck, she was hot in the uniform.

Shifting in my seat, I focused on the road ahead and cursed myself for not jerking off right before I left my apartment. "Yes, favorites. Like, what's your favorite color?"

"You mean your fabulous instincts didn't tell you?" she teased.

"Ha. If I had to guess, I'd say...pink." *Don't think about her pink parts. Really, dickhead. Just don't.*

"Good guess. What about yours?"

"Green. Just like my babydoll's eyes." I gave her an over-the-top adoring look.

She slapped my arm. "Is green your real favorite color or what?"

"I don't have one," I said, chuckling. For someone who struggled with insecurity, she had a feisty streak a mile long. My eyes strayed to her legs again as I wondered which side of her personality came out in bed.

For fuck's sake. Stop it.

I cleared my throat. "Favorite food?"

"Hmm. Maybe Italian? I love meatballs."

It killed me to let that one go by, but I did. "Me too. Favorite restaurant?"

"Andiamo," she said without missing a beat. "I love the tiramisu there."

I nodded. "Good to know. Favorite movie."

"Uh uh. I'm making you guess this one, smartypants." She crossed her arms. "I gave you the last few."

A smile pulled at my lips. "Let me think." I rubbed a hand over the stubble on my chin, gave her a critical glance. "Well, it's definitely something romantic with a happy ending, although you probably cry every time you watch it."

"Guilty," she said with a sigh. "My friends are always teasing me about how emotional I get at movies. But who doesn't like a happy ending? There's nothing wrong with that, is there?"

He laughed. "Believe me, I love happy endings. And I never said it was wrong. It's sweet, actually."

"Only you could make 'sweet' sound like an insult."

"It wasn't an insult, I promise. OK, let me think about this. Which chick movie is your favorite...I'd say Titanic, but I bet you hate that he dies."

"He might not die!" she exclaimed. "We didn't *see* him die, not exactly, so he might have lived!"

"Um, I think death was strongly implied."

She jerked her chin at me. "Guess again."

I thought for a minute. "Casablanca?"

"Nope. Too dreary at the end. But I do love that movie."

"Is it some sort of Disney princess movie?" I asked, thinking that her taste might run close to my nieces'. Their favorite color was pink, too.

"It does have a princess in it, but it's not a Disney movie." She clapped her hands gleefully when I remained silent. "Haha, I stumped you!"

"I'm not stumped. Just give me a minute." I pulled into the parking lot of the banquet hall and circled around to valet so Claire would only have to walk about ten feet, under a canopy, to the door. "OK, it's not a Disney movie, but it has a princess and a happy ever after. Aha!" Putting the car into park, I grinned at her. "The Princess Bride!"

Her face fell. "Dammit! I thought I had you."

God, she was so fucking cute. "You do have me. For a whole three hours."

Her smile returned, a little smug this time. "During which you will not make fun of my taste in movies, clothes, colors, or anything else. You will say only nice things, so everyone will think you're crazy about me."

I couldn't resist. "As you wish."

INSIDE THE HALL, we checked Claire's coat and found our place card, which indicated we were at table 12. I let Claire lead the way, admiring her ass in front of me. Suddenly she stopped and turned around, and I thought for sure she'd caught me looking at her butt, but instead of scolding me she put a hand on my chest and whispered in my ear, "Twenty bucks says that's the singles table." She nodded toward a table of awkward, miserable-looking people.

No one was talking, and everyone was staring at their phones, save the one guy who was making some sort of swan out of his napkin. "Wow," I said. "I should have charged you more."

She gave me her favorite dirty look and poked me in the chest. "Behave. Hey, what's your last name, anyway? I never asked, and I'll have to introduce you."

"Woodcock."

Her eyes narrowed.

"What? It's a real last name."

"But is it *yours*?"

It wasn't, and I'd promised not to lie to her, but this was a hard line for me. I *never* used my last name.

Plus...Woodcock. Come on, that's fucking awesome.

"It is tonight," I told her.

She sighed. "OK, whatever. I just hope they don't ask to see your license."

"If they did, I'd show it to them."

"You have a fake license?" She held up one hand and shook her head. "No, don't tell me. I don't want to know."

"Good. You ready for the show?"

Her face paled a bit. "I have stage fright."

I took her hand and kissed the back of it just for fun, pleased with the way her cheeks went pink. "Break a leg, darling."

We found our table and Claire made the introductions. Although there may have been a raised eyebrow or two at my last name, Claire's co-workers were too polite to laugh or request proof. After shaking hands and saying hello, I asked her if I could get her something to drink. She was perched ramrod on the edge of her chair, twisting her fingers in her lap. "Yes, wine," she said. "A big one."

"One big wine coming up. Red?" I guessed.

She nodded gratefully.

I turned to the rest of the table. "Anyone else need a drink?"

One other woman said she'd take a glass of wine too, so I stood in line at the bar and brought two glasses of cabernet back to the table.

"Don't you want anything?" Claire asked when I sat down.

"I'm driving." I couldn't tell her I didn't drink, since that was probably something she'd know if we'd been dating for a few months.

She nodded and took a few healthy swallows of wine. "Thanks for this."

"My pleasure." I lowered my voice and leaned over to whisper in her ear, one arm draped across the back of her chair. Her hair smelled amazing. I wanted to swim in it. "You doing OK?"

"Yes," she whispered back, tugging on one earlobe.

"Are they all looking at us?"

"Yes."

"Good. Sweet nothing, sweet nothing, sweet nothing."

She giggled. "Thanks."

Reluctantly, I sat up straight again...but I left my arm across her chair.

"So, Theo," said Fran, one of the women at our table. "Did Claire tell you about the art projects she had the Girl Scouts do for Operation Gratitude?"

I looked at Claire for my cue, and her cheeks went pink.

"The greeting cards and bracelets in the care packages," she said, a little too loudly. "For soldiers overseas?"

"Oh, right! She did." I shook my head like I couldn't believe I'd forgotten. "She's so giving, sometimes I lose track of all her good deeds."

"She *is* giving! She organized the Halloween candy collection for the packages too," added Fran.

"Fran, enough. You'll embarrass me," said Claire.

"I'm just making sure he knows what he has, dear. You're much too modest."

"I agree," I said, tapping Claire on the shoulder. "I'm always telling her she needs to stop giving away her artwork and start selling it." I wasn't positive she gave things away, but it seemed like a good bet.

"Exactly!" Fran nodded excitedly. "I tell her that all the time. She gave me this beautiful little painting of a magnolia tree after I had to cut mine down, and I cherish it. You have to work on her, Theo. Get her to see how talented she is."

"I'll try," I said, smiling over at Claire, who looked like she wanted to disappear, but not before gouging my leg with her butter knife.

But once it was apparent no one suspected anything strange about our relationship, Claire relaxed a bit, sitting back in her chair, smiling more readily, laughing more naturally.

I loved her laugh. It was bubbly and girlish, and it made me want to pick her up, put her in my pocket, and carry her around with me just so I could hear it all the time.

She didn't have an unkind or gossipy thing to say about anyone, and it was clear she was as good a teacher as she was an artist. Her friends at the table praised her creativity, her caring nature with students, her dedication to her job.

She blushed prettily and brushed off the compliments, saying she just loved what she did, that's all.

So fucking sweet.

Yeah, she is. Which is why she'd never be interested in someone like you—a drifter with a criminal record, a questionable moral compass, and a history of bolting. So don't even think about it.

The voice in my head was right—beyond sex, I had nothing to offer a girl like Claire, and I didn't want to be anyone's boyfriend.

But why the hell hadn't some nice guy with a good job, a good heart, and good genetics swept Claire off her feet already? Built her up? Made her fall in love? She was beautiful and talented and kind. It baffled me that she was still single and didn't want to be. Something wasn't right.

I thought about it all through dinner and dessert. I had plenty of time, since when I was with a client, I liked to let her take the lead. If someone asked me a question directly, I responded, but all inquiries pertaining to the relationship, I artfully deflected to Claire, who seemed to be enjoying the act, now that she'd relaxed. She even impressed *me* with her performance, answering questions without hesitation, providing cute little anecdotes about us, saying nice things about me at every opportunity.

Well, the fake me, anyway.

"We met at the art gallery where I work, but we really bonded over Italian food. Theo is a fantastic cook."

A fantastic cook? I could boil water. Push buttons on the microwave. Order pizza. That was about it.

"He had blond hair when we met, isn't that crazy? He's like me, likes to change things up every now and then. And he looks great no matter what."

I actually look fucking terrible with blond hair, but I wasn't going to tell her that.

"When I found out he played the ukulele, I thought it was so cute! And he has a great voice."

What the fuck? The *ukulele*?

"Oh, I love the ukulele," gushed Fran. "And he sings to you too, Claire?"

"All the time." Claire's eyes sparkled as she patted me on the leg. "He's amazing. I'm so lucky."

She looked so happy I felt horrible that the me she described didn't exist.

Without thinking, I leaned over and did something I'd never done to a client—I kissed her cheek. It was warm and soft beneath my lips, and I hated that it was the only time my lips would touch her skin. *What I wouldn't give for just a taste of her.*

Claire was delighted. "Shall we dance, sweetheart?"

"As you wish," I said, making her smile even wider.

Rising to my feet, I offered her my hand. She took it, and I led her to the dance floor, where the band was playing an old Sinatra ballad. Claire went into my arms so easily, and fit there so naturally, it made me feel off balance. Off rhythm. I made sure to keep her at a slight distance, holding her a little closer than I'd hold another client, perhaps, but not allowing the lengths of our bodies to touch. She was off limits for way too many reasons, and I didn't want to give my dick any reason to think otherwise.

But God have *mercy*, she smelled good.

"Theo, this is so fun!" she said in a loud whisper, tipping her head back to look up at me. "I can't believe I was so nervous about it. We totally have them thinking it's real."

There is something real here—the way I want you. I forced myself to smile. "You're a much better actress than you led me to believe. You don't give yourself enough credit for anything."

"Hey." Her brow furrowed. "No scolding me. I still have at least twenty minutes of Nice Theo left."

"I'm not scolding. I'm encouraging. Because I don't understand why someone as talented as you doesn't sell her artwork somewhere. Or at least display it."

She sighed and looked away from me. "I'm waiting until I create just the right piece to submit somewhere."

"Are you working on it now?"

"No. I don't have the right inspiration yet."

"That's an easy way out, isn't it? Blaming a lack of inspiration."

Her eyes snapped back to mine. "What do you mean?"

"You have plenty of beautifully-inspired pieces already. Why not submit one of those?"

"Because it has to be perfect," she said. "You don't understand."

"Actually, I understand perfectly. You don't think you're good enough."

She opened her mouth and closed it again, struggling with a defense.

"But you are, Claire."

"What if *they* don't think that?" She shook her head. "It doesn't matter what I think or what you think. They might tell me I'm no good. And it will crush me."

"So what? You can't let that scare you into never taking a chance. I get that it's not easy for you to put yourself out there that way. You're not guaranteed the happy ending. But Claire." I stopped moving and forced her to look at me. "I know how it ends."

"You do?" Her eyes were wide and trusting, like she really believed I might be able to tell the future.

"Yes. Everyone dies."

She rolled her eyes. "I can't believe I fell for that."

I gave her a sheepish grin. "Sorry, couldn't resist. But it's true, Claire. Life is short. Do you really want to live yours this way? Never taking a risk? Never testing your limits?"

"No," she admitted. "But I don't know how to make myself do it. I don't know how to be different than I am. Even though sometimes I really, really wish I was."

"Believe me, I get that." Fuck yes, I got that. "But *you* don't have to be anyone else. You just have to stop staring over the edge and jump."

She looked up at me with huge eyes that said *I want to trust you.* "You make it sound easy."

"It could be. You just have to want it badly enough."

She lifted her chin slightly. "I do. I do want it."

Neither of us moved. Suddenly it felt like we were talking about something other than art. *Oh, fuck. Her lips are so close to mine. I could kiss her right here, right now. Just once. No one would even question it. And I want to—I really fucking want to. Just to know what it feels like.*

Her lips fell open and she rose on tiptoe. Cursing myself, I stepped back. "Hey, give me a minute, OK? I need to use the bathroom real quick."

She blinked at me in surprise. "Oh. Of course. I'll meet you back at the table."

I left her standing there and took off for the lobby, but instead of going into the men's room, I went outside, hoping the cold air would clear my head.

What the fuck was I thinking? I couldn't kiss her. Not here, and not ever! Not only would it break the contract, it would confuse her. Claire wasn't the kind of girl who messed around. She didn't just give her kisses away—it would mean something to her. *I* would mean something to her.

And she might mean something to me.

I couldn't let that happen.

TEN

Claire

WHOA. *Whoa.*

I'd almost kissed him. My rent-a-date.

I touched a hand to my stomach and caught my breath. My pulse was thundering in my ears. Had I lost my mind? He didn't want to kiss me—this was all just a show! And I'd been enjoying it way too much. The private smiles we'd exchanged, the sweet things he'd said about me, the arm around the back of my chair, the kiss on the cheek. I was starstruck by him, a little girl with a crush on her favorite actor. How embarrassing that I'd puckered up like that!

And how maddeningly unfair that the first guy I'd felt a spark with in years was only spending time with me because I was paying him.

Suddenly I realized I was standing there alone on the dance floor like a statue, and I quickly headed for the lobby bathroom. Through the glass entry doors, I saw Theo standing outside near the valet stand, and for a moment I was terrified that I'd freaked him out so much he was going to take off on me.

You idiot! I shoved open the ladies room door and locked myself into a stall. *Were you thinking it was real? It's not! Everything tonight has been fake!*

At that moment, I realized part of me *had* been thinking it was real. On one level, I'd known why he was here, but on another, I'd felt real chemistry with him. A real attraction. I'd started to hope for more.

And wasn't it just like me to get caught up in this as if it were one of my Hallmark romances! But it wasn't. And those things didn't happen to me. Despite the red lipstick and the lacey dress and the tumble-down hair, I was still Claire French, art teacher. Girl Scout volunteer. Wallflower.

His voice echoed in my ears. *You don't have to be anyone else. You just have to stop staring over the edge and jump.*

Theo didn't get it. He'd probably never been scared of anything in his life. He was so cool and detached, just wandering around the country flying planes and escorting lonely women to weddings. He didn't understand what it was like to have your whole heart set on something and be too afraid of failure to go for it.

Even the near kiss felt like a failure, one I wasn't sure how to recover from. Did I just pretend it hadn't happened? I closed my eyes and leaned back against the stall door, fighting tears. Things had been going so well—in fact, it was the most fun I'd had on a date in... Jesus, maybe ever! And it was all fake.

Get over it, Claire. This thing is done. You're never going to see him again, and that's that. What could ever come of it, anyway? He's not what you want. Now buck up enough moxie to get out of this bathroom, face him, and go home.

Sighing, I pushed myself off the wall and left the stall, stopping for a moment to wash my hands. In the mirror over the sink, I noticed some lipstick on my teeth and watched my cheeks flame with embarrassment. God, couldn't I do anything right? I grabbed a tissue and wiped off the smudge, then angrily tried to rub off as much of the color as I could. Who was I kidding? I'd never been audacious a day in my life.

I tossed the tissue in the trash and left the bathroom, doing my best to hold my head high, even though all I wanted to do was curl up on my couch with a fuzzy blanket, the remote, and a box of Moose Munch.

At least Theo hadn't left. He was sitting back at the table, and he stood when I approached.

"Hey," he said, his mouth curving into a smile. "I thought I'd lost you."

"Oh, she'll never let *you* get away," said Fran. "It took her too long to find you."

I managed a wry smile, even though it sort of felt like a joke at my expense. "Sorry. I was in the bathroom."

"Better not leave this one alone for too long," teased Fran. "I noticed a lot of women checking him out."

"I only have eyes for Claire." Theo winked at me, but I was over this game.

"I'm actually not feeling very well. Are you ready to go?" I asked him as I picked up my purse from my chair.

"Of course. Are you OK?"

"I'm fine." *Not that you really care.*

Turning to my colleagues who were left at the table, I said goodnight and told them I'd see them Monday. Without waiting for Theo, I began marching toward the coat check. I heard him say it was nice meeting them and he hoped to see them again soon—ha!—and felt his hand inside my elbow a moment later.

"Hey," he said, gently pulling my arm. "What's wrong?"

"Nothing." Even I was surprised at my poker face. "I'm just ready to go home." His face fell, and for a moment I felt a twinge of doubt. Maybe he did care. But a second, later his expression was blank.

"Whatever you want," he said. "You're the boss."

Right. And you're my employee. The reminder of the exact nature of our relationship was enough to ground me solidly in reality. "We must be over the three hours, anyway."

Theo looked at his watch. "Just barely. I didn't even notice."

"Time flies when you're having fake fun."

His brow wrinkled. "What's going on with you?"

Dropping the icy facade, I felt my shoulders droop. "I just want to go home." *Before I fall apart.*

"OK. I'll take you." Ever the gentleman, Theo retrieved my coat and held it up while I put it on. He even tipped the coat check woman and the valet driver who brought the car around.

"I'll pay you back for that stuff," I said, digging in my purse as he pulled out of the parking lot.

"Don't worry about it."

"No, here." I held up a ten-dollar bill.

"I don't want it."

"Take it," I snapped, tossing the money onto his lap. For some reason, it bugged me that he was so nice. It would have been better if he'd been mean. Maybe not serial killer mean, but something other than what he was.

He glanced at me, but said nothing.

The two of us remained silent the entire ride home. I spent the twenty minutes chastising myself for all the dumb decisions that had led me to this humiliating episode, starting with lying to Elyse. I should have known better.

I peeked over at Theo a couple times, but I had no idea what he was thinking about. He just kept rubbing one finger along his lower lip, his expression grim, his jaw tight.

He pulled into my driveway, and I was about to get out when he put a hand on my leg.

"Claire."

"What?"

"Did I do something to offend you?"

Yes. Made me think you could care. "No."

"Was something wrong about the way tonight was handled?"

Jesus. Was he worried about his business? "Don't worry. I'll give you a glowing review, just like the rest of them."

"I'm not worried about that. I'm worried about you."

"Ha."

"Ha?"

"Ha!" I said again, louder this time. "Why would you be worried about me?"

"Because we're...friends."

"We're not friends! We're not anything! No, I take it back, we're boss and employee right now, but in a minute when I go inside, we'll go back to being nothing, and I'll never see you again. It's my fault for getting caught up in this stupid charade. For thinking something real was there." *Shut up, shut up, shut up! You're only making it worse!*

Theo threw the car in park, but left it running as he shifted in his seat to face me. "Is that what this is about?"

Wrapping my arms around myself, I stared straight ahead.

"Hey." Putting his fingers beneath my chin, he forced me to look at him. "Talk to me, please."

I jerked my head away. "No."

"Why not?" His soft voice was breaking me down.

"Because I'm embarrassed."

"About what?"

"About...what I just said. About what I almost did on the dance floor." I lowered my voice to a whisper. "I almost kissed you."

His silence stretched out so long, I finally had to look over at him. In the dark, his expression was hard to read, so his next words shocked me. "I promise you, Claire, what you almost did on the dance floor was nothing compared to what I want to do to you right now."

My jaw dropped. "What?"

"But Claire." Whatever he said next was swallowed by the thunderous pounding of my heart.

"Wait a minute. Wait a minute." I held up one hand. "What do you want to do to me right now?"

His jaw twitched. "It's a long list."

"Start at the top."

"No."

"Please, Theo." My heart hadn't slowed down one bit. In fact, it was galloping wildly out of control, and taking my imagination with it.

"*No*. I can't."

"Why not?"

He laughed grimly. "That list is almost as long."

"Is it because of the Promise?"

"There's that."

"And what else?"

He ran a hand over his stubble, and my stomach flipped as I wondered what it would feel like on my skin.

"Theo, you have no idea how bad I feel about myself tonight. Just tell me I'm not crazy. Tell me it wasn't all pretend."

"You're not crazy."

"Tell me something else," I whispered. "Please." His words were like a drug—I needed more. Even if the high was only temporary. Even if the crash would hurt.

He looked at me. "I've never met anyone as beautiful as you."

My toes tingled, and it wasn't the cold. "Really?"

"Really. And I've never wanted to kiss anyone as badly as I wanted to kiss you on that dance floor."

The tingle moved up my legs. Was he leaning closer to me? "Really?"

"Really. And I've never wanted to taste someone the way I want to taste you."

The tingle nestled between my thighs. He was slowly closing the distance between us, his eyes on my lips.

"But it's a bad idea," he said, his mouth so near mine I could almost feel his breath. He took my face in his hands. "Such a fucking bad idea."

"And you're scared," I whispered. "You don't know what will happen."

"Actually, I do know what will happen." He rubbed his lips against mine, so gently I wanted to scream. "Because I'm not good at stopping."

A little sound of want and frustration escaped the back of my throat. "Theo," I begged. "Jump."

Strong hands angled my head as his mouth closed over mine, wide and full and warm. His tongue stroked between my lips, setting my entire body on fire. He tasted like winter, and I could smell the season on his skin—something woodsy and smoky and sweet. His kiss was powerful and deep, and it stirred something inside me that I hadn't felt in forever—*desire*.

I clung to it, let it build, pulled my gloves off to thread my fingers through his hair, breathed him in. I struggled to get closer despite all the barriers between us—clothing and coat and seat belts. I needed more. I needed skin.

I surprised myself by asking for it. "Do you want to come inside?"

He groaned and rested his forehead against mine. "You know I do. But I shouldn't."

"Listen. I'm usually the first person to do what I should, but tonight, I want to do something else." I remembered his words from earlier. "I want to test my limits a little. You can test yours."

He groaned again, louder this time. "You're killing me. *I'm* usually the first person to take a dare, but I'm trying to do the right thing here."

"What's the worst that could happen?" To help persuade him, I let one hand wander up the top of his thigh. When he didn't stop me, I moved it between his legs, and my thumb brushed over the tip of his erection. I kept it there, rubbing my thumb back and forth over the ridge pushing against his pants. I don't know where I found the nerve, but I was damn glad I had.

"Fuck," he whispered. "Are you sure?"

"Yes."

He fisted his hands in my hair so hard and fast I gasped. "Good. Because I have no limits to test, but I'll be *damn* happy to test yours."

My heart raced as we bolted from the car to the house. While I struggled to unlock the front door, Theo reached beneath my coat and dress, sliding his bare hands up the sides of my thighs. His mouth descended on my neck, his tongue hot on my skin. My fumbling fingers finally managed to get the key in the lock, turn it, and push open the door.

We moved inside the house with Theo pressed against my back, his hands already moving to the buttons on my coat. Tilting my head to one side, I reached up and grabbed a handful of his hair. His tongue was doing things to my throat that made my legs wobble. Somehow we made it into the living room, which was lit only by the colored lights on my Christmas tree.

When my coat was unbuttoned, he pushed it down my arms and tossed it aside. Immediately his hands returned to my thighs, yanking up the bottom of my dress and taking my shapewear with it. One hand moved between my legs, his fingertips touching me intimately.

He went still. "You're not wearing underwear?"

"No. That dress is too tight."

"*Fuuuuuck,*" he said, dragging the word out. "Good thing I didn't know this sooner. It was hard enough to keep my hands off you all night." He slid one long finger along the soft, slick seam, making my breath catch. I angled my head so I could kiss him, and his tongue slipped into my mouth just as his finger slid inside me. My knees trembled— it had been so long since anyone had touched me this way.

Theo's other hand closed over one breast, kneading it beneath his palm. I wanted to stop and take my dress all the way off, but I didn't want him to stop what he was doing. He teased my clit with wet fingertips, mimicking the stroke of his tongue against mine. Then he pushed two fingers inside me. My hips moved of their own accord, and I clung to his neck. Behind me I could feel his cock rubbing against my lower back.

"You're so wet, it's so fucking hot." Theo's voice was

different, raspier, needier. No teasing lilt of laughter in it. "I want to bury my head in your thighs, get my tongue right here," he said, torturing me with soft, quick swirls over my clit. "Then I want to fuck you with it. Would you like that?"

"Yes," I whispered, shock mingling with excitement. No one had ever talked to me like this before.

A second later, Theo spun me around and picked me up, my legs wrapping around his torso, my dress riding above my hips. He brought me over to the couch, set me on the cushions, and knelt down in front of it. "Don't move."

I watched him wrest the coat from his shoulders and take off his tie, my insides tight with anticipation. His eyes held mine as he unbuttoned the top few buttons of his dress shirt and rolled up the cuffs, exposing one thick wrist and then the other. His chest looked broad and muscular, I was dying to touch it. But when I reached out, Theo put a hand on my chest and shoved me against the back of the couch. Then he parted my knees, reached underneath my thighs, and yanked me to the edge so that my chin nearly rested on my chest. "Patience, princess."

"But I want to touch you." I moaned as he kissed his way up one trembling leg.

"I'm going to let you." His lips and tongue traveled up the other leg. "But not until I make you come."

My breath caught as I felt his tongue stroke up my center and circle slowly over my clit. My fingernails scraped at the upholstery on the couch.

"Not until I make you scream." He slid two fingers inside me, so deep I gasped.

"Not until I make you beg." His mouth closed over my clit and sucked greedily as he fucked me with his fingers. My insides clenched up so tight my feet came off the floor, as if the energy in my body was drawing itself in, a wave retreating before the surge. Just when I was at the peak, he pulled his hand from me and slipped his tongue inside. I gasped at the decadent heat of it, the startling intimacy, the shocking sensation of being devoured inside and out. My fingers found his hair and curled inside it, my jaw resting on my chest as I watched him bury his face between my legs. He rubbed his thumb hard and fast over my clit as his tongue thrust inside, driving me to a place of want so fierce it frightened me. Impulses I'd never felt had me grinding against him. Sounds I'd never made, frantic and feral, escaped my throat, the pitch rising higher and higher as I reached the breaking point. And when I finally exploded, my body pulsing with years of pent-up frustration, I screamed so loud and long I thought the windows might shatter.

"Two down." Theo straightened up and touched the back of one hand to his mouth while my entire body shivered with aftershocks. Or maybe it was anticipation—would he let me touch him now?

I sat up and reached for his belt and he closed his hands over my wrists. "Not so fast, princess."

"What?" I asked breathlessly.

"I haven't heard you beg yet."

ELEVEN

Theo

JESUS. That escalated quickly.

I hadn't meant for this to happen. I hadn't meant to tell her the truth, hadn't meant to kiss her, hadn't meant to take her home and fuck her with my tongue next to the Christmas tree.

But the road to hell is paved with good intentions. (And several strands of multi-colored lights.)

And she was impossible to resist. When she'd admitted to feeling something real tonight, my walls had crumbled a little. I was used to women wanting my attention, but I wasn't used to feeling this kind of chemistry with them. But Claire had this strange effect on me—she made me want to fuck her and protect her from guys like me at the same time. She made me want to break my rules. She made me wish I was someone else...someone worthy.

I was an expert liar, and I didn't often feel bad about it, but even I couldn't bring myself to lie to Claire when she asked me to tell her she wasn't crazy—even if it would have made things easier. Simpler. Cleaner.

Too late now—things were about to get dirty as fuck.

"Beg?" she asked a little nervously.

"Uh huh." I got to my feet and backed away from her. If she got her hands on me, there was a chance I'd say to hell with testing her limits and fuck her into next year like I wanted to.

"I don't know what to say." Self-conscious now, she closed her thighs and tried to bring her dress down.

Such a fucking good girl. She'd probably never uttered the filthy words I wanted to hear her say. But I had a feeling they were there in her head. Claire knew what she wanted —her hand on my dick in the car told me that—she just had to get over her fear. "Yes, you do."

"I don't," she said, sounding a little panicked. "I—"

"Do you want something from me?" To help her out, I unbuckled my belt.

She stared at my crotch. "Yes."

"What?"

"You," she said nervously.

I undid my pants and slipped my hand inside. "Come on, Miss French. You can do better than that." My dick was hard and hot in my palm, and I moved my fist up and down my shaft, enjoying the way her eyes popped.

"I want to do that. What you're doing."

Jesus. We were going to be here all night.

"You want my cock in your hand?" I let my pants fall open a little, so she could see what she was missing. MacLeod men might be emotionally fucked and criminally irresponsible, but physically we were well-endowed and not particularly humble about it.

"Yes." Claire nodded with wide eyes and started to get up.

"Stay there." I stopped her with my other hand out. "Where else do you want it?"

She licked her full lips and touched the bottom one with her fingertips. "Right here."

Oh, Jesus. I had to slow down with the hand or I was going to come all over myself. "Say it," I said, a little louder. "All of it."

"I want...your cock in my hand." She took a breath, her voice a little softer, but more intense. "I want your cock in my mouth."

"Good girl." My dick thickened inside my fist, and I ached to slide it between those plump red lips. "Tell me more."

"I want your cock inside me."

She was getting braver, I could hear it. She liked the sound of the words, liked the feel of them in her mouth. That first taste of the forbidden was always so sweet—the flavor of her still lingered on my lips, and I licked them again. "Where?"

"Where?" she repeated.

"Show me."

She hesitated, but she sat on the edge of the couch and spread her knees, her dress still at her hips, her heels still on her feet. Slowly, she ran her hands down the tops of her thighs and let them rest on her knees, open to me completely.

Fuckfuckfuck, this was even hotter than I'd imagined it. I stopped moving my hand, and my dick twitched threateningly within my fingers. But I pushed her some more. "Touch yourself where you want me, and say the words."

Would she do it? My heart clattered against my ribs as

she weighed what she wanted against her self-conscious-
ness. *Come on. Don't be scared.*

Then something shifted in her mind and in her body.
She spread her legs wider. Sat up taller. Arched her back.
Dared me with glittering eyes to watch. One hand moved
along her inner thigh toward her pussy, and my entire body
tensed. When her fingers reached the center of her body,
she stopped and rubbed herself lightly. "Here. I want your
cock right here." She tilted her head coquettishly. "How's
that? Do I get what I want?"

My jaw, which had gone slack with surprise as she
spoke, snapped shut. I swallowed hard as I fought off the
urge to come. "Fuck yes, you do."

She stood up and I rushed for her, our mouths colliding
as her hand replaced mine on my erection. I was so aroused
already I could have lost it the moment she touched me, but
I willed myself to hold back until I could get inside her. I
reached between her legs, felt how warm and wet she was,
and my knees nearly buckled.

"God, I want you," she whispered, sliding her hand up
and down my cock as we kissed feverishly, frantically. "I've
never wanted anyone the way I want you. I feel like I'm
losing my mind right now."

I knew exactly what she meant. Usually, I spent more
time messing around before sex—the art of foreplay is one I
rather enjoy, and I've been told on several occasions my
technique is unparalleled. Don't get me wrong, I love a good
orgasm as much as the next guy, but I don't like to rush
them. Sex was like my favorite game, one I didn't play very
often so when I did, I liked to take my time. Show off my
best moves. Exhibit a little finesse before I put the puck in
the net.

But tonight, any plans I might have had for finesse were

off the table—I was coming out of my skin with the need to get inside Claire, to know what she felt like. I managed to get my shirt off with her help on the buttons, but I didn't even bother with my pants or her dress.

I picked her up like I had before, our breath hot on each other's lips as her legs twined around my hips. I went down on my knees on the floor, tipping her onto her back, and reached into my pocket for my wallet. Sex was the one thing I did responsibly, having seen firsthand that fatherhood was not something MacLeod men were good at. Better to go home and jerk off than risk being an asshole absentee dad.

Thankfully, I had a few in there, and I wasted no time putting one on. Claire drew her knees up as I positioned my cock between her thighs, rubbed her clit with the tip. That first touch sent bolts of electricity screaming down my legs. My entire body vibrated with tension, and I couldn't wait one second longer. I buried myself inside her, watching her eyes flutter closed, hearing her sharp intake of breath, feeling her hands grab my ass.

I'd intended to go slow. I'd intended to whisper filthy things in her ear and make her say filthier things back to me. I'd intended to be creative and clever. Impress her with my size and skill and stamina. Give her something amazing to remember me by, an unforgettable experience that would linger in her mind long after I was gone.

I did none of those things.

Instead, I fucked her like a testosterone-fueled teenager on the living room rug, without words, without artistry, without control, my pants still shackling my thighs.

What was she doing to me?

TWELVE

Claire

SO DEEP it hurts was an expression I'd heard from friends and read in books and vaguely imagined when I was under the covers with my vibrator (the Cosmopolitan from the Sex in the City line by Pure Romance, featured heavily in Coming Alone), but I'd never experienced it on a personal level. I'd thought people were exaggerating.

I'd only been intimate with a handful of guys, and none of them had even come close to *so deep it hurts*. And though Cosmo was skilled at his job, discreet, and dependable, size and strength were not his forte.

But Theo. *Theo.*

The man had everything. When he first slid inside me, I couldn't even breathe. I don't know if it was because I hadn't had sex in so long or because Theo was really that much bigger than anyone I'd ever been with, but I felt the exhilarating thrill of losing my virginity all over again with none of the first-time awkwardness. (Am I doing this right? Will I bleed on the sheets? What's that smell?)

As he moved inside me, those four words kept repeating in my brain—*so deep it hurts*—but the pain wasn't like any I'd ever felt before. At first it was sharp, and I'd gasp every time he pushed inside me, my eyes tearing up. Then its edges started to soften, and I felt my body adjusting to his, my hips tilting to take him even deeper.

The muscles on his shoulders and abs flexed as he bracketed my head with his forearms. His breathing matched mine, hard and heavy and hot. I ran my palms over his back, raked my nails down his skin. Two hands weren't enough—I wanted to feel every inch of him all at once. And damn this dress! I'd been so anxious to get him inside me that we hadn't even stopped to take it off, but now I was desperate to feel his hands and mouth on my breasts, the warmth of his chest on my skin. What if I never got another chance?

But I didn't want him to stop. Something was happening inside me that I'd never felt before, a tightening at my core that intensified with every rhythmic thrust of his hips. I chased it, digging my fingers into his ass, pulling him tighter to my body. I wanted to tell him how good it felt, how big he was, how hard, how hot, how he was going to make me come again, how badly I wanted to feel him come too.

But I forgot every word except one.

"Yes," I panted, over and over again, my lips brushing against his throat. "Yes, yes, yes..."

Theo groaned, almost as if he was in pain. "Goddamn it, I'm gonna come." He sounded angry about it, but I cried out in bliss as the knots inside me unraveled in glorious, pulsing pleasure. Above me, Theo's body went stiff, and I felt his orgasm echo my own as his cock throbbed inside me.

"Oh my God." I could barely speak, my heart was beating so fast. My body didn't even feel like my own. (And I'd have to retitle my memoir. Or at least add an afterword.)

"Oh my *God*." Theo still sounded mad. "I'm such an asshole."

I froze. Was he sorry already? Was he going to run out? My head fell back onto the rug. "What's the matter?"

Bracing himself on his hands, he lifted his chest up and looked down at me. "That was not supposed to happen so fast."

Relief had me giggling. "I obviously didn't mind."

"I didn't even do half the things on the list."

"Well, then..." I lifted my shoulders and willed myself to be brave. "Stay."

He didn't say anything at first, just studied me from above. The tree lights lit his face just enough to show his indecision.

Maybe I can persuade him.

"Stay," I whispered, running my hands up his chest.

He swallowed. "I want to, Claire, but—"

I put a finger over his lips. "Stay. I want to cross some more things off that list."

He smiled. "You do?"

"Yeah. And maybe I have a list of my own."

"Listen to you," he said appreciatively.

"Just trying to be brave." My heart refused to stop pounding. And it was exhilarating to speak my mind like this, even if I was risking being turned down. But what did I have to lose?

Exhaling, he shook his head. "You're making this very difficult."

"Good." I crossed my ankles behind him. "Because I don't want you to go."

"I don't want to go, either. I just..." Theo hesitated, like he wasn't sure how to phrase what he wanted to say. "I'm worried about what happens tomorrow."

He was thinking about *tomorrow*? "I predict I will be very sore, but I promise not to complain too much."

He smiled, but barely. "That's not what I meant. It's more that I'm worried about...expectations."

"Expectations?"

"Yes. You and I are different, Claire. I like being with you, but...I'm no good for you."

"What makes you say that?"

"It's the truth."

I let that sink in for a moment, trying to think of this from his point of view. "Because I'm looking for a relationship and you're not?"

"That's part of it."

"What are the other parts?"

"I'm not sure how long I'll even be in town, or when I'll be back. My...other job often involves traveling at the last minute."

I nodded slowly, realizing how little I knew about him. Not even his real last name. "So maybe all we'll ever have is tonight?"

"Not maybe, Claire. Definitely."

So we wouldn't see each other again. I was disappointed, sure, but did that mean our night had to end? When I'd invited him in, I hadn't done it because I wanted to bring him home to meet Mom and Dad. I'd done it because I was attracted to him, and I wanted to have some fun.

I liked Theo; I felt safe with him. Even better, I felt *sexy* with him—sexier than I'd ever felt in my life. Why not take advantage of that while I could? A one-night stand wasn't exactly romantic, but it sure as hell beat going to bed alone tonight. Maybe I'd even learn a few things that would help me be more confident. *I bet there's a lot he could teach me.*

I looped my arms around his neck and pulled him down for a kiss. "Then we shouldn't waste any more time talking. I'm not looking for a boyfriend here, Theo. Just a good time."

He smiled against my lips. "OK then. Got any chocolate syrup?"

I DID HAVE CHOCOLATE SYRUP. But Theo got even more excited about the tube of crescent rolls I had in the fridge. "Oh my God, I have the biggest craving right now."

"For what?" I asked, throwing my hair up in a sloppy bun on top of my head. Theo was probably going to complain about that, but if he was going to cover me in chocolate syrup or something, I wanted to avoid getting it in my hair. While Theo cleaned up in the bathroom, I'd run upstairs, taken off the dress and slip, and put on a white t-shirt and pajama pants. After debating underwear, I'd gone with my gut and left them off.

Theo pulled the rolls out of the fridge and turned around to face me. He was barefoot and wore just his pants and his white dress shirt, unbuttoned and cuffs rolled up. "Tell me you have marshmallows."

His face was so serious, I had to laugh. "I have marshmallows."

"Butter?"

"Yes."

"Cinnamon and sugar?" His eyes were getting bigger with every ingredient.

"Yes, but what are we making?"

"My grandmother called them Magic Marshmallow Puffs or something. Oh my God, they're amazing. I haven't had them in years, not since she died. Turn the oven on to..." He looked at the tube. "Three seventy-five."

"Got it." I wanted to ask him more about his grand-mother, but I wasn't sure if I should. He guarded his privacy so closely, and I didn't want to spook him, make him think I hadn't meant what I'd said about being OK with just one night.

While I preheated the oven, Theo started opening my lower kitchen cupboards, which were so old the hinges were coming off. "These aren't in very good shape." He dropped down to examine one, balancing on the balls of his feet.

"Yeah, I know. It's on my list of things to work on this winter. What are you looking for?"

His brow furrowed as he examined the hinges closer. "Uh, one of those pans with the holes in it."

"Holes?"

He frowned and looked up at me. "Not holes exactly. A pan that you'd make cupcakes in."

"Like a muffin tin?"

"Yes! A muffin tin."

I laughed as I reached for a high cupboard, rising up on tiptoe to grab the muffin tin. "Here you go."

"Perfect." He shut the cabinet door, but it was crooked. "You know, if you have a drill, I could fix that for you."

"That's sweet, but if I only have you for one night, there's only one kind of drilling I'm interested in." My cheeks burned as I said it, but I loved the way it made his eyebrows arch in surprise, his mouth hook up in a slow grin.

"As you wish."

I smiled. "So what can I do?"

"Grab a bowl and melt some butter in it."

"Like how much?"

He thought for a second then held up his hand, thumb and forefinger about two inches apart. "About this much."

I burst out laughing and went to the fridge for a half-stick of butter. "You really don't cook, do you?"

"Nope. Sorry. I know the fake Theo cooks for you all the time."

Something in his voice made me look over at him. He was peeling the wrapper off the tube of rolls and seemed to be concentrating hard on the task. Was he jealous of his fake self? "Hey. I'm not interested in fake Theo."

"No?"

"No." I shut the fridge and grabbed a bowl to melt the butter in. Once it was in the microwave, I went to him and slid my arms around his waist. I was so short in my bare feet, I had to tip my head way back to look at him. "Why would I be, when I have the real thing right here?"

"I don't know. Fake Theo is a pretty good guy."

"Real Theo is better."

He smiled. "Even though he doesn't cook?"

"He's got...other talents."

Theo lowered his lips to mine and softly stroked them with his tongue. "Yes, he does. And he's going to use them." As the kiss grew deeper, his hands wandered down over my butt, inside my pants. He groaned. "You're still not wearing underwear?"

"No. Did you want me to put some on?"

"Don't you dare. I like you this way." His mouth moved down the side of my throat, making me shiver. "I just might get a little distracted while I'm trying to cook."

"No complaints here." I loved his hands on me. And his lips and tongue and anything else he wanted to touch me with. He kissed his way down my neck and chest, making my nipples perk up and poke through the thin cotton. Bending down, he lowered his head and sucked one into his mouth, shirt and all. He took it between his teeth, and my clit started to tingle. The microwave dinged, signaling the butter was ready, but neither of us cared. I took his head in my hands, threading my fingers into his hair as he moved his mouth to the other breast and his hand to the first. *Oh my God, if it feels this good with a shirt on, imagine how incredible it will feel when it's off.*

My lower body was humming, and I wondered if he was hard. I had my answer a moment later when he turned me toward the counter, pulled my pants off, and flattened himself against my back. One hand remained on my breast and the other snaked between my legs as he rubbed his cock along my lower back. "I can't get enough of you." His breath was warm on the back of my neck and sent gooseflesh rippling down my arms. He dipped one long finger inside me and brought it to his mouth. "The sweetest thing I've ever tasted."

I was mesmerized watching him suck his finger clean. "Really?"

"Yeah." He slipped two fingers inside me, slid one foot between mine, and kicked it out wider. His fingers moved deeper.

I gasped and flattened my palms on the counter for stability. Suddenly I felt shaky on my feet.

He moved his fingers in and out of the silky wetness between my legs and rubbed it over my clit. His cock bulged against my spine, and I wanted it inside me again. "Theo," I whispered, looking over my shoulder at him with pleading eyes.

He kissed me, gliding his tongue along mine, pinching my tight, tingling nipple with his left hand and bringing me closer to orgasm with his right. "Can I fuck you in the kitchen?" he asked, his voice low and raw.

"Yes," I panted. "You can fuck me in every room of this house if you want to." *Oh my God, did I just say that?*

"Then I better get started." His hands left me only for the amount of time it took him to grab a condom and put it on. Then he was back between my legs, guiding the tip of his cock inside me from behind, filling me slowly, deliciously, completely.

Instinctively, I rose up on my toes and arched my back, bracing my hands on the counter. Theo's breath was ragged as he began to move with slow, deep, rhythmic thrusts. His hands gripped my hips so hard I'd have bruises, but I didn't care. It would be evidence that this night had really happened, proof that I was capable of being uninhibited, unashamed, unafraid. I'd cherish those black and blue marks like gifts.

Theo moved one hand between my legs and circled his fingertips over my clit, burying his cock so deep inside me my toes nearly left the floor. Then he pulled the elastic from my hair, causing it to tumble down my back. Grabbing a handful of it, he yanked my head back, pulling my hair so hard, tears sprang to my eyes. But the sharp-edged sting on my scalp was in perfect contrast with the swirling, spiraling pleasure he wrought at my center.

"Was this on your list?" he rasped. "Being fucked by a stranger in your house?"

My pulse skittered away from me. "Stranger?"

"Yes. You don't know me."

My eyes were wide. Was he playing a game or was he serious? I wasn't sure I liked it that either could be true.

Suddenly he stopped to whisper in my ear. "Play along, princess. It's more fun that way."

He's acting.

Relief mingled with arousal, sending a shiver through my body as he began to move again. For a second, I panicked that I didn't know how to play along—that I wouldn't be good at these games. I was creative, yes, but with art I could take my time. I was kind of on the spot here. Closing my eyes, I tried to think about fantasies I had when I was alone. There were scenarios that turned me on, but I'd always kept them private. Could I go there with Theo? What if he didn't understand?

"You're so wet for me. I think you wanted this." The sexy growl in his voice pushed me over the edge.

"I don't," I gasped. "You should leave." But I arched my back even more, pushed my ass back against him, hoping he'd follow me.

He laughed, sinister and seductive. "Not going to happen. I told you I wasn't good at stopping."

"Please!" I begged, trying to keep a smile off my face. Damn it, did Giselle have to get all the acting talent? I wanted to play the role fully, but I was so excited it was hard not to show it.

"You don't really want me to stop. You weren't even wearing underwear. You wanted me to fuck you. You wanted my hands on your pussy. You want me to make you come all over my cock." His hand moved faster and harder over my clit, making my stomach feel weightless, my legs go numb. "Don't you?"

"No." My voice was as weak as my knees, because I wanted it so badly. I was already on the edge, the tension in my body coiled tight. One second later, I was writhing against him, riding out the most intense orgasm I'd ever felt, my muscles contracting repeatedly around his cock. He kept his hips still, which meant I could feel the tip of him in that deep, hidden spot that electrified every fiber of my being.

As soon as I collapsed forward on the counter, he grabbed my hips again. "Such a bad girl," he snarled, fucking me hard and fast. "To want me this way."

"But I'm a good girl." Getting the words out was a struggle.

"That's just a show. You want this." He was close. I heard it in his voice, felt it in the way he moved. "You want me to come."

"Yes," I breathed, unable to think beyond the truth of my desire. "I want it. I want it—give it to me."

His body stilled as he surged inside me, his hands tight on my hips. I closed my eyes and grabbed one of his wrists, circling it with my fingers. It was crazy, but I'd never felt so close to someone during sex before. Maybe it was because I'd had the courage to act out a fantasy with him. Maybe it was because he seemed to know me better than he should. Maybe it was the way he'd said *I'm no good for you*, as if he wished he were.

Why couldn't he be?

Before my heart could answer the question, my head spoke up.

Because he doesn't want to be. He said as much.

You have tonight, and that's it.

Make the most of it.

THIRTEEN

Theo

"GOT THE CINNAMON AND SUGAR READY?" I lined up the bag of marshmallows, the bowl of melted butter, and the crescent roll dough, which Claire had placed on a plastic cutting board.

"Yes," she said, holding a little white bowl with two hands. After we cleaned up, she'd put on pastel pink flannel pajama pants with little gray bunnies on them (I'm not making this up) and traded the white t-shirt for a fitted gray tank top that showed off her breasts. Her hair was back on the top of her head, and every time I looked at it I remembered taking it down and watching it spill down her back like honey. "Where does it go in the assembly line?"

"Right here." Ignoring the twitch in my pants—*take a break, asshole*—I made space between the butter and the cutting board, and she set it on the counter. "OK, ready?"

"Ready."

I pushed my cuffs up a little higher. "So you take a

marshmallow, and you give it a bath in the melted butter."
Taking a marshmallow from the bag, I rolled it around in
the butter, and the memory of doing this hundreds of times
as a kid hit me like a freight train. I could hear my grandmother's voice, smell her house, see the blue ceramic mixing
bowl she always used for the cinnamon and sugar. I'd taken
that blue bowl when Josie, Aaron and I cleaned out the
house. But I didn't bake, so it sat unused and gathering dust
in my kitchen cupboard. Same with her electric mixer and a
set of spatulas that I recalled licking batter off. Those were
the good years—the cake batter years.

"And then what?" Claire prompted.

I focused on the present. "Then you cover it with
cinnamon and sugar." Melted butter dripped from the
marshmallow as I rolled it around in the little white dish.
"Now get one of those little triangles of dough ready."

Claire laid out one raw crescent roll. "Just flat?"

"Yes." I placed the sugar-and-cinnamon-coated marshmallow at the wide end of it. "Now you have to wrap it up
with the dough and seal the edges." My fingers were also
coated with butter, sugar, and cinnamon, so I watched as
Claire folded the pointed end of the triangle over the top of
the marshmallow and then pinched all the edges of the
dough together.

"Like that?" She looked up at me.

"Yes. Just make sure the seal is really tight, or they
explode in the oven and all the magic drips out."

She laughed. "Got it. So the marshmallow melts, is that
it? That's the magic?"

"Don't try to look behind the curtain, Claire. Sometimes
believing in magic is better than the truth."

"OK, OK. So now what?" She held up the dough-
wrapped confection.

"Now dip the bottom of it in the butter and drop it into one of the holes in the muffin thing."

She did as instructed and looked at me. "How's that?"

"Perfect."

"I really want to lick your fingers right now. Is that one of the steps?"

I grinned. "It wasn't when I made these with my grandmother, but help yourself."

With a twinkle in those sage green eyes, she took my right arm by the wrist and held my hand up like a lollipop. She looked at me as she closed her lips over the base of my thumb and slowly pulled it out, her tongue swirling over the tip.

My dick took interest, hopping around in my pants like a little kid in line for the merry-go-round, impatient for his turn. She licked the next two fingers just as slowly, savoring every drop of butter and grain of sugar. And the way she kept her eyes on mine, oh my God, my imagination was out of control. My pants grew uncomfortably tight.

Gently I took my hand from her grasp. "Uh, I could watch you do that all night, but I'm going to lose all interest in baking these things if you keep going, and I really want you to taste them."

She giggled. "Will you let me lick them again once they're in the oven?"

"You can lick anything you want to once they're in the oven."

"Deal."

We worked together, and even though there were some spontaneous finger-licking breaks, we managed to get them in the oven in about ten minutes.

She set the timer for ten minutes and I rinsed the bowls in the sink. "Should I put these in the dishwasher?" I asked.

"I'll do it." She pushed me gently to the side and took my place in front of the sink. "You tell me about your grandmother."

Leaning back against the counter, I crossed my arms. I wasn't in the habit of talking about my family, but I'd opened my big mouth about my grandmother already. And I couldn't believe I'd missed that damn Barbie doll when I'd cleaned out my car. I was usually so careful. "She was good to me."

"Were you close?" Claire loaded the bowls into the top rack of the dishwasher, which looked about as old as the house. For that matter, so did the linoleum floor, which was clean but cracked and faded. She had a lot of work ahead of her, fixing this place up.

I could help her.

Immediately, I shoved that notion from my mind. I was out of here tonight and I couldn't come back. "Yeah. We were, for a while anyway. She basically raised me from eight to eighteen."

"Really?" She flicked a glance at me. "What happened to your parents?"

I hesitated, but figured what the hell. "My mom left when my brother and I were young. Dad was in and out of the picture for a while, but eventually decided out suited him better."

"Ah." She shut the dishwasher door and wiped her hands on a kitchen towel. "Did you grow up around here?"

"Not far."

"Where's your brother now?"

"That's a good question."

She faced me with the towel still in her hands, a quizzical look on her face.

Shit. I shouldn't have said that. Now what? "Like my father," I said carefully, "my brother struggles to stay put."

"You said you're a drifter, too," she pointed out.

I gritted my teeth. "I don't have a wife and three kids, with a fourth on the way."

Claire's jaw dropped. "Wow. Those are the nieces you mentioned?"

I nodded.

"And his wife is pregnant?"

My hands clenched into fists beneath my arms. Every time I thought about Josie and those girls, I wanted to punch something. But Claire didn't need to hear about it. "Yes. But she's fine. They're all gonna be fine." I said it with much more conviction than I felt.

Claire folded the towel and left it on the counter. "I bet you're a fun uncle."

"I am pretty awesome at tea parties."

"You play tea party with them?" She put a hand on her heart. "That's so cute. Do you get to see them much?"

When I paused, she went on quickly.

"I'm sorry, I don't mean to pry. I'm just...curious."

"It's OK." Again, I spoke carefully, keeping emotion out of it. "I don't see them as often as I'd like."

She nodded slowly. "I hope their dad comes back."

"Me too. You close to your folks?" I asked, veering the conversation away from the dysfunctional MacLeods.

A huge sigh escaped her. "Yes. Too close. They only live like a mile away, and my mother loves to drop in."

"Should I be nervous?" I glanced over my shoulder, which made her laugh.

"No. She's in bed by now, I'm sure. She goes bananas at Christmas, and tomorrow starts the three-day countdown." She shook her head. "She drives me crazy this time of year."

"Must have been nice when you were a kid. Before I moved in with my grandmother, we never even had a tree."

Her face fell. "That's terrible. God, I'm sorry. I'm such a brat to complain about anything. I have great parents."

I grimaced. What the hell was I doing? Not only was I telling her private stuff, I was being depressing as fuck. "Don't be sorry. That's my fault for saying that, and it really wasn't that big a deal. We had nice Christmases later on. My grandmother didn't have a lot of money, but she made up for it in other ways. I think she always felt she'd fucked up with my dad, so I felt like a second chance for her."

"What about your grandfather?"

"I don't really know. He was in the military, I think, but he was long gone by the time Aaron and I moved up here, and she never talked about him." I shrugged. "Another drifter, I guess." She nodded slowly, and I could see her processing things. *Like how fucked up my family is compared to hers. I bet her parents adore her. I bet they all have matching pajamas they wear on Christmas morning, and they sit around watching each other open gifts and sipping hot chocolate from matching mugs that say Proud to be French.*

"Think your brother will come home in time for Christmas?" Claire asked.

"I fucking hope so, but I'm not sure. I want to bring a tree over there for them tomorrow."

She perked up. "That's a great idea! Can I—"

The oven timer went off, and I was glad for the distraction. I had the feeling she'd been about to ask if she could meet the girls or help with the tree, and I had to stick to my one night only rule. I had to.

For her sake.

Claire had the kind of heart that was big enough to let anybody in, even me. I couldn't let her do it.

"Oooooh!" Claire squealed as she took the rolls from the oven. "They look so good! And no explosions. The magic is safely contained."

"Good."

She set the pan on the table. "Do we need plates?"

"Nah. Let's just eat them right from the pan. That's what I used to do." I dropped into one of four chairs around the table and pulled her onto my lap. "Come here."

Laughing, she sat across my legs. "Can I try one now?"

"No. They have to cool a little. Learned that lesson the hard way. Scorched the fuck out of my tongue."

"Want me to kiss it better?"

"Actually, yes."

Her mouth on mine, her hands in my hair, her ass in my lap, the scent of magic in the air...there was nothing about this moment that wasn't perfection.

She pulled away and inhaled deeply. "Oh my God. They smell so good. *Now* can I try, please?"

"Yes." I grabbed one and took a bite, and the taste turned back the clock twenty years. "Oh man. That's like heaven."

She took a bite and moaned. "It is," she said, her mouth full. "Oh my God."

"Told you." I finished mine in two more bites and reached for another.

"It's like—oh crumb, look what I just did." She tipped her chin to her chest and giggled. "The magic just dripped onto my cleavage."

"Please allow me." Angling her body so I could lick her chest, I swept my tongue across the top of her breast. *Actu-*

ally, this is like heaven. I don't need to turn the clock back—I just need to stop it right here.

She shivered. "That feels good."

"I'm so glad you think so," I said, "because you just gave me a fucking fantastic idea." I bit into the puff in my hand and let the syrupy insides spill onto her chest on purpose.

She giggled as I licked it up, and my dick started to swell. "When's it my turn?"

"Go for it," I told her, eating the rest of the pastry. "Better hurry, because the magic disappears fast."

One night only.

"Say no more." She finished the puff in her hand and stood to grab another one, then she straddled me. "Let's see if I can do it right." With her eyes on mine, she took a small bite, pushed my shirt aside and tipped the sticky sweetness onto my chest. It dripped over my left nipple, and my cock surged when her tongue hit my skin.

She closed her eyes and licked the syrup off slowly, each stroke of her tongue making my blood rush faster. I ran my hands over her ass as she circled my nipple with her tongue, sucked it into her mouth. She did the same to the other one even though she'd spilled nothing on it. Then she kissed her way up my chest, sliding her hands over my shoulders beneath my shirt. I'd never felt anything like the softness of her mouth on me, and no one had ever kissed me this way— tenderly, slowly, asking nothing in return. When her lips reached mine, I wrapped my arms around her, holding her close.

I'd never forget the taste of this kiss as long as I lived.

"WHAT TIME IS IT?" I asked as we put ourselves back

together. We could now cross Have Sex On Vintage Kitchen Table off our lists.

"Um." Claire pulled her shirt over her head and squinted at something behind me. She was sitting on the table, her legs criss-crossed like a kid's. Those fucking bunny pants were killing me. So much about her was youthful, even childlike—her exuberance, her trusting nature, her excitement over small things—but she was all woman, too. She had curves that made me dizzy, and once she gave herself permission, she moved her body in ways that left no doubt she knew what she wanted and how to get it.

I'd been more than happy to give it to her—but my time was about up. As enticing as she was, I was not a stayer.

"It's after midnight," she said. "Has your car turned back into a pumpkin?"

"Probably."

"Good. Then you have to stay." She smiled devilishly and fluttered her steepled fingers. I'd pulled her hair loose again, and it hung in thick waves past her shoulders. I fucking loved that hair.

"I've really corrupted you, huh?" I buttoned up my shirt. "I'm starting to feel bad. You were such a sweet girl before I got my hands on you."

"I'm making up for lost time. And I'm learning."

"You're a star student. Teacher's pet."

She smiled back, a little color blooming in her cheeks.

I cleared my throat. "Your table can sure take a hell of a beating. It's pretty sturdy for an antique."

"Yeah, not too bad for a fifty-dollar garage sale find."

"Really? That's all you paid?"

"Yeah, and that even included the chairs." She glanced at the one we'd been sitting on. They were wood with upholstered cushions, the fabric faded and threadbare.

"Which need to be re-covered, of course, but this whole place is a work in progress. That's what my mother doesn't get—she comes over here and sees what it's become over time because it hasn't been taken care of, but I see what it could be. The bones beneath the dirt and dust are beautiful, they just need a little love." She ran a hand over a tiny gouge in the wood. "Anyway, sorry for running on." She laughed gently as she hopped off the table. "I get a little carried away talking about this house and things in it."

"Don't apologize. It's good you see the potential beyond the surface of things. That's a gift."

Suddenly she looped her arms around my waist. "What's your gift?"

"My gift? You mean besides my superhuman sexual skills?"

She giggled and slapped my ass. "Yes."

"Hmm." *I'm an excellent liar. A damn good thief. And I'm a pro at a clean getaway—usually.* Although tonight I was having trouble with that. "I'll go with my instincts. I think I read people pretty well."

She sighed. "You read me right, that's for sure."

"You were easy." I gave her a little squeeze. "You wear your heart on your sleeve."

She tipped her head back and looked up at me. "I do?"

"Yes. And someday, some lucky guy is going to come along and steal it." I didn't love the idea, which annoyed me.

"He sure is taking his time."

"Lucky for me."

She smiled. "I had an amazing time tonight, Theo."

"Me too." Time to make my exit. Her smile was putting weird thoughts in my head. "But I should get going."

In the living room, I put my jacket on, slung my tie around my neck, and slipped into socks and shoes. Claire stood near the door, one foot on top of the other, her arms wrapped around herself like she was cold. The thought of it made my chest tight. *It's freezing tonight. Maybe I could just—*

Are you nuts? What's with you tonight? Get the fuck out of here.

Buttoning my coat, I moved for the door. "See you," I tossed off as I passed her. It was an asshole move, but sometimes the shoe fits.

Five seconds later, I was alone on the porch with the door shut behind me. *Fuck.* It was like going from a steaming hot shower into an ice bath. Frowning, I braced myself against the bitter cold, icy air stinging my nasal passages and lungs as I hustled through the freezing dark to my car.

It would have been so easy to turn around and go back inside, stay the night in her cozy little fairy-tale house with its Christmas lights and delicious scents and her warm, soft body next to mine. *It would feel so good.*

But I couldn't do it.

I threw the car in reverse and backed out of the driveway, then shoved it into drive and took off down the street, tires spinning in the snow.

FOURTEEN

Claire

WOW. OK then.

I stood there for a moment, staring at the front door, a little in shock that he'd actually just walked out so abruptly, with barely a glance in my direction. In all honesty, I kind of thought it might be one of his games. Like he might knock on the door a minute later and say he'd only been kidding and sure, he'd stay.

So I kept standing there.

One full minute ticked by. A car door slammed.

Another minute. The engine came to life.

A third minute. Headlights flashed through the living room window as he backed out of the drive and pulled away.

Well. I guess that's that.

My mouth turned down as I realized that he was really gone. Maybe it had taken him some additional willpower as he sat there in his car, but in the end, he'd left. It was amazing to me that a person could change gears like that. One moment, he was hugging me in the kitchen and saying sweet things, and the next he was bolting for the door like he didn't even care that we'd never see each other again.

Of course, that was assuming a few things.

That he even *had* feelings.

That he hadn't been pretending.

That tonight had been more than just business as usual.

I really had no evidence that any of those things were true. What I did have was sore muscles, tangled hair, and memories of what had been the hottest night of my life. In fact, if I hadn't *had* the sore muscles and tangled hair as proof, I might have thought I'd dreamed it.

Slowly, as if I was moving through mud, I turned off the kitchen light, the Christmas tree lights, and plodded into the bathroom.

What are you moping about? I asked my reflection as I brushed my teeth. *You got exactly what you wanted. You fooled everyone at the wedding, you didn't have to sit at the singles table, and you had an unbelievable night with a hot guy who gave you like eleventy orgasms. What more do you want, greedypants?*

I scowled at myself, toothpaste froth all over my mouth.

You knew all night long this was a one-time thing. He told you it was, flat out. You said it was fine. You said all you wanted was a good time. You said no expectations.

After rinsing my toothbrush, I washed my face, turned off the lights and dragged my sorry ass upstairs, continuing to berate myself.

Did you think it would go another way? Did you think your hired hottie would turn out to be The One? What the hell would you tell your kids? "Daddy and I met the night I paid him three hundred dollars to be my pretend boyfriend so I wouldn't look like a loser. Isn't that romantic?"

Angry with myself, I got into bed and pulled the covers over my head, curling into a ball on my side. Maybe I was doomed to be unhappy. No matter what I did, it backfired. I played it safe, I didn't meet anyone I like. I took a risk, I met the wrong guy. Unfortunately, I happened to like him.

I flopped over to the other side. It just seemed so unfair. Finally, *finally*, after years of trying, I felt the *thing* with someone, and we'd never see each other again. Had it been one-sided?

Maybe it had. A guy like Theo probably had all kinds of beautiful women panting after him everywhere he went. What would he want with a girl who might wear red lipstick and talk dirty on a Saturday night but wanted to cuddle in bed on a Sunday? Who said she had no expectations but was crushed when he left her at the door? Who believed in soul mates and *wanted* to be tied to someone?

When the dirty talk was over, he'd want nothing with a girl like that.

A girl like me.

FIFTEEN

Theo

AFTER A SHITTY NIGHT'S sleep during which I swear I kept smelling Claire next to me, I woke up in a bad mood. Why, I had no idea. I'd had a great time, a bunch of great sex, and even enjoyed a little trip down memory lane to one of the happier times in my life. Then I'd gotten out without disappointing her. What the hell did I have to be grouchy about?

I went to the gym and worked out, hoping a good, punishing sweat would make me feel better. It didn't.

I decided it must be concern for my brother's family making me feel down. So after cleaning up, I thought I'd go get a little Christmas tree for Josie and the girls. Seeing their happy faces and watching them decorate it would cheer me up. Maybe I could try to figure out what each of them wanted from Santa, and if Josie hadn't gotten it all taken care of—which I doubted—I'd go shopping for them.

Before I left, I checked my email and calendar, where I

noticed a reminder to invoice Claire for the balance of her date. Frowning, I deleted it. Somehow I'd give her hundred bucks back too—now I felt bad that I'd even taken it.

On the way to the tree farm, I stopped to grab a cup of coffee and a donut, and as I sipped the scalding hot dark roast, I remembered watching Claire rush into Great Lakes Coffee, nervous and flustered and much, much prettier than I'd expected. If I were the kind of guy who said things like, *She took my breath away*, that's what I'd say about Claire. Probably I should have introduced myself right away, but in those situations I liked taking a few minutes to size people up, see what my intuition told me about them. It gave me the upper hand.

The donut was OK, but it didn't taste half as good as those magic things she and I'd made last night. Funny how some things from childhood—your favorite movie, that song you loved, the fucking beanie you thought made you look cool but only made you look like a dipshit—don't have the same appeal later in life. But that sweet taste had been just as good as I'd remembered, if not better. I wondered if Aaron had ever taught the girls to make those. Probably not, since he hadn't really been around when our grandma and I were making them. *Maybe I'll pick up some groceries too. Do a little baking with the girls. They'll love that.*

My spirits lifted.

At the tree farm, I chose one I thought would fit in their living room, helped the guy tie it to the top of my car, and then hit Meijer for a tree stand and some strands of lights in case theirs didn't work. I also grabbed crescent rolls, marshmallows, butter, sugar, and cinnamon, my excitement building. On the way to my brother's house, I briefly wondered what Claire was doing today. Was she working on her house? Painting? Had she slept late? Or had she, like me, been restless all night and woken up early?

"Enough," I muttered as I pulled into the driveway. "Put her out of your fucking mind already."

That was easier to do once the kids spotted the tree. I heard them shouting and banging on the window as I untied it from the car, and a minute later all three came racing out the front door with their boots on but no winter coats. They all talked at once, and I couldn't keep the grin off my face.

"Is that for us?"

"Is that a real tree?"

"Did you chop it down?"

"Can we help decorate it?"

"We never had a real tree before!"

"Does Mommy know?"

"Daddy's home!"

At that one, I stopped what I was doing and looked behind me. "What did you say?"

"We never had a real tree before," said Ava, her blue eyes wide.

"No, after that." I scanned their faces, thinking I must have heard wrong. I'd just been here two days ago. No sign of Aaron. "Did someone say your dad is home?"

"Yes!" Hailey jumped up and down, smiling proudly that her voice had been heard. "He's back!"

"Girls!" Josie's voice carried from the front door. "Get in here without your coats on! It's freezing!"

I looked at her, the question on my face. She nodded and smiled.

I turned away.

The girls scurried back into the house, and I returned to the task of freeing the tree, my hands moving a little slower now. I always felt this weird mix of things when my brother came home. Relief that he was home safe. Happiness that his wife and kids had him back. Anger that he'd left them again in the first place. Frustration that he couldn't seem to overcome his problems. Guilt because so much of his pain stemmed from the abuse he'd suffered at the hands of our father, abuse he'd taken to protect me while I hid upstairs or in the basement or in the yard, covering my ears and wishing I could fly.

And underneath it all, so shameful I didn't even want to acknowledge it, was resentment that my role in his family would now be reduced. It was so stupid, and I hated myself for feeling it, but some secret part of me enjoyed being the man his family depended on. Enjoyed the responsibility of taking care of people. Enjoyed the way they looked at me, trusting and grateful. When my brother was gone, I got to feel that for a while. When he was home, all that was gone.

Immediately I felt like shit.

Don't be a dick. They're not your family. It's not your house. You don't even want a wife, let alone kids or a home. How the hell would you make that work, anyway? What if you got caught in a scam and sent back to jail? How do you think your family would feel about you then?

I braced two hands on the frame of my SUV and took a few slow, deep breaths, trying to get my head on straight.

But I didn't feel right in my skin.

INSIDE THE HOUSE, I put the groceries away in the kitchen—my earlier excitement about baking with the girls had been snuffed out—and set up the tree stand in the corner of the front room.

Josie shushed the excited kids. "Daddy's still sleeping," she said, putting a finger to her lips.

I kept quiet as I hauled the tree inside and fixed it in the stand, thinking it should be Aaron doing this for his family and not me. Aaron wondering if his pregnant wife had made her doctor appointment yet. Aaron asking how Peyton's ears were and if the medicine had worked.

"Yes. She's better." My sister-in-law lowered her voice. "And I haven't made the appointment yet, but I'm going to."

I frowned but held my tongue. Scolding her wasn't my place. "Can you hold the tree?"

"Sure." Josie held the tree steady while I got beneath it to make sure it wouldn't tip over in the stand.

"Mommy, where are the ornaments?" Ava asked.

"In the basement. Why don't you go down there and see if you can find the boxes?" she said brightly.

The girls traipsed into the kitchen and down the basement steps, leaving us in silence. When the tree was secure, I got to my feet and glanced toward the closed bedroom door.

"When?"

"Yesterday." She still looked tired, but her cheeks were flushed with pink. Her hair had been washed.

I crossed my arms over my chest. "He sober?"

"Yes."

"He OK?"

Josie nodded. "Looked a little rough when he got in, but he cleaned up. He's just tired now, but he's so glad to be home."

I fought off the anger and tried to focus on the relief. On moving forward. "So what now?"

"He says he's going to do better. Get a new job."

"Is he going to go to rehab?"

Her eyes dropped. "We can't afford that."

"I've told him a thousand times I'd pay for it."

"He won't go. He's too proud."

"Meetings then. AA. He could get a sponsor."

"I...I don't know if he would. He always says he doesn't need them."

"You have to tell him that's the condition, Josie. If he keeps drinking, he's going to keep doing this." My voice rose. I didn't mean to be hard on her, but sobriety was the only hope Aaron had. Without it, he'd never heal enough to take care of his family. I didn't even want to think about what gutter or cell I'd be in if I hadn't quit drinking.

"Shhh. I know." Her eyes were glassy with tears. "But he just got here, OK? I didn't want to say anything that would make him angry or ashamed. I just wanted him to stay."

The bedroom door opened, and my brother appeared in jeans and a black t-shirt, his hair combed. At the sight of him, my chest got tight. Without thinking we walked toward each other and hugged. No matter what, he was my brother and I loved him. We'd been through so much together, and I didn't want to give up on him, but fuck—he had to try harder.

"Glad you're back." I stepped back from him and assessed his appearance. We were built alike, both tall and muscular, thick through the chest with strong arms and hands. His nose was crooked, since it had been broken more than once, and his beard was longer, but we had the same brown eyes and short dark hair.

"Me too." He cleared his throat. "Thanks."

From downstairs we heard the shouts of the girls and some banging noises, and Josie sighed. "I'll go help them. They're probably making a big mess."

As soon as we were alone, I spoke. "Josie said you're sober?"

"Yes." Aaron shoved his hands in his pockets.

"Tell me you're going to stay that way."

"I'm gonna try."

"You have to do more than try, Aaron." I tried to keep my voice down, but it was hard. "This shit can't happen anymore. You've got a pregnant wife and three daughters."

"You think I don't know that?" My brother's eyes filled with tears, and he struggled to hold them off. "Every day I was away from them was agony. I kept drinking just to numb myself from the pain of missing them. They're everything to me."

"Then act like it," I snapped, surprising even myself. I wasn't normally this hard on him. "Where the fuck were you?"

"Different places."

"Working?"

"Some construction jobs here and there."

"Josie needed you. Those kids needed a father."

He closed his eyes. "I know. Thanks for being here for them."

"Well, I'm not doing this anymore." It wasn't true. I'd always be there for them, but my brother needed to hear some hard words. If he thought I'd always be there to step in for him every time he bailed, he'd never have a reason to change. "Get your shit together and be a husband. Be a father. Be a *man*."

"I will." He took a breath. "I need to get a job."

"You have to stay sober to get a job."

"I *told* you, I'm gonna try." His hands came out of his pockets, fingers curling into fists. "But every time I make a promise, I can't fucking keep it, so I'm not making any more promises. I just set myself up for failure."

I inhaled and exhaled through my nose, jaw clenched tight. "Whatever you have to do, whatever you have to tell yourself, make it happen, Aaron. Or you're going to end up alone."

"Josie said she would never leave me," he said stubbornly.

"Good thing one of you can keep a promise." I heard the kids chattering excitedly as they came up the steps, but suddenly I wasn't in the mood for Christmas. Josie and the girls would want time alone with Aaron, and he needed time with them. It needed to sink in how lucky he was to have all this to come back to. "I gotta go."

I heard him calling to me as I went out the front door, but I didn't turn back. Two minutes later I was speeding down the street, no idea where to go, no place to put all these conflicting feelings, and no one to talk to about it. Moving around and keeping to myself as much as I did meant I had a lot of acquaintances in various places, but no close friends. Josie and Aaron were really all I had.

The longer I drove around, the more worked up I got. I was mad at my father for taking out his rage on his children, for not teaching us how to be men. I was mad at my brother for fucking up the best thing in his life—his family. I was mad at Josie for not standing up for herself and her kids. I was mad at myself for being resentful that Aaron had come home. And I was mad at the mother I didn't remember, whose only lesson to her sons was that love wasn't enough to make someone stay. How dare she leave that note? Sometimes I thought the note had fucked me up worse than her leaving.

About the only person I could think of that I wasn't mad

at was Claire. As soon as she entered my mind, my entire body thrummed with heat, my insides pulling tight. I wanted to feel the way I had last night. I wanted that warm, sexy magic. I wanted to lose myself inside her, be surrounded by her sweetness, see her smile, hear her laugh. I wanted to smell her hair, taste her kiss, touch her skin. I wanted to undress her, whisper dirty words, play our little games. I wanted her to look at me again like she had last night, like she trusted me, like I was worthy of her trust.

I wasn't an idiot. I knew nothing could come of it. I wasn't worthy of her or her trust—it was all pretend.

But damn, it had made me feel good.

I needed to feel good again.

SIXTEEN

Claire

WHEN I LOOKED at my phone the morning after the wedding, I noticed I'd missed five texts from Jaime and three calls.

7:52 PM Hey, how's it going?

9:07 PM Hellooooo? Are you alive?

9:32 PM Missed call.

10:25 PM Either you're having a great time or you're stuffed in a trunk and I'd really appreciate knowing which one it is, thanks.

10:30 PM Missed call.

10:50 PM I just sent Quinn to your house.

10:56 PM Missed call.

11:24 PM Quinn says there is a car in your driveway, lights on in your house, and no sign of foul play. If you are not dead, I'm going to kill you because you promised to keep in touch.

Oops. I'd forgotten all about that promise what with all the excitement (and by excitement I mean orgasms). I texted her quickly that I was fine, I was sorry, and I'd call her with details after I made coffee.

Her reply: **Boo you whore.**

Smiling for the first time since Theo had left, I got the coffee going, picked up my phone, and called her.

"Hello?"

"Hey, it's Claire. I'm sorry."

"You should be, I was having heart attacks all night imagining all the terrible places your lifeless body could be stashed."

"I'm fine."

"Are you? You don't sound that fine."

Sighing, I leaned both elbows on the counter and watched the coffee brew. "I'm alive and unharmed, I mean."

"What happened with the guy?"

"We had a good time."

"Did anyone suspect he was a fake date?"

"Not that I know of. And actually, it kind of turned into a real date."

"What?! Details. Stat."

"Well, at some point in the night, things just started to feel...real, I guess." My stomach flipped as I recalled the moment on the dance floor.

"And then what?"

"And then when he brought me home, I asked him to come in."

Jaime squealed. "Did he?"

"Yeah." I closed my eyes, feeling him sink into me again and again. "He did."

"And? You're killing me!"

"And we had fun."

"How much fun?"

"A *lot* of fun."

Jaime gasped. "How many times did you have fun?"

"Three. Once on the living room floor and twice in the kitchen." Pride made me smile a little bit—I could just imagine her eyes bugging out of her head at how un-Claire that was. *Turns out I am audacious. At least with Theo.*

"The *kitchen?*" she shrieked.

My smile widened. "Uh huh. The last time was on the kitchen table." Something clattered in my ear.

"Sorry," she said a moment later. "I dropped my phone. I'm in shock. So that was his car Quinn saw?"

"Yes." The coffee pot hissed as it finished brewing, and I grabbed a mug from the cupboard that said *The earth without art is just "eh"* on it, a gift from a former student. I poured myself a cup and opened the fridge to grab the cream. "And I get it. I even shocked myself."

"But you had a good time, right?"

"A great time. Best I've ever had with any guy."

"So why do you sound like you regret it?"

After pouring in a little cream, I added some sugar. The sight of it reminded me of licking Theo's fingers, and my body went weightless for a moment. "I definitely don't regret it. I just wish he wanted to see me again."

"Why doesn't he?" Jaime sounded outraged.

I put the lid on the sugar bowl and returned the cream to the fridge. "Because he made it very clear right from the get-go that he was not looking for anything more than fun."

"But if it was so good, and if you're both just looking for fun, why not see each other again?"

Leaning back against the counter, I took a small sip of coffee. "He said he's not in town very long and doesn't know when he'll be back."

"Why? What does he do?"

"I don't know," I admitted. "I thought he was a pilot, but that turned out to be more of a hobby. I actually know very little about him—not what he does, not where he lives, not even his real last name."

"What the fuck? He didn't give you his last name?"

"Well, he gave me *a* last name." I almost laughed at the memory. "Woodcock."

"*Woodcock*? That can't be real."

"No, I don't think it is. Although it fits him."

Jaime didn't laugh. "This is weird, Claire. Why is he so secretive? What's he got to hide? A wife, you think?"

"No, I don't think it's that."

"Then what?"

"I don't know. Maybe he's just really serious about his privacy."

"Maybe he'll come around. Get in touch again."

"I doubt it. We didn't even exchange numbers. The only place we ever communicated was through the Hotties for Hire site."

"Sounds like you communicated pretty well in the kitchen too."

I glanced over at the kitchen table. Would I ever be able to look at it again and not think of the way he moved? The way he drove me to clutch and claw and beg? The way he made my body yearn and stretch and quiver? "Yeah."

Jaime sighed. "I'm sorry, Claire. I mean, I'm glad you had a great time, and I'm proud of you for coloring outside the lines a little, but I wish you were happier about it."

"I'm happy about it." It wasn't entirely a lie. "It did feel good to be a little daring. And I learned some things about myself."

"Such as?"

I thought for a moment. "I like a dirty mouth."

She snickered. "Me too."

"And I shouldn't be ashamed of what I want."

"Fuck no."

"I can wear red lipstick."

"Wait—red lipstick? You don't wear red lipstick."

"I did last night. I've been thinking about Margot a lot, about the night she threw those scones. I wanted to channel some of that badassery."

Jaime laughed. "I think you succeeded."

"But I also learned I'm not good at the whole 'no expectations' thing. I told him it was OK and I just wanted to have a good time for a night, but when it was time to say goodbye, I was sad. I wanted there to be a next time."

"God, I used to be great at the no-expectations-sex thing. But you know what? I've learned to embrace the expectations. I don't always live up to them and neither does Quinn, but we try and we forgive and we make it up to each other. There's something to be said for that give and take. Don't feel bad for wanting it."

"I guess I don't." I tried to find the bright side. "I had fun. That's more than I expected. And what happened between us didn't have to mean everything, I only wish it had meant *something*."

"I'm sorry. Want to hang out this afternoon? Go shopping? See a movie or something?"

"Actually, I have some things around the house I need to work on today. Maybe tonight?"

"I'm having dinner with Quinn tonight. He's cooking."

"Oh." Of course she was. Saturday night was for boyfriends.

"Why don't you join us? He's making pierogi," she said temptingly.

"No, thanks. Quinn's cooking is always delicious, but I'll just be in the way."

"Claire, come on. You're always welcome here. And I hate to think of you alone and sad."

"Really, I'm fine," I said, although I wasn't, not really. I felt oddly close to tears, in fact. "I've got a ton of stuff to do today. I'll catch up with you tomorrow."

"Invitation is always open if you change your mind."

"Thanks. I'll talk to you later."

"OK. Bye."

I hung up and set the phone down, then took a deep breath and a big gulp of hot coffee to keep my cool. No need to cry over this disappointment. I still had friends and family and the house to work on, and maybe later I'd paint or sketch a little. That always made me feel better.

AFTER TWO CUPS of coffee and a blueberry muffin, I threw on some old clothes, put my hair up, and tackled the kitchen cabinets. I had the next two weeks off school for winter break, and I planned to spend as much time as possible working on the house.

Luckily the kitchen wasn't too big, so there were only eight doors. I liked the original finish on the wood, but it was faded and speckled. My mother had tried to talk me into painting them white to create a brighter kitchen (as well as hiring someone to do the work), but a dark stain felt more authentic to me. I didn't mind that the kitchen wasn't bright —its earth tones were warm and natural. Plus I was planning to lay a light-colored tile on the floor, and that would brighten things a little.

After laying an old sheet down in the empty dining

room, I took the cabinet doors off and set them on top of the sheet. Then I took everything out of the cupboards and washed out the insides. After that, I removed the hardware and cleaned the doors and facing with a mixture of TSP and water. While I waited for them to dry, I did some laundry, changed the sheets on my bed, and cleaned the bathroom.

Despite the fact that I was trying to use the work as a distraction, Theo was constantly present in my mind. Maybe because he'd offered to work on the cabinets last night or because we'd spent so much time in the kitchen, or maybe just because I was still bummed about never seeing him again when we'd had so much fun. I kept picturing his smile, his chest, his hands. Hearing his laugh. Tasting his kiss. Feeling his hands in my hair.

Get over it, Claire. Quit thinking about him.

But as I sanded and dusted the cupboards, I thought about his offer to fix the crooked ones last night. When I mixed an ounce of the stain into a gallon of varnish and painted it on, the color reminded me of his eyes, dark and shiny. And when I applied a coat to the cabinet facing, I stood right where I had last night and thought, *Right here. This is where I stood when he pulled my hair and whispered in my ear and made me come so hard my knees buckled.*

Such a bad girl. To want me this way.

His cock pounding into me again and again.

Right here. Right here. Right here.

My core muscles clenched, and I knew if I touched myself, I'd be wet.

I had to get out of the kitchen. Better yet, out of the house. At that point, I had to wait at least two hours for the varnish to dry anyway, so I decided to clean up and head over to Jaime and Quinn's. Maybe some wine and conversation would get my mind off Theo.

I took a shower and dressed in jeans and a white cami. Once my hair was dry, I'd add a soft gray poncho sweater. I was coming down the stairs with my wet hair hanging down my back when I heard three loud knocks on the front door.

I paused, one hand on the banister, wondering who it could be. Jaime? My mother? But I barely had time to think before I heard three more sharp raps.

"Coming," I called out, hurrying the rest of the way down the stairs. I pulled open the front door, and a rush of cold air swept in.

My breath caught—it was Theo.

"I need you," he said, stepping across the threshold and taking my head in his hands. "I need you."

SEVENTEEN

Theo

SHE WAS EXACTLY the salve I'd hoped she would be—the moment I crushed my lips to hers, I felt the conflict in my body resolve. The anger dissipate. The sadness lift. All of it was swept aside, replaced only by the desire to get closer to her.

I drew her into my body, thrilled when she wrapped her arms around my waist. Leaning back against the door to push it shut, I brought her with me, stroking her damp hair, sliding my palms down her bare shoulders.

"You're here," she said breathlessly, tipping her head back to look up at me. Surprise and delight lit up her face, which was devoid of any makeup.

"Yes." I kissed her mouth, her cheek, her jaw, her throat. Buried my face in her neck and inhaled the sweet, clean scent of her skin. "I couldn't stop thinking about you."

"I feel the same," she whispered, tilting her head to give me better access to her neck and chest.

My lips brushed across her collarbone, over the top of her breast, and I felt her shiver. She ran her hands up the front of my chest, and I hated that I couldn't feel her touch through the leather.

"Let's go upstairs," she whispered, backing up and taking me with her.

I shrugged out of my coat and dropped it at our feet, then I picked her up, groaning as she wrapped her legs around me and slipped her tongue between my lips. I carried her up the stairs into her bedroom, breaking the kiss only long enough to make sure I'd reached the top and wouldn't bump into anything. To my surprise, this entire level of the house was one open area, her bed at the back and a little art studio set up in the front by the east-facing window.

I moved quickly for the bed and tipped her onto her back, taking a second to ditch my boots. She scrambled to her knees and grabbed the bottom of my Henley and t-shirt, lifting them up. I helped her get them over my head, then did the same to her little white top. Reaching behind her, I unclasped her bra and she flung it aside, immediately throwing her arms around my neck.

I crushed my mouth to hers, moaning at the feel of her bare chest pressed against mine. Last night's sexual escapades had been a blast, but they'd been frantic and fast —we'd never even taken the time to get all the way undressed. This time I didn't want to leave any inch of her skin unexplored. I was determined to feel every part of her against every part of me.

"You feel so good," she breathed, running her hands all over me. "I can't get enough."

"Try," I told her.

She laughed lightly and kissed a path down my chest,

her hands moving to the button and zipper of my jeans. My heart beat hard in my chest as she pushed them and my underwear down. I kicked them all the way off, breathing heavily as she spread her knees wider, lowered her head in front of me and looked up.

Fuck yes.

The late afternoon light spilled in through both windows, which were far enough away that no one could see us, but close enough that I could make out the devilish expression on her face. She braced herself on one hand and used the other to grip my shaft and run the tip of my cock over her lips, tracing the shape of her full mouth. When I felt her tongue sweep over the crown, I sucked air between my teeth, making her smile.

She took her time, relishing every decadent swirl, every velvet stroke, every impatient throb. When she finally slipped her lips over the tip, sucking gently, I groaned, my hands moving automatically to her hair, holding it out of the way so I could watch her.

As if she was in no particular hurry, she lavished a few minutes on just the crown, driving me insane with the need to feel her plush, hot lips sliding over my entire cock. Her fucking mouth was incredible, soft and silky and full.

"Claire." A growl and a plea.

She laughed from the back of her throat, but she obliged, lowering her head, those plush, petal-smooth lips sliding down my shaft, warm and wet and snug. My knees trembled, and I widened my stance for stability, my jaw dropping in ecstatic disbelief as she worked her mouth up and down my cock, one hand gripping the base.

"Fuck, you can take me so deep." I was riveted by the sight of her head bobbing slowly in front of my hips, elated at the sounds she made, at the way she seemed to be enjoying herself. My eyes traveled over her whole body, the hair streaming down her bare back, the curve of her waist, the perfect ass in tight jeans sticking up in the air. My hands tightened in her hair.

She moaned and took me in as far as she could, her hand pumping up and down what her mouth couldn't handle. I struggled to maintain control, allowing myself only the smallest thrusts between her lips. Inside me a battle waged between a monster desperate to do unspeakable things to this angel on her knees for me, and a man who wanted to maintain control. The pressure inside me was building, pushing me toward the edge, and I kept pulling back, pulling back, pulling back, because I never wanted this to end. And the more I fought the release, the harder she worked me. *Goddamn, she's good at this! How is she so good at this?*

Just when I thought it couldn't get any better, she pulled my dick from her mouth and flipped onto her back, her hair and head and neck hanging over the edge.

She reached for me. "I want to make you come like this. Let me."

I almost lost it.

Willing myself to hold on for one more miraculous minute, I guided my cock between her lips, watching as she took me in deep. Jaw-dropping, mind-blowing, eye-popping deep. Her hands gripped my hips, moving me in and out, while I looked on in amazement and fought the insane urge not only to come but to tell her I loved her, propose marriage, and offer to father her children if only she'd just keep doing what she was doing. For a moment, I was paralyzed with pleasure, but then my body took over, my hips rocking with the rhythm she set, my cock pumping hard and quick into her mouth.

What the fuck is she doing to me? I can hardly breathe! What's that sound? Is that my pulse? It sounds like a marching band is in the room. I think I'm having a heart attack. It's beating way too hard. I'm going to die. This is it. This is it! Oh my fucking God, this is iiiiiiit…

I didn't die. But I did come harder than I ever had before, in several seconds of earth-shattering bursts, grunting and gasping as my cock throbbed between her lips. As my vision clouded with silver, I imagined the way I was filling her mouth, sharing myself in the most intimate, most erotic, most dominant way possible. But it was the craziest thing—she was powerless beneath me, yet I felt vulnerable to her.

What the fuck was happening?

When I could see straight again, Claire was still gasping for breath, her head on the bed again. Wait, she'd swallowed? Maybe I *would* propose.

OK, I wasn't *that* crazy.

But there were other things I could do.

"Miss French, you are a very naughty girl." I walked around the side of the bed, staring down at her. "Where did you learn to do that?"

She propped herself up on her elbows and smiled. "I read it in a book once. Did you like it?"

I grabbed her by the ankles and yanked her legs toward me, rotating her body so she lay across the bed. "I think you just swallowed that answer."

She licked her lips.

"And now," I said, unbuttoning her jeans and peeling them off, "it's my turn." I pulled her toward the edge of the bed and dropped to my knees.

"You don't have to."

I flung her legs over my shoulders and gave her a look. "Are you fucking kidding me?"

"No. I did that because I wanted to, not because I expected anything in return."

"Good, because I'm not doing this for you. I've had a very bad day and the only thing that will make it better is the taste of your pussy and the sound of you screaming my name while I make you come. Got a problem with that?"

She smiled. "No."

"Good." I stroked up her center and felt the tremor in her legs. "Now let's get started."

WHEN WE FINALLY WANDERED DOWNSTAIRS AFTER a ninety-minute nap (neither of us had slept well last night), it was about six o'clock and both of us were hungry.

"My kitchen is a mess," she said, picking up my coat from the floor at the foot of the steps. I followed her through the living room, where she tossed my coat on the couch, and into the dining room. "I started the cabinet rehab today."

"Wow, you did." I switched on the light and examined her work. "Nicely done. I like the stain. Needs another coat, huh?"

"Yeah, that was the plan, but I got—"

"Naked?"

She giggled. "I was going to say distracted."

"Not sorry."

"Me neither."

Our eyes met, and something happened inside my chest, a quickening. It was slightly terrifying, and also kind of nice. "What if we order in and get that second coat on tonight?"

She smiled. "Sounds good to me. Pizza?"

"Perfect."

She ordered pizza and a salad and opened a bottle of wine while I retrieved the paint brushes from the basement sink, stirred up the varnish, and got started. "Want a glass?" she called from the kitchen.

"No, thanks. Actually, I don't drink." It felt like a safe piece of myself to share, and for some reason, I wanted to share a few pieces with her. Just a few.

"At all?" She stood in the doorway between the kitchen and dining room, a glass of red wine in her hand.

"Nope."

"Are you...recovered?"

"You could say that." I painted the cabinet doors with long, even strokes.

"How long?"

"I never went through rehab or anything. But I quit drinking about six years ago. Right after my first niece was born." Another safe piece.

"That's...that's great." She paused. "But now I feel bad for drinking in front of you."

I looked at her guilty expression. "You don't have to feel bad. I don't drink because I didn't like how it made me behave. It was hard to stop once I got started, and I made really bad decisions when I was drunk. But I don't miss it."

"You're sure it's OK?"

"Yes. Promise."

I got all eight doors coated by the time the food arrived, and Claire did the facing in the kitchen. While I washed out the brushes in the basement, she set the kitchen table with dishes from a box in one corner of the room.

"So what's next after the cabinets?" I asked her as she filled two bowls with salad.

"The floors, I think. I want tile, but I haven't picked it out yet. Know any good tile places?"

"Actually, I do." I sat down and opened the pizza box, placing a slice on Claire's plate and then on mine before closing it up again. "I'll write the name down for you. Or I could take you there."

"Really?" She went completely still, salad bowl in her hand.

"Um. Yeah." It had sort of just slipped out, but it was the kind of thing I enjoyed—helping out someone who needed it. Josie and the girls had Aaron to take care of things at their house now, but Claire was all alone. Just like I was.

Still, I needed to rein myself in. She was going to get confused if I kept sharing things about myself and offering to help her.

"Wow, thanks. That would be great." She set the bowl down in front of me. "What can I get you to drink? Water? Vernor's? Cranberry juice?"

"Vernor's sounds good."

She plunked a few ice cubes in a glass and poured me some ginger ale, then sat across from me and lifted her wine glass. "Cheers to a second date—I haven't had many of those lately."

"Me either." Or first dates. Not real ones, anyway.

Claire set down her glass and picked up her fork. "By the way, I still want to pay you for your time last night—at least the time you spent at the wedding. It's only fair."

I stuck a tomato in my mouth and gave her a look. "Don't be ridiculous. I don't want your money. In fact, I need to give you your hundred bucks back."

"But it's your job." She picked up her wine again and took a quick swallow. "Isn't it?"

"Yeah." It wasn't a complete lie. More of a half-truth. "I also have a carpentry business." Another not-lie.

Her face lit up like I'd given her a gift. "You do?"

"Yes. I've never really been able to make much of it, but I like the work."

"And you're good with your hands." She gave me one of those smiles that chipped away at my rules.

"Thanks."

"I could definitely use your help around here. I have lots of projects."

"I'd be glad to help you." I added quickly, "But I might not be in town too long."

"That's right. You move around a lot. It's one of the only things I know about you."

I cocked a brow. "I'd say you know a few other things about me."

Her eyes met mine. "I know how you taste."

Fuck. I swallowed with difficulty. "Yes. You do."

She focused on her food. "I'd like to know more, but you're such a private person."

"So ask me something," I said, hoping I wouldn't have to lie. Part of me wanted to open up a little, but it didn't come naturally to me.

"What's your last name?"

Crap. Of course she'd want to know that, but it made me searchable. My conviction was public record. But Claire was so trusting, I didn't think she'd race to do a background check. "MacLeod."

She smiled radiantly, as if I'd just given her an amazing gift. "MacLeod. So you're Scottish?"

I shrugged. "No idea, actually."

She took another bite of her salad. "I did a family tree when I was in school. I got back eight generations on both sides."

"Yeah? What'd you find?"

"I'm English, French, Irish, Dutch, and a little German."

"A mutt." I cocked my head. "Suits you."

She kicked me under the table. "Jerk."

After that, she was quiet for a moment, but I could see her struggling with something. Finally she asked, "So are you not a pilot, then? I'm not trying to be nosy, I'm just... trying to get to know you."

I thought about it for a second and decided to answer honestly. "I have a recreational pilot certificate. I don't use it much, though. I wish I did."

"What made you get one of those?"

"Just always wanted to learn to fly."

"But you didn't want a career as a pilot?"

I hesitated before lying. "No. I don't like strict schedules. It wouldn't have suited me. But I do love flying."

"I hate it." She shuddered.

"Why?"

"It's terrifying. I don't understand how something that heavy can even get off the ground, let alone stay up there."

I laughed. "You don't have to understand something to enjoy it, do you? I don't know how to make pizza but I enjoy the hell out of a good slice."

"I'm telling you, just the thought of being on an airplane gives me a panic attack." Her eyes were wide and serious. "My mother is the same way."

"What are you afraid of?"

"Dying!" she said, like duh. "Falling out of the sky!"

I shook my head. "You do know that the odds of dying in a car accident are much, much higher, right?"

"That's different." She sniffed. "I have control in the car. And even if I'm not the driver, at least I know what all the noises and bumps are."

"What happens when you want to go somewhere you can't drive to?"

She sighed. "That is a problem. Because I *do* want to go places like that—Paris. Florence. Madrid..." Her head tilted to one side. "Maybe I'll take a boat."

I laughed. "That's a long boat ride. Can't you just get over your fear long enough to get on a plane and take a sleeping pill or something?"

"I don't know. Maybe someday." Her cheeks flushed slightly. "You probably think it's silly to be so afraid of something."

I shrugged. "Not necessarily."

"What are you afraid of?"

Not wanting to leave here tonight. "Nothing, really."

"I knew it. You're a thrill seeker, huh? I bet you love rollercoasters."

"Uh huh." I swallowed the bite in my mouth. "But not as much as skydiving."

"Skydiving!" she shrieked. "You mean you have purposely jumped out of a perfectly good plane?"

"Many times. Nothing like it."

She looked at me like I was nuts. "What's so great about it?"

"The way it makes you feel. Totally free. Like you could do anything. No limits."

She shook her head slowly. "You're brave. I could never. I'm too afraid of falling, always have been."

I liked it that she called me brave. I liked it that she

thought I was good with my hands. I liked the way it felt to sit at her kitchen table and share a meal and talk.

I liked it so much that I began to be afraid of falling too.

But later, she asked if I wanted to stay.

And I said yes.

EIGHTEEN

Claire

IT WAS BETTER than my fantasies, falling asleep next to Theo. The sheets were sweatier and my hair was messier, but I'd had way, *way* more orgasms, and he was hotter than any man I could have dreamed up. Taller, stronger, dirtier. More handsome, more fun, more complicated.

I still had no idea what had made him come back here tonight, but I was scared that asking him would break the spell. *I need you*, he'd said. What had he meant? Just sex, or something more?

He was an enigma—so open and generous with his body but so closed off when it came to anything personal. I was amazed that he'd shared a few personal details with me tonight. I ran through the list of things I'd learned—last name, quit drinking six years ago, had a pilot license but wasn't a pilot, had a carpentry business on the side, liked skydiving. And last night, he'd mentioned that he was raised by his late grandmother. Parents had both taken off. He had a brother who struggled to stay put, a sister-in-law, and three nieces he played tea party with.

And he fucks like a rockstar.

It was an intriguing picture, but it wasn't very complete. Like a painting with random details drawn here and there, maybe even some color, but other parts of the canvas left blank.

I had no idea how to complete the sketch, no experience getting a man who guarded himself so closely to open up, no way to know how this would play out. All I had were more questions. Who was he, really?

"Theo?"

"Hm?"

"What were you like as a kid?"

He groaned. "More questions?"

"Sorry, sorry." I kissed his chest. "I was just lying here trying to picture you."

"I was a typical kid."

"What did you like to do?"

"Ride my bike. Throw rocks. Make fun of girls."

I poked him in the side. "Tell me about one nice childhood memory from when you were small."

It took him a long time to think of one. "There was a tire swing in our yard when I was little. When I wanted to escape my house, I used to like playing on it."

"We had a tire swing up north at the cabin," I said excitedly. "It's still there, actually."

"Oh yeah?"

"Yeah." I laughed. "You probably won't be surprised to learn I was scared of it at first."

"Of the *tire swing*? Why?"

"Because it was just a rope tied to this skinny old branch. I always thought it would snap."

"Even if it did, you'd only fall a couple feet."

"What can I say? I'm delicate."

"Uh, I beg to differ."

I poked him in the side again and then snuggled closer. "Why'd you want to escape your house?"

He shifted, as if he was uncomfortable. "I don't know. Just didn't like being cooped up, I guess. I still don't."

That made sense. He liked his privacy *and* his freedom.

One thing I knew for sure was that I couldn't pressure him, couldn't make demands, couldn't set limitations or conditions. And honestly, I didn't really want to. He'd told me as soon as he walked in the door he didn't know where this could go, and it had taken me all of three seconds to realize I was OK with that. Even if all he had to offer was orgasms and conversation right now, I'd go with it. I'd be patient.

But lying there, wrapped in his arms, cuddled against his side with my head on his chest, listening to his heart beat, our feet tangled together, the blankets cradling us with warmth...I was dizzy with hope, drunk with possibility.

NINETEEN

Theo

IN THE MORNING, I woke up first, and for a moment I forgot where I was. It happened to me all the time because I moved around so much, but what rarely happened was the smile that took over my face when I realized whose bed I was in.

Claire was facing away from me, curled into a ball. I moved close behind her, tucking her into the crescent of my body, one arm around her stomach. Her breathing changed and she hugged my arm, wriggling back against me.

"You're still here," she said softly.

"I'm still here." I was as surprised as she was, actually.

"Somehow I thought I'd wake up and you'd be gone."

I'd done that a lot in my past. Honestly, I could count on one hand the number of times I'd spent an entire night in a woman's bed. And I was always sorry and just wanted to get the fuck out of there in the morning.

Today was different. I didn't want to leave her. What the hell was that about? My muscles tensed up.

Um, it's about sex, asshole. Duh.

I relaxed again. "This bed is way too comfortable to leave. Especially with you in it."

"Mmm." She was quiet for a moment. "You're the first to sleep in it."

"Am I?"

"Yes. I'm not in the habit of asking guys to stay." She giggled. "Now *you* should feel special."

I pinched her butt. "You're gonna pay for that, little girl." Scenes from last night started filtering through my mind—we'd played stranger again, in the bedroom this time—and my dick decided to wake up too, tapping against her butt as it grew hard.

She took my hand from her stomach and brought it to her breast. My breathing grew ragged as I kneaded the flesh in my palm, teased her nipples into stiff little peaks, and rubbed my cock on her ass. She moaned when I swept my hand down her stomach and between her legs, finding her wet and warm. My fingers moved over her clit, rubbing gently at first and then harder and faster. I took my cue from the sounds she made, the way she moved against my hand. When she came, she cried out my name, and I nearly lost it and shot my load all over her back. Her perfect, smooth, vanilla-skinned back, unmarked except for a little crop of freckles near her tailbone.

Jesus. I want to come on her back.

Claire probably wasn't the kind of girl who enjoyed that sort of thing, but once the thought took root, I couldn't ignore it. Without a word, I flipped her onto her stomach and knelt above her with one knee on either side of her thighs. We'd used the last condom in my wallet after coming upstairs last night, so this would be better anyway—as long as she was OK with it. Should I ask? I glanced at her profile on the pillow and saw that her eyes were closed and she was smiling blissfully.

Nope, not asking.

I took my cock in my hand and rubbed the tip of it over each plump little ass cheek and up and down between them. Fuck, would I have loved to squeeze right in there—but that would have to wait. Instead I wrapped my fingers around my dick and moved it up and down the shaft, over the crown, feeling my lower body heat up.

"Your skin is so perfect," I whispered, my breath coming fast. "I want to mess it up."

Her smiled curved higher. "Do it. I want you to."

With my free hand, I pushed her hair out of the way and ran my palm from her shoulder blade down her back over the curve of her hip. "God, I love your body." Her skin was pale and soft, untouched even by the sun. I felt like a god that she'd let me sully her this way, that she *wanted* me to.

"Talk to me," she breathed. "I can't see you. Help me imagine it."

Goddamn, she was awesome. "My cock is so hard," I told her, working my hand a little quicker. "The muscles in my stomach are flexing. I'm fucking my hand and thinking about you."

She moaned and arched her back a little, her ass rising between my thighs. "Yes...I can see it."

"It's the hand I just had on you. My fingers are wet."

She moved a hand underneath her and began to touch herself. "Now mine are too."

"Oh God." My voice cracked. It was so fucking amazing, I was paralyzed for a moment, and all I wanted to do was watch her. But my dick was aching inside my fist, the tip covered not only with Claire's arousal but my own. "You're so fucking hot."

"And wet," she whispered, her ass moving up and down as she rubbed herself on her hand. "You make me so wet."

My arm, giving up on my brain, seemed to move of its accord, jerking hard and fast above her. I fell forward, bracing the other hand on her headboard, my eyes wide and my breathing strained. "Fuck, I'm gonna come so hard."

"Yes!" she cried out in anguish.

I realized she was bringing herself to climax, and it pushed me over the edge. My orgasm unfurled from bottom to top inside my body, and I felt it build like a volcanic eruption and watched it explode in thick, hot ribbons that flowed like lava over her back. I had no words to describe it, not that I could have talked anyway. All I could do was moan in agony and delight and gratitude and shock that any man should get to do this.

Let alone me.

I BROUGHT up a hand towel I'd found in the hall closet downstairs and wet with warm water. "Don't move," I told her.

She stayed on her stomach, her arms folded beneath her chin, while I gently cleaned her up. "Thank you."

It was insane that she was thanking me. "Believe me, it's my pleasure." When I was finished, I kissed her shoulder. "There. All clean."

She smiled at me over one shoulder. "For now, anyway. Here, give me that." Sitting up, she took the wet towel from me. "I'll put it in the laundry."

Going over to her closet, she slipped into a fluffy floor-length white robe with her initials embroidered on the chest. I laughed as I tugged on my jeans. "That thing is huge."

"I know, I love it. It's like being inside a cloud." She snuggled inside it. "It was a gift from my friend Margot."

"The one who lives on the farm?" She'd told me about her two closest girlfriends last night. I'd never had friendships like that. I was close to Aaron, but that was different—our bond was in blood, and we'd been born to it. The bond between friends was different. You chose each other.

"Yes. And the one getting married in February."

"Should I book the date? I could offer you a frequent flier discount or something." As soon as I said it, I was sorry. One, I didn't want to hurt her feelings, and two, I had no idea if I would actually be around to take her. February was more than a month away. I'd learned not to make promises like that.

But Claire got the joke. "Asshole," she muttered, punching me on the arm as she passed me on the way to the stairs. "I'm never hiring a Hottie again. You can't get rid of them!"

I smiled as she disappeared down the steps, then looked around for my underwear and shirt. I'd thrown my jeans on before going down to grab a towel, but nothing else. As I dressed, I wondered what I should do today. Go to Aaron and apologize? Did I owe him that? I considered it. Maybe I'd been wrong to lash out. Maybe my anger at him was less about his inability to commit to sobriety and more about his inability to commit to staying with his family. Maybe I was taking out my anger at our parents on him.

Fuck...was that it?

Frowning, I sat on the edge of her bed and pulled on my

socks. The truth was, I was much better at perceiving how other people felt than I was at self-reflection. Looking too hard at myself made me uncomfortable, and I was an expert at sweeping shit under the rug.

As I was lacing up my boots, Claire came up the steps. "Hey, are you hungry? I need to keep going on the project list today, but I'm in the mood for some pancakes or something. Want to get breakfast?"

"Sure." Eating pancakes with Claire sounded a lot better than eating crow with my brother. And his family didn't need me today—they had him back. Claire, on the other hand, needed my help. "Maybe after that, we could hit the tile store."

"I'd love that!"

"What are you thinking for the counters? Replacing the Formica?"

Claire went to her closet, slipped off her robe, and hung it on a hook. "I want something natural, like stone. I'm not sure which kind yet, but I'm leaning toward slate."

"Good choice. We could check out some options at a stoneworks place where I used to work. It's not far from the tile store."

"Really?" she squealed, going over to a small dresser. She pulled out something tiny and white. "That would be amazing."

I watched her pull on her underwear, slip into her bra, shimmy into her jeans, and throw a sweater over her head. I'd never watched a woman dress this way before, in her own bedroom, morning sunlight coming in the windows, her movements graceful and feminine. So different from furtive, awkward, post-sex yanking on of clothing in a dark hotel room. It felt personal, like she was letting me in on a secret.

Because she trusts you.

I fucking loved that.

One more day with her. That's all I needed.

"TELL me why your day was so rough yesterday." Claire sipped her coffee, which she'd doctored with so much cream and sugar it was almost as light as her skin.

I brought my cup to my lips and tipped it up slowly, giving myself time to consider how to handle this. I supposed talking about my family was OK. *Better to clue her in on Aaron's shortcomings than my own.* "My brother came home."

Her eyes widened. "But that's great! Isn't it?"

"Yes and no." I took one more sip and set the cup down. "He does this—comes home, claims he's going to stay sober and find a job. Fills his wife and kids with hope. But it never sticks."

"Maybe this time will be different," she said hopefully. "Give him a chance."

"He's had so many chances, though. And I know his alcoholism is a disease and I shouldn't blame him for it, but at what point do you stop putting the pillows under him when he falls down?"

She shook her head. "God, I don't know. I can see both sides. You love someone, so you don't want them to feel pain. But if he doesn't feel pain, he won't stop."

"Exactly. And the thing is, he *does* feel pain. He feels horrible—but the only escape he knows is the bottle."

Claire was silent a moment, setting down her cup and looking at me intently. "What's he escaping?"

I exhaled. "Fuck. A lot of shit." *History. Genetics. Abuse.*

"How's his marriage?"

"Josie idolizes him and he adores her. They've always been crazy about each other. It's not that."

She bit her lip. "Childhood stuff?"

I nodded slowly, my eyes dropping to the menu in front of me but not seeing the words. Instead I saw blood on Aaron's shirt. Heard the sickening thump of a punch landed. Felt winded as I ran up the stairs to hide under the bed like my brother had told me to do. The familiar shame of it slammed into me like a fist—I'd escaped then. Who was I to prevent Aaron from escaping now?

"Hey." Claire's hand reached out and covered mine. "You OK?"

"I'm fine." I cleared my throat, burying the shame somewhere I couldn't feel it. "But yes. Our childhood was not good. And Aaron took the worst of it to protect me."

"I'm sorry," she said. "I can't imagine how awful that must have been."

"I don't even want you to."

The waitress came over and took our orders, then returned a moment later to pour more coffee. When we were alone again, Claire spoke quietly. "I don't know what the answer is with your brother. But I do know that when you're struggling with something inside, talking about it can help."

"Yeah." But I'd talked too much already. I needed to shut up.

She reached across the table and touched my wrist. "And I'm here for you. I know we just met, but I want to be your friend."

"My friend, huh?" I stared at her fingers on my skin. Every time she touched me, my body warmed.

"Yes." She looked nervous, pulling her hand back. "Is that OK?"

"Uh, sure." Friend was fine, right? Friend was casual. Friend didn't come with any expectations or pressure to be someone I wasn't.

You could have fun with a friend, say goodbye at the end of the day, and not feel guilty that you weren't sure when you'd hang out again.

Of course, friends didn't usually have trouble keeping their hands to themselves the way Claire and I did, but I wouldn't worry about that today.

"So," I said. "Tell me what you're thinking about for the kitchen floor."

TWENTY

Claire

IT WAS A PERFECT DAY.

After breakfast we hit the tile store, and Theo was totally patient with me as I walked up and down each row, checking out everything they had to offer and comparing prices. Eventually we left with several samples, and I couldn't wait to get home and see how they looked with the wood.

At the stoneworks warehouse, Theo introduced me to a former work acquaintance named Zack, who seemed surprised but glad to see him.

"You in town for long?" he asked, his feet planted wide, hands on his hips.

Theo shrugged. "I'm not really sure."

"Thought maybe you bought a house or condo or something."

"No, the stone is for Claire. She's redoing her kitchen."

"I'm just browsing today," I explained. "Trying to get a feel for the choices."

"Great. Well, go on back and let me know if you need help. And if you ever decide you want your old job back, we'd love to have you. This guy's an amazing salesman," Zack said to me. "The best."

I smiled. "I believe it." Another reason I loved today was because I was learning more about Theo, and after hearing about his painful childhood, it made more sense to me why he was so private. He probably had a hard time trusting people, especially people who were supposed to care. No wonder he never dated anyone.

Theo thanked Zack and clapped him on the shoulder before leading me into the cavernous warehouse full of giant stone slabs from all over the world. I was in awe.

"Look how beautiful this is!" I exclaimed, running my hand over a gorgeous slab of charcoal gray granite with swirling white veins and one slash of red. "A geological event forever captured in stone! A work of art done by Earth, thousands of years ago, and preserved here almost like a photograph!"

Theo laughed at my enthusiasm. "I never thought of stone as art. And I thought you wanted slate."

"I haven't made up my mind yet." I turned in a slow circle, overwhelmed by all the choices. "God, I could be here all day."

"Take your time." Theo tucked his hands in his pockets. "I don't have anywhere I need to be today, so I'm all yours."

Something about the way he said it made me wonder if tomorrow would be a different story, but I brushed off the concern. Instead I gave him an impulsive kiss on the cheek. "Thank you. This means so much to me."

"My pleasure. So do you just want to browse, or do you

have a specific idea about what you'd like?"

I bit my lip and squinted at a piece of marble across the aisle. "I want it to look flowy."

"Flowy?"

"Yes, I know it's stone, but I want it to have movement. Flow. The pattern in it, I mean. Some of these are more static—the ones with flecks or spots. Others, like this one behind me, have veins reminiscent of water flowing. I like that."

"Got it. Come with me." As we walked, he explained that while slate was durable, non-porous, and stood up well to heat, it probably didn't have the look I wanted. "Granite is higher maintenance for sure, but I think it's going to be what you want. In terms of looks, it's more striking, and has that quality of movement you're looking for."

"The pretty ones are always high maintenance, aren't they?"

He grinned, elbowing me in the side. "Not always."

AFTER WE WERE DONE at the stoneworks, we went back to my house, where we attached new hardware to the freshly stained cupboard doors and hung them again.

"They look great. Are you happy with the color?" Theo asked.

"Yes. I love it!" I clapped my hands. "I know it's dark, but that makes it more authentic. Let's look at the tile samples for the floor."

He laid them out at the base of the cupboards, and we stood back to inspect them. "I like the idea of the hexagonal, but if you're going to make a statement with the counters, I'd probably go with the large square travertine."

"I think you're right. I might—"

I was interrupted by a knock on the front door. A voice rang out. "Yoo-hoo! Claire?"

"Mom?" Theo and I exchanged a glance.

"You shouldn't leave your door unlocked, dear. Someone could walk right in." She appeared in the entrance to the kitchen and noticed Theo. "Oh, hello!"

"Hello." Theo nodded.

"I'm sorry, I didn't realize you had company." But her smile told me how happy she was about it. She set down the shopping bags she carried and smoothed her honey-colored bob.

"Mom, this is my friend Theo MacLeod. He's helping me with the kitchen rehab."

"How wonderful!" My mother came into the kitchen and pulled off her gloves. "Nice to meet you. I'm Carol French."

Theo shook the hand she offered. "Nice to meet you, Mrs. French." Then he stuffed both hands in his pockets.

"Oh, please. Call me Carol." She clasped her hands at her waist and looked delighted. "I just dropped by to bring you some groceries. Last time I was here, your fridge was nearly empty." She was talking to me, ostensibly, but she never took her eyes off Theo.

"Thanks. We were just checking out our work on the cabinet doors. Didn't the stain come out beautifully?" I stepped aside so she could admire them.

"Mmm, nice." She gave them a cursory glance and beamed at Theo. "What do you do, Theo? Are you a builder or something?"

His cheeks colored. "No."

"Just handy, then?" She winked at me. "That's always helpful. Your father is a disaster in that area. I practically have to call someone every time I need a picture hung or a light bulb changed!"

"Dad's a judge, Mom. He's good at other things."

She waved a hand in the air. "I suppose. Anyway, Theo, are you a teacher, then?"

Theo, who was looking a little panicked, threw me a look that I recognized as a question. *Oh, right. He wants to know what to say.* I hadn't thought about this yet—what was our story? I decided to go with something close to the truth.

"Theo owns his own business."

"An entrepreneur! How nice." Her eyes drifted over Theo's face, his broad shoulders and chest. "And so handsome."

Theo's face turned a deep shade of purple. He seemed completely unnerved by my mother, which I found kind of funny. He was so cool when playing a role, but being himself around people was a challenge. *Poor guy.*

"How cute, he's blushing!" My mother's tinkly laugh rang out. "Claire, he's too adorable for words. Where have you been hiding him, you silly girl?"

"Mom, that's enough. I haven't been hiding him anywhere." I tried to meet Theo's eyes to reassure him, but he wasn't looking at me. And was I imagining things, or was he slowly inching toward the back door?

"Well, how long have you been dating?"

"Not that long."

"A month?"

"Something like that." Flustered, I tried again to make eye contact, but he had this strange blank look on his face as he stared at the wall behind me.

"Theo." She turned to him, her hands clasped. "What are you doing tomorrow night for Christmas Eve?"

"Uh." He swallowed. "I'm not sure."

"You must come by the house. Claire can tell you where it is." She gestured toward me. "Claire's father and sister would love to meet you, and I make a delicious glazed ham."

"Mom, don't pressure him."

She dismissed me with a click of her tongue. "Nonsense, I'm not pressuring him! I'm simply extending an invitation. It's not often you have a boyfriend to bring to Christmas dinner." She turned back to Theo. "Au gratin potatoes. French bread. Onion tarts. Candied pecans. Sound good?"

Oh, Jesus. "OK, that's enough." Taking her by the shoulders, I turned her around and marched her through the dining room into the living room. "I'm sure you have to be on your way now. Lots of prep to do for tomorrow night."

"OK, OK, I'll leave you two alone." She called out to Theo. "Nice meeting you, dear. Hope you can make it to dinner."

"Nice meeting you, too." Theo came into the dining room and lifted one hand in farewell.

I walked my mother to the door. "Thanks for the groceries."

"You're welcome." She lowered her voice to a stage whisper. "He's so good-looking!"

I frowned at the surprise in her tone. "Does that shock you or something?"

"Well, he's much better looking than anyone else I've ever seen you with."

"Thanks." I opened the front door. She was right, I should keep it locked.

"Where's his family from?"

"Connecticut," I lied. It was surprisingly easy.

"Connecticut!" Her eyes lit up. "What about college?

Do you know where he went? Was it somewhere out East? Yale's in Connecticut. Was it Yale?"

"Bye, Mom." I practically pushed her out. "Thanks for dropping by."

"Bye, dear." She blew her air kisses at me and pulled on her gloves. "I'll let dad know you might be dating a Yale man. His alma mater—he'll be thrilled!"

"Night." I shut the door. I think she was still talking.

When I turned around, Theo was standing in the living room too.

With his coat on.

"Are you leaving?" I asked in surprise.

"Yeah. I can't—this was—" He stopped, his lips pressed together, one leg twitching restlessly. "I have to go."

"Why?"

"I can't do this. Sorry."

"Can't do what? Look at tiles?"

"No. Date you."

I stuck my hands on my hips. "I never said we were dating."

"You mother said it. You didn't correct her."

My eyes narrowed. "What was I supposed to say? 'No, Mom. We're not dating, I hired him to pretend to be my boyfriend for Elyse's wedding. Now we're just fucking and painting cabinets.' It's just a word, Theo. It means two people are spending time together, that's all."

He struggled for a reply, his entire body jittering with urgency. "What was all that stuff about Yale?" he finally blurted. "And your dad's a *judge*? You never told me that."

"Because it never occurred to me that it would matter! What difference does it make what my father does? You don't have to date *him*."

"There's that word again," he accused, his hands curling

into fists. "I told you from the start, I don't date. I don't date, I don't do mothers and Christmas Eve dinners, and I sure as hell don't do judge fathers."

"I never asked you to! My *mother* was the one who invited you to Christmas Eve dinner, not me!" I exploded, my arms flailing. This was unbelievable! He was ruining the perfectly nice day we'd just had and treating me like I'd done something wrong. "You know, *you're* the one who came here saying you need me. I was fine with one night only." It was a complete lie, and my ears started to tingle, but I kept going. "What did you even mean by that? Need me for what?"

His jaw was clenched tight, his neck muscles taut. "I was wrong. I don't need you or anybody else for anything. This was a big fucking mistake." He stormed past me and out the door.

I was bursting with fury, my blood boiling. He was lying! He was a horrible actor when he wasn't playing a part, but what good would it do to chase him down and call him out on it? He was so damn stubborn—he'd never admit he was wrong or tell me the truth about why he was so freaked out.

"Fuck you, Theo MacLeod!" I yelled at the door he'd slammed behind him. A moment later, I heard his car start and the engine revving. "I don't need this in my life! Take your secrets and your lies and your big dick and get out. And stay out!" I finished loudly before turning on my heel and bolting up the steps.

In my bedroom, I threw myself face down on the sheets that still smelled like him, and screamed into the mattress. This was so unfair! I'd played by his rules! When he'd showed up at my door with sad eyes and grasping hands and searching lips, I hadn't questioned it one bit! *I need you,* he'd said, his voice raw with emotion. I'd never heard him sound that way. But did I ask why? Did I ask what happened to make him change his mind? Did I lay out a bunch of conditions for sex? No! I'd pulled him in out of the cold and done my best to take away whatever hurt he was feeling. I thought I'd done a pretty damn good job of it, too! I'd never heard a man moan so loud before.

And I hadn't asked about a next time, either—all I'd done was suggest pancakes. It was Theo who'd offered to help me with the house and take me shopping, Theo who'd said *I'm all yours today*. Had the appearance of my mother really spooked him that much? Did the word *date* trigger some sort of instinct to run, like prey flees from a predator? It wasn't my fault she was excited to meet him. She was only trying to be kind inviting him to dinner. And why the hell did he care what my father did?

I flipped onto my back and stared at the ceiling. If he'd been moody and sullen all day, I might think the panic had been building in him and my mother had caused it to burst. But he hadn't—he'd been relaxed and happy. Smiling. Laughing. A little sad when he'd talked about his brother, but he hadn't gone into a funk about it. What was I missing? Where had I gone wrong?

This is bullshit. I didn't do anything wrong.

Tears slipped from my eyes, making me angrier. I didn't want to cry over him. I'd known him for less than a week, for God's sake! Why did I always have to be so damn emotional?

But the loss of him cut deeper than it should have, because when he left, he took more than just himself. He took away hope. He took away possibility. He took away a little piece of me that still believed in the fairy tale.

There were only so many of those pieces left.

TWENTY-ONE

Theo

YALE?

Fucking *Yale*?

Panic had been rising in me like helium fills a balloon, and the word Yale popped it wide open.

Suddenly I couldn't remember why I was there or what I was doing or how I was going to get out—but I knew that I had to.

From the moment Claire's mother had walked in, I'd felt on edge. I didn't do mothers. What mother wants her daughter dating someone like me?

An *entrepreneur*? Fuck me!

And her dad was a judge. A goddamn judge. In my experience, judges weren't particularly fond of people who'd committed a felony, even if it was almost ten years ago and I'd ostensibly served my time. That was such bull-shit. I might have spent only one year in a cell, but those fucking bars followed me everywhere and they always would. People would continue to judge me for that mistake for the rest of my life. I'd never be free of my past—never. Not to mention insurance fraud and money laundering. My present wasn't too shiny either.

"Fuck!" I banged a hand on the steering wheel as I sped away from Claire's house.

Why couldn't Claire have just said we were friends, like she'd said to me at breakfast? I was fine with being friends. If she hadn't confirmed her mother's belief that we were dating, I might not have bailed so fast. But I didn't date anymore. Ever.

Dating meant a relationship. A relationship meant you had to be honest with someone. You had to let them in. You owed them the truth. You owed them time. You owed them trust.

I couldn't do it.

So then why the hell did you go there last night?

I squirmed in my seat. I didn't want to answer that question. I just wanted to go home and forget about this.

Forget about her.

TWENTY-TWO

Claire

THE MORNING OF CHRISTMAS EVE, I met Jaime and Margot for coffee.

"How's Jack holding up staying at your parents' house?" Jaime asked Margot.

She smiled. "He's OK. Muffy keeps asking him questions about the layout of her garden, even though I told her he's a farmer, not a landscaper. In her mind, dirt is dirt."

Jaime laughed. "At least she's trying."

"She is. And Jack's a good sport about it." Margot tucked her blond hair behind her ears. "He was more put out by the custom suit fitting."

"I bet. But at least he agreed to wear it."

Margot sighed. "I think he'll be very glad when the wedding is over. He is not enjoying the planning that much. Sometimes I feel like he's dreading the whole thing."

"Because he's a *guy*," Jaime said, rolling her eyes. "And he's not social, so he's probably nervous about being the center of attention that day. Just tell him all eyes will be on you."

She laughed. "He says that all the time when he's trying to get out of wearing the fancy suit and shoes."

"He'll be fine. Everything coming together like it should?"

"Yes, although I've redone the seating chart a thousand times. It's amazing how many people aren't speaking to each other in that crowd." Margot sipped her coffee and gave me a funny look. "Claire, is everything OK?"

"Yeah," I sighed. "I'm just tired." That was true—I'd hardly slept last night.

"How did it go with the rent-a-date the other night?"

"It went fine. Better than fine, actually."

"Turns out, they were *very* compatible," said Jaime, her lips twitching.

Margot's brows arched. "Oh?"

"Yes. We had a good time that night." I paused. "And the next night."

Jaime almost spit out her coffee. "The next night! You didn't tell me about that."

"I haven't really had a chance." I shook my head, staring into the foam on my latte. "It was the craziest thing. On Friday night, he made it very clear that we were a one-night-only thing, even though we'd had an amazing time. Then Saturday night, he shows up at my house and says 'I need you.'"

"What?" Jaime set her cup on the saucer with a clank. "That *is* crazy."

"But really sweet," said Margot.

"It was. And he said he didn't know where this could go, and I said I was OK with that, and we had another great night. Then yesterday, he offered to take me shopping for tiles and to look at options for counters. Apparently he used to work for this stoneworks place. And he also has his own carpentry business."

"Does he have a last name now?" Jaime's eyes were wide.

I almost smiled. "MacLeod."

Margot pursed her lips. "Hmm. Doesn't ring a bell. Is his family from around here?"

"I don't think you'd know his family. He was raised by his grandmother, but she's gone now. A brother lives somewhere close, and he has a wife and three kids." I kept the rest of the details about his family to myself—Theo had trusted me with them, and I wouldn't feel right disclosing them, even to my friends.

"Tile shopping, huh?" Margot's eyes sparkled over the rim of her cup. "How romantic."

"You know what? Somehow it was." I tilted my head. "Well, it was and it wasn't. We didn't hold hands or kiss or anything, but I love that he wanted to help me. He even stained the kitchen cabinets Saturday night and hung them back up yesterday."

Jaime blinked. "When's he moving in?"

"Never. Because my mother showed up as we were looking at tile samples for the floor, and he freaked the fuck out."

"Why?" they both asked at once.

I shrugged helplessly. "Could have been anything. He seemed really nervous the whole time she was there, which was all of five minutes. I introduced him, and you know how my mother is, she was so excited to meet him and started fawning all over him. She scolded me for hiding him and asked how long we'd been dating and I made something up—I think I said a month. He didn't like that, apparently."

"Didn't like what?" Jaime asked.

"That I let her assume we were dating. He doesn't like that word."

She rolled her eyes. "What the hell were you supposed to say?"

"That's what *I* said. But he was all spooked by it. And by the fact that my dad is a judge."

"Why would that matter?" Margot wondered.

"I have no idea. I asked him why he'd even come back, why he'd said he needed me."

"What did he say?" Jaime asked.

"He said it was a mistake. He doesn't need anything or anybody. Two seconds later, he was out the door."

My friends were stunned silent. But what could they say?

"What's wrong with me, you guys?" Out of nowhere, tears threatened, and I propped my head up at the temples. "Why did I get my hopes up after two stupid days? Why didn't he feel what I did?"

Jaime rubbed my back. "I don't know, hon. But I don't think he would have come back if he didn't feel *something*. Let alone spend an entire day working on your kitchen. It doesn't make sense."

"You know," Margot said slowly. "Maybe it wasn't so much the word *dating* that freaked him out as the fact that he realized he likes you as more than a fuck buddy."

"Or he has a wife," Jaime added. "I'm still not convinced he doesn't."

"I'm not convinced of anything at this point." I picked up my latte again. "I don't *think* he has a wife, but he definitely makes it tough to get close to him."

"Jack was like that too," Margot said. "It took him a while to open up, and even after he did, he tried to push me away. As soon as he realized he had feelings for me, he shut down."

I nodded glumly. "I remember that."

"I tried to push Quinn away too," Jaime said through gritted teeth. "As soon as I realized I was in love with him."

"Theo's not in love with me," I said wryly. "Not even close."

"Maybe not," she admitted, "but even the first little inkling of feeling might be enough to spook a guy like him."

"Maybe."

"I think he's just scared." Margot's voice was confident. "I'll bet you a hundred bucks he comes back and apologizes within a week. By New Year's."

"I'll take that bet," I said, thinking of the hundred bucks Theo had given back to me at breakfast yesterday.

I'd gladly give it to Margot if she was right, but I had a feeling I'd be a hundred bucks richer come January 1st.

CHRISTMAS EVE AT MY PARENTS' house had all the usual sparkle, but I wasn't feeling it.

I ate all the traditional foods she served every year, the glazed ham and the potatoes au gratin, the caramelized onion tarts, the roasted brussels sprouts with balsamic, the freshly baked bread. But it was oddly tasteless this year. Even Grandma Flossie's chocolate pudding lacked the usual flavor, and I hadn't gotten the texture quite right.

"Sorry," I mumbled when my sister commented on it. Then I said what I was really thinking—a first. "You know, you could always offer to make it if you think you can do better."

"Doesn't matter," she said, pushing the dish away from

her. "I shouldn't eat it, anyway. I need to lose some weight for a part I just got."

"That's wonderful, honey," said my mom. "And Claire, don't worry about the pudding. Your mind was probably elsewhere when you were making it." Her eyes twinkled.

"Like where?" Giselle wondered, dipping her finger into the pudding she'd just rejected and sucking it clean.

"Like on her handsome new boyfriend."

Giselle's mouth dropped open. Even my dad looked up from his pudding, and there wasn't much that could distract my father from desserts.

"Boyfriend?" my sister echoed.

"Yes. She's been hiding a hunk from us." My mother giggled, her cheeks rosy from the wine.

Speaking of wine, I reached for mine and took a big drink.

"You *have*?" Giselle asked, clearly shocked. "Who is he?"

"His name is Theo," my mother bubbled, "and he's just adorable. I went over there Sunday and he was at her house helping her redo the kitchen cabinets. Although I do think you should have gone with white, dear."

"I like them dark," I said, trying to think of a way out of this without having to say there was no Theo anymore.

"So what does he look like?" my sister asked.

"So handsome," my mother gushed. "He owns his own business, he's from Connecticut, and he might have even gone to Yale."

"Really?" My father perked up. After football and birds, Yale was his favorite thing to talk about.

"He didn't go to Yale," I said.

The table was silent, and I took a deep breath, preparing to tell the truth and be pitied. Or mocked.

And then.

"He went to Ohio State. Played football there," I added, giving my dad a smile. Theo had mentioned he played football in high school and college, although he hadn't elaborated. I had no idea if he'd even gotten a degree or not.

"Did he?" My dad beamed. "That's a good program."

"Yes," I said, my mind working furiously to stay one step ahead of my tongue. My ears began to tingle.

"So is he built like a football player?" Giselle asked.

"Totally." I drank some more wine. "He doesn't play anymore, but he's in great shape."

"He seems very sweet to her." My mother nodded happily. "And you can just tell by the way he looks at her how much he cares."

I swallowed hard. "It's still pretty new."

"Is he coming over tonight?" my mom asked hopefully.

"No, he's at his brother's house tonight. He's got three nieces he just adores."

"Sounds like a real catch," Giselle said. "I'd like to meet him. What are you guys doing for New Year's? Why don't we all get together?"

"Oh, we can't. We're going away for New Year's." I thought fast. "I meant to ask you, actually, Mom, if I could use the cabin for a couple days? I want to show it to Theo."

"Of course!" my mom said brightly. "I'll give you the keys tonight. I was just up there last week, so the pantry is stocked. You know how to turn the heat up and everything?"

"Mmhm." I finished off the last of my cabernet, congratulating myself on a performance well played. I'd head up to the cabin for a couple days, come home, and say we'd had a big fight about something. Then I'd tell everyone at work the same thing when school was open again. It would mean taking time off from the restoration of my house, but maybe the little vacation would be good. I could sketch or paint, take walks in the woods, enjoy the solitude. If I stayed home, where even my own bed reminded me of Theo now, I'd probably just wallow.

After helping my mother with the dishes while Giselle and my father played Scrabble in the next room—"Dad, spanx is totally a word"—, I went up to bed, the keys to the cabin tucked in my hand.

I always spent Christmas Eve at my parents' house, in my old room, in my old bed. It was sort of silly, but it meant a lot to my mother, who still played Santa, setting out gifts for my father, Giselle, and me under the tree. In the morning, tradition dictated we all put on a Christmas sweater and open gifts together, after which my dad made eggs and bacon for everyone, and my mom and I baked cinnamon rolls. Later, we'd make real hot chocolate and watch *It's a Wonderful Life* as we drank it from these oblong coffee cups my mother called "hug mugs" because you had to cradle them with two hands.

I often rolled my eyes at my mother's goofy traditions, but in my heart I knew I'd probably do the same things for my children one day.

If I ever have them. Depressed, I snapped off the lamp and pulled the covers up to my chin.

In the distance, I heard the familiar sleigh bells CD that my mother had played every year after Giselle and I went up to bed in the effort to convince us there really was a Santa Claus.

But there was no Santa Claus. No Easter Bunny, no Tooth Fairy, no Prince Charming coming to wake me in the morning with a kiss.

"Asshole," I muttered. Then I flopped onto my belly, squeezed my eyes shut, and went to sleep.

TWENTY-THREE

Theo

NOTHING WAS MORE DEPRESSING than being alone at Christmas. I knew, because I'd spent many a holiday in a crummy hotel room, eating Chinese takeout and watching *A Christmas Story*. I never got tired of watching that movie. After I saw it for the first time as a kid, I used to daydream about having a family like that—a gruff but funny dad like the Old Man; a sweet, loving mother; a brother close to my age to play with. I wanted to be Ralphie. I wanted that feeling he experiences when his dad tells him there's one more gift behind the tree. I wanted my biggest problem to be broken glasses. I wanted to beat up Farkus. I wanted to look back at my childhood and recognize the best present I'd ever gotten.

My grandmother had gotten me some nice things. Toys I wanted, clothes I needed, books I mostly ignored. I liked Legos best, especially sets that built a plane or a helicopter. She'd also baked cookies and roasted a chicken, served with mashed potatoes and gravy. It was good, but my mouth watered every time I thought about that meal Claire's mom had described. I wondered what Claire would say about me at dinner. Would she tell them the truth?

Not that she *knew* the truth.

I frowned as I mindlessly flipped through channels on my old TV. Every time I thought about how I'd bolted on her, I felt like shit. I was always going to walk out—I'd just done it a little more suddenly than planned. I'd said some harsh words, too. Her feelings had clearly been hurt. Knowing I'd hurt her made my chest cave in. She hadn't really done anything wrong, and I'd made her feel bad. God, I was an asshole.

I found the station showing the Christmas Story marathon and watched it for a few minutes, but even that didn't cheer me up. Sighing, I switched off the TV and tossed the remote on the couch.

Both Josie and Aaron had called and texted, inviting me to come over tonight. **The girls are excited to see you**, Josie had messaged. **They have a gift for you. Please come.**

I had presents for them too, which I'd planned on bringing over tomorrow, but tonight loomed long and lonely before me. Maybe watching them tear the paper off the Royal Dreams Dollhouse I'd gotten them would cheer me up.

After a quick shower, I got dressed and loaded one bag and one big box into my car. Before pulling out, I texted Josie that I was on my way and asked if there was anything she needed from the grocery store. While I waited for a reply, I noticed there was a text message on my phone from John Salinger, which was the alias used by the guy who hired me out for con jobs. Usually I was excited by the prospect of an influx of cash, but today I stared at his name and the series of numbers he'd texted with a mixture of regret and unease.

How long could I keep doing this and not get caught? I was good at what I did, but deep down I felt it was only a matter of time. And helping Claire out the last couple days, being at the stoneworks yesterday, had reminded me how much I'd liked that kind of work. I'd felt useful. Skilled. Necessary. Honestly, I couldn't even remember why I'd quit. Probably I'd just gotten restless and felt like it was time to move on.

Giving up on a good thing was my specialty.

Claire's face popped into my head, and I closed my eyes, inhaling deeply and wishing I could smell her. I fucking *missed* her. I was sorry I'd hurt her. I wished things could be different—wished *I* could be different—but I couldn't.

Josie texted back that she was all set and I told her I'd be there soon. I committed the number John Salinger gave me to memory, deleted the text message and backed out of my parking space. Maybe I'd call him later.

On my way to Aaron and Josie's house, I rehearsed what I was going to say. I'd apologize for yesterday and make the offer to pay for rehab again without being insulting or demeaning. Aaron already felt so bad about himself. But if the answer wasn't to cushion him and it wasn't to abandon him, there had to be something in between that would work. Some way to help him without being an enabler.

If you were to stay here permanently, you could be more of a support.

Frowning, I shelved that thought for now, even though I

knew it was true. But it would mean everything had to change.

I pulled into their driveway and noticed it had been shoveled after last night's snow. That was a good sign. I hoisted the girls' present from the back of my car onto my shoulder and walked up to the house. Through the window I could see the lights on the tree, and I heard music playing too. Kids laughing. I smiled. *All good signs.*

After knocking on the door, I opened it a crack. "Anyone here?"

"Uncle Theo!" shrieked a little voice.

"Hey!" I entered the living room and kicked the door shut behind me. "Look what I have!"

"What is that?" Three little girls circled me like puppies, jumping up and down with excitement.

"I don't know! I found it outside on the porch. Let's look." I set it down, and they immediately put their hands on it.

"There's writing on it," said Ava, her eyes lighting up. "To Ava, Hailey, and Peyton!" She looked up at me. "I need help with the rest."

I ruffled her dark hair. "It says, 'I had to bring this a little early, and I'm afraid it didn't fit down the chimney. Ho ho ho! Love, Santa.'"

Three smiles got even wider. "Can we open it?" Hailey asked.

"Sure." I stood back and watched them tear off the paper, unable to keep a grin off my face. This was exactly what I'd needed.

"What's this?" My brother came in from the kitchen, wiping his hands on a towel.

"Santa brought us...a dream castle!" Ava shouted. Deafening cries of joy pierced my ears. "Look how big it is! And it has furniture!"

Tomorrow morning, there would be three dolls under the tree for them too. Maybe I'd come over early and watch them open gifts.

"It's from Santa, Daddy!" Hailey announced.

"Wow," said Aaron, dropping to his knees to admire the gift. "Santa must know how good you've been this year."

"Open it?" little Peyton asked.

"Sure." Aaron got to his feet. "Maybe Uncle Theo will help with that while Mommy and I get dinner finished."

"Oh, I think I can manage that." I took off my coat and tossed it onto the couch. "Let me get a knife. Be right back."

I left the kids touching the box lovingly and followed my brother into the kitchen. "Hey, Josie."

She was at the stove, and turned to greet me over one shoulder. "Hey. I'm so glad you came. Brought some excitement with you, huh?"

"Wasn't me, it was Santa," I said, grabbing a knife from the holder.

"Thanks." My brother clapped me on the shoulder and spoke quietly. "You didn't have to do that."

"I wanted to."

"You made their night."

I glanced into the living room, where they were still smiling. "They made mine, too."

LATER, when bellies were full and pans were soaking and kids were desperately fighting sleep in their beds, my brother and Josie and I sat with cups of decaf in the living room. They shared the couch and I took the chair across from them.

"When they're asleep, I have a few more things to bring in for them," I whispered.

"You're too much." Josie shook her head, tucking her legs beneath her. "After all you've done for us the last couple months, you did not have to buy them gifts."

"I wanted to."

Aaron set his mug on the table and leaned forward, elbows on his knees. "It's my intention to pay you back for everything you've given us. And it goes without saying how grateful I am, although I want to say it. Josie's been telling me how much you did for her and the kids while I was gone."

"They're my family too." *And they needed me.* I sipped hot coffee, trying not to let even a drop of resentment surface and ruin what had been a nice night. The nicest Christmas Eve I could remember.

"We are," said Josie firmly.

"How are you feeling?" I asked her.

"Great. And before you ask, I'm seeing the doctor on Friday before work," she said.

"Good."

"I went to a meeting yesterday," Aaron said.

I stared at my brother. "You did?"

He nodded. "And again today, and I'm going tomorrow."

"That's awesome, man." I noticed how good he looked as well. Clear eyed and level-headed. "I'm proud of you."

"You were right. I wasn't acting like a husband or father. I wasn't acting like a man. Not the man I want to be."

I nodded. "You can get there."

"Thank you," he said, his eyes shiny. "For not giving up on me."

I struggled to reply. My throat had gone tight. "You're welcome."

"So tell me what you've been up to." My brother leaned back and picked up his coffee. "Working any jobs?"

"A few here and there. One just came in, actually."

Josie frowned sadly. "I wish you didn't have to do that."

"Josie," my brother warned. "We don't need to judge."

"I'm not judging." She shook her head, touching her hand to her chest. "And believe me, I'm grateful for the financial help he's been able to give us. But I worry every day that..." Her voice trailed off.

"I know," I admitted. "I worry sometimes, too."

"Do you? You always seem so cool and calm about it."

"Because there's no sense in worrying. It doesn't change anything. But lately..." Fuck. Did I want to do this?

"Lately what?" she pressed.

I decided to brave it. "Lately, like just over the last few days, I've been thinking about my carpentry business. I kind of miss it."

"You were so good at it," my brother said with conviction. "I never understood why you gave up."

"I didn't make as much doing it as I made...doing other things. And I always felt so fidgety and unsettled when I stayed in one place too long. But maybe...I don't know. Maybe I'm outgrowing that."

"Why don't you try again?" Josie asked.

"I could." I rubbed the back of my neck. "I'll give it some thought."

"I'd help you," Aaron offered. "I'd go in with you if you wanted a partner. I don't have any money to put up, but I could apply for a loan once I got a job. We could save up.

Invest in some more equipment. Advertise. I know a lot of contractors who might hire us."

"I think that's a great idea," Josie enthused. "You guys would be a fabulous team."

"I'll give it some thought," I said again. I'd probably have to get a legit job in the meantime too, until we got on our feet. Maybe the stoneworks would take me back part time.

"What made you start thinking about that again?" Josie wondered.

"I've been helping a friend of mine redo her kitchen, and I'm really enjoying it."

"*Her* kitchen? Hmmmm." Josie's eyebrows rose. "Very interesting. Who is this friend?"

"Just someone I met recently."

"Is the someone pretty?"

My neck got hot, but I answered truthfully. "Yeah."

"Are you...dating her?" The disbelief in my brother's voice told me how well he knew me.

"No." I sighed and closed my eyes for a second, Claire's hurt expression still fresh in my mind. "We were just hanging out. But I fucked it up. As usual."

"Want to talk about it?"

"No. I don't know. Maybe." Did I? Would I feel better if I talked this through? Maybe if I told them what had transpired, they'd be able to tell me I'd done the right thing, validate my decision to end things the way I had.

Josie laughed sympathetically. "The look on your face is pure agony."

"Talk," my brother said. "What did you do?"

I decided to try it. "I really like this girl. I just met her last week, but right away, something about her got to me. She's really different than anyone I've ever met."

Josie smiled. "How so?"

"She's just...nice. Sweet. Smart. Fun. And so damn talented. She's an artist and she creates the most incredible things, but she has no confidence in herself. Doesn't think she's good enough to sell what she makes, so she doesn't even try."

"How does she support herself?" asked Aaron.

"She's an art teacher at an elementary school. And she's really good at that, too. I took her to this wedding on Friday night, and all her co-workers were saying how incredible she is at her job."

"Wow," said Josie. "Sounds like a good catch."

"She is. Totally different from me in so many ways, but we really hit it off." *And hit it hard.* "We have...great chemistry."

"So what's the problem?" Aaron asked.

"The problem is that I was at her house last night and her mother showed up. Claire introduced me to her, and she started asking all these questions about me. It made me nervous. Her dad's a judge, for fuck's sake. I didn't know that."

"Ah." My brother understood. "You haven't told her about the conviction."

"No. Somehow I never worked up the nerve." I shook my head, hating the part that came next. "So I bailed. I said some asshole shit and took off."

"Why? Do you think it will be a deal breaker if you told her the truth?"

"Maybe. And I'd understand if it was. But it's more than that," I admitted. "The way she looks at me, the way she trusts me—it's crazy how good it makes me feel."

"And you don't want to lose that," Aaron said. "You think if she knew the truth she'd never look at you that way again. Never trust you."

"Why should she?"

"Because you'll earn it." Josie set her cup down and leaned forward. "I'm not saying it will be easy, but if you really like her, it's worth a try, right?"

"But what's the point?" I argued. "Why go through the trouble of getting her to trust me when I'll just fuck it up another way later on? When have I ever been able to keep a good thing going?"

"I don't know the answer to that," she said. "But I've also never heard you talk this way about anyone."

"Me either," said Aaron.

"Do you want to be with her?" Josie asked.

"I think so." I ran a hand through my hair. "Yes."

"Then give her the chance to accept you," she urged. "And give yourself the chance to be happy with her. To keep the good thing going, like you said."

"You mean go to her and tell her the truth? Ask for another chance?"

"Yes," she said firmly. "But you have to apologize for being an asshole and you have to mean it. You have to ask for another chance to do things right."

"But won't I just give her the chance to shoot me down?"

She shrugged. "Guess that's a risk you'll have to be willing to take. And don't do this if you don't want to follow through." Her voice got a little sharper. "No woman wants to be lied to, Theo. If all you want is sex and hanging out, say it. Maybe she'll be cool with that. But if she wants more and you don't—"

"I think I do, though," I blurted. It was kind of a relief to say it out loud, to admit that I actually had feelings for her that went beyond sex. "But I need to be sure. I don't want to hurt her again."

"Take some time to think, then." She smiled. "You'll figure it out."

Aaron stood up. "I'm going to check on the kids. If they're asleep, we can bring out the gifts."

After he left the room, Josie spoke softly but her tone was steel. "Be a man, Theo. Just like you told Aaron to do. Be a man who owns his mistakes and takes responsibility for who he is. For who he wants to be."

Aaron came back in the room, smiling. "Out cold."

I rose to my feet. "Thanks," I said quietly to Josie. "I appreciate it."

Following Aaron to the basement, I helped him carry up the presents, and we spread them around under the tree while Josie took the plate of cookies and carrots the girls had set out into the kitchen.

"Not much, is it?" My brother grimaced. "I'll do better next year."

I put a hand on his back. "It's more than we had at their age. And they're happy kids, Aaron. I've never seen them happier than they were tonight."

"I don't deserve them, or Josie." His voice was raw with emotion and he sniffed. "I knew just what you meant when you talked about the way that girl looks at you. I'm so damn lucky."

"You are," I agreed.

"Ever think about it? Having a family?"

"No."

"You'd be a kickass dad."

I laughed a little. "Nah."

"You would. You're amazing with my kids."

"That's being an uncle. Being a father is..." I shook my head. As much as I enjoyed playing dad sometimes, twenty-four-hour-a-day responsibility for eighteen years—*per child*

—was daunting. "I can't imagine how hard it is. You're totally responsible for real human beings at all times, not just occasionally."

"True. But along with that responsibility comes a lot of good stuff. There's something to be said for being depended on that way. Being needed that way. Being loved that way. I never want to lose that again." His voice wavered.

I glanced sideways at him. "You're scared you will?"

"Every fucking minute," he whispered, staring straight ahead. "I don't want to be him."

My chest got tight, and I put an arm around him. "You're not. It's gonna be OK," I told him. "And I'm here for you. I'll always be here for you."

Josie came back in the room with the plate, which was now scattered with crumbs. "Look convincing?"

I dropped my arm, and Aaron took a step back. "Very. I have a few more gifts for them in the car. Can I put them under the tree?"

"Sure," Josie said. "Would you like to stay over? Watch them open gifts in the morning?"

I thought for a second. "Sure. Thanks."

Josie brought me a blanket and pillow, and I stretched out on the couch. When all the lights were off except the tree lights and the house was quiet, I lay there in the dark and thought about Claire. Wondered if she was asleep or awake. Wondered how dinner had gone. Wondered if she missed me. Wondered if I had the courage to go to her and ask for another chance.

Would she accept me?

I thought about what my brother had in Josie and the girls, and how nice it was to see him stepping up to be the person—husband, father, man—he wanted to be.

It gave me hope.

TWENTY-FOUR

Claire

FIVE DAYS AFTER CHRISTMAS, I packed two bags—one with clothing, one with art supplies—and headed out of town. I was reluctant to leave right in the middle of my kitchen restoration, but I wasn't getting much joy out of the work anyway. It had been a lot more fun with Theo around.

I was loading the bags and an easel into the car when my phone buzzed in my coat pocket. I didn't recognize the number. Who'd be calling me at nine A.M. anyway?

"Hello?"

"Claire, it's Theo."

My traitorous heart beat quicker. "What do you want? And how did you get this number?"

"From the Hotties for Hire site. It's on your membership application."

I frowned. "I need to cancel that."

"Yes, you do." A pause. "I need to see you."

"I thought you didn't need anything or anybody." I

didn't even know why that hurt me so much—he'd told me flat out the day we met that he had no ties to any person, place or thing and liked it that way. Had I honestly thought I might be the exception? I was such a fucking fool.

"I'm sorry I said that. I didn't mean it."

What? I hesitated. "It took you a week to realize that?"

"Yes, actually. It did. But I want to talk to you about it in person."

Part of me wanted to give in and see him, but I'd learned my lesson with Theo. "Well, I can't. I'm going up to the cabin for a few days."

"What cabin?"

"My family's."

"Alone?"

"Yes, alone," I snapped, aggravated that *now* he cared about my plans. "Want to know why? Because I couldn't bear to let you ruin my Christmas Eve dinner by announcing our breakup, so I made up a lie that we were going on a romantic vacation together."

"Let me come with you. For real."

"Why? So you can fuck me and leave me again?" It wasn't like me to be so crass, but he pushed all my buttons. *Now* he wanted to be real? Too late!

"No. Please Claire, I just want to talk. I won't even touch you."

"Ha! I don't believe you, Mr. I'm Not Good At Stopping."

"There's a lot of snow headed our way. The roads will be bad—you shouldn't drive alone."

"I'll take my chances."

He exhaled noisily. "What do I have to do to convince you to hear me out?"

"I don't know, Theo. I really don't." I hung up.

Then I burst into tears.

THE DRIVE to the cabin usually took about four hours, but snow started to fall about an hour in, so it took me closer to six. I spent the time trying to take my mind off Theo by listening to an audio book. However, my audio library was full of nothing but romance, and three hours into the story, I was annoyed and frustrated with the heroine's reluctance to commit to the amazing guy who wanted her.

"Grow up!" I shouted at her. "Do you know how many women would love to have a man like that fall for them? I can't even take you right now!"

I turned it off in favor of catching up on NPR podcasts, but I was still grumpy when I pulled in the long driveway that led to my family's vacation house.

My mood improved slightly when the cabin came into view, covered with snow like frosting on a gingerbread house. We'd always called it "the cabin," but the only cabin-like thing about it was that it was built from logs and located in the woods. In reality, it was four thousand square feet of luxury. Since my mother is afraid to fly but my father loves to get away, they built the cabin after they got married to have a place to go. My sister and I had spent every summer here growing up, and my parents planned to retire here.

Summers were beautiful, but I'd always loved winter up here too—the snow made it look like a wonderland, and the play of light and shadow as the sun shone through the bare branches of the birch trees was exquisite. I was always inspired by it, and by the tiny bursts of color when a cardinal or bluebird or robin stopped to eat at one of the bird feeders my father and I hung in the trees. First thing, I wanted to walk one of the hiking trails through the woods, but I needed to get some winter gear on first. The snow was a foot deep.

After deactivating the alarm, I let myself in the front door and locked it behind me. I took the bag with my clothes up to my room and left the bag with the supplies by the giant floor to ceiling windows overlooking the woods and frozen lake. A quick check of the pantry, fridge, and freezer told me I had plenty of staples but I'd have to hit the grocery store for milk and fresh produce. Not right this second, though—I was antsy to get outside and move my legs after the long car ride. A quick walk would be perfect, then I'd brave the slippery roads again.

I tugged on ski pants and snow boots I found in the mudroom, traded my wool coat for a ski jacket, and rummaged through a bin for a warm hat, scarf, and mittens. Tucking my phone and the cabin keys into one pocket, I set out, inhaling deep breaths of fresh cold air, watching snowflakes on my tongue. It was so quiet—all I could hear was wind through the trees, birds singing, and the crunch of snow beneath my feet.

But I couldn't find peace or inspiration. Both eluded me as I walked, pausing only when I came to the tire swing that still hung from a tree not far from the house. I gave it a push and watched it sway back and forth, but I didn't get on it. Instead I imagined a little boy clinging to the tire...a beautiful little brown-eyed boy trying to escape what was going on inside his house. My throat tightened.

Had I been too hard on him? He'd had a rough start in life. I wished he'd been more open with me about it, but he'd only seemed willing to talk about his brother's issues. Maybe if he'd shared some of his own experiences or feelings with me, I'd understand him better.

Sighing, I walked back to the house, giving my easel a sad glance before grabbing my car keys. I didn't feel inspired enough to paint, so I might as well go get some groceries for the next few days.

The next seventy-two hours loomed long and lonely in front of me.

SNOW WAS FALLING EVEN HEAVIER NOW, and the roads were worse. It was dark when I finally got back from the store, and I was chilled to the bone. I put on a pot of sweet potato chili, and while it was simmering, I took a long, hot shower and put on my flannel pajamas. That was one good thing about being up here—I could lie around in comfy pants all day.

I was just cozying up on the couch with my Kindle and a soft blanket when I heard a knock on the front door.

What the hell? Who could that be?

Warily I approached the entrance and peeked through one of the windows that flanked the big wooden door. It was dark outside, but motion sensors had triggered the porch light.

It was Theo.

Immediately a battle broke out inside me, one side clamoring to let him in and hear him out, the other desperate to defend its uncompromising position.

He looks so good! And it's so cold and snowy out there, and he drove all this way to find you!

Who cares about how he looks! He uses his hotness as a weapon—don't be fooled! He can probably melt snow with one glance.

I backed away from the window, but not before he saw me.

"Claire," he shouted through the door. "Please let me in."

"No!" I crossed my arms. "Why should I?"

"I drove eight hours through a blizzard to talk to you."

"Then you wasted your time. How did you even find me?"

"I called your mom's house."

My jaw dropped and I yanked the door open. Snow swirled in on a frigid gust on wind. "You did *what?*"

"Thank God. It's fucking freezing out there." He pushed the door shut behind him and inhaled. "Jesus Christ, it smells so good in here. And it's so warm, and you're so beautiful."

I would not be swayed by flattery. But since my heart did not appear to get the message and was beating madly, I stepped back, crossing my arms over my chest again. *No entry.* "You called my mother?"

"I had to. To get the address of this place."

"And she gave it to you?" I rolled my eyes. "Thanks, Mom! Scold me about locking my doors but give out my location to a virtual stranger!"

"But I'm not a stranger. I'm your boyfriend, remember? And you were so disappointed that I had to meet you at the cabin instead of drive with you because of a last-minute business trip to Chicago, so I wanted to send you flowers to make it up to you before I arrived." He took a step toward me, and I put out my hands.

"Stay right there."

"OK." He stopped moving and just looked at me. "I missed you."

"I can't believe my mother fell for that."

His mouth hooked up on one side. "I'm very charming when I want to be."

"It's not charm, it's lies. And it won't work on me anymore." Although that crooked smile had my stomach fluttering. "I was playing the game by your rules, and you stomped all over me."

His smile fell away, replaced by a grave expression. "You're right. I'm sorry."

"I didn't even want to play that game."

"I know."

"So if you're here just to ask me to play another round of sex-without-expectations, the answer is no."

"I'm not. I want more."

"You do?" I blinked. Was this for real?

"Yes."

I stood there, momentarily struck dumb. I had no idea what to do.

"Can I come closer?" he asked.

"I guess," I said cautiously, twisting my fingers together at my waist.

He closed the distance between us until we were nearly chest to chest. His eyes were sincere, his tone solemn. "I'm sorry I walked out like that the last time I saw you. I never should have treated you that way."

"Why did you?"

"Because I panicked. I'd convinced myself that what we were doing was just a temporary thing—I wasn't going to stay in your life. That meant I didn't have to tell you things about myself I don't like sharing."

"Like what?" I gasped. "Oh God, you have a wife."

His forehead wrinkled. "What? No. I don't have a wife."

"Then what is it?"

"Well, lots of things."

I tapped my bare foot. "I'm listening."

"I've fucked up every good thing in my life by giving up on it. Running away from it."

"And?"

"And the reason I don't let anyone get close to me is because I know I'll disappoint them."

Something tugged at my heart, but I did my best to ignore it. "And?"

"And there are things in my past I'm not proud of."

"Such as?"

He looked me right in the eye. "Nine years ago, I was convicted of a felony and served a year in prison for it."

It was as if he'd punched me. A solid blow right to the gut. "What?" What was a felony? Was that like...*murder*? I backed away from him a little. "What did you do?"

"Stole a car," he said matter-of-factly, his face grave. "It was a stupid, fucked-up, drunken night with friends that got out of control. I'm ashamed of it, and I hate talking about it, but I can't change it."

"Why didn't you tell me sooner?" I asked. My mind was reeling. How did I feel about all this? What else was he hiding? No wonder he'd been so reluctant to talk about himself! But I sympathized too—he was revealing some deeply personal fears and feelings. That took a lot of guts.

Theo put his hands in his jacket pockets. "I didn't think I needed to. We'd just met, and that's something I don't put out there right away."

I guess I understood that, but still. "What about after that? What about the night you came back? What about the entire next day we spent together?"

"I could have done it then," he admitted, "but I didn't see the point."

"The point was that I trusted you, and you didn't trust me!" I yelled, pointing at his chest and then mine.

He grimaced. "You're right. And deep down, I know that part of the reason I didn't tell you was because of that trust you had in me. The way you looked at me, I..." He shook his head and shrugged helplessly. "No one's ever looked at me that way before. And it made me feel so good. I didn't want to give that up."

"You thought I wouldn't trust you after that?"

"Yeah. I mean, why should you?"

"Everybody makes mistakes, Theo. You're not your past. And I'm not a judgmental person. But you didn't even give me a chance to tell you that! You were too busy keeping me at a distance so you could ditch me and feel nothing later!"

"Because I thought I was no good for you, Claire." He came at me and took me by the shoulders. "I told you that from the very start."

"That was *my* decision to make," I said through clenched teeth.

"I know." He closed his eyes for a second. "I'm sorry for not trusting you, and for bailing on you. I'm not good at... letting someone in. I never have been."

I appreciated his honesty, but I was still wary. How did we move forward from here? "So now what?"

"Now I ask for another chance with you."

A lump formed in my throat. I was a believer in second chances, but I was scared. "I don't know, Theo." Tears welled in my eyes, and I struggled to speak. "Twice now you've walked out and left me wondering what's wrong with me that I keep getting my hopes up. I don't want to get hurt."

"Come here." He pulled me closer to his chest, and I let

myself give in to the urge to cry, weeping quietly as he spoke. "I've made a lot of mistakes in my life, and I'll probably keep on making them. Driving up here tonight, I kept asking myself why the hell you should give me another chance. And the truth is—I've got no fucking idea."

In spite of everything, it made me laugh a little through my tears.

"But I know that you should. Not because I deserve it. Not because I'm the perfect man. Not because you couldn't do better—God knows you could." He paused. "But I've never felt magic like I do when we're together. And I have to believe that doesn't happen very often."

I sniffed. "I don't think it does."

"So what do you say? Can we try again? Give ourselves a *real* beginning this time, instead of a fake one?"

I wanted to. Deep in my heart, I wanted to. But I needed a moment. I needed to think. And I *really* needed a tissue. "Give me a minute, OK?"

He let me go, and I went into the downstairs bathroom. After going through half a box of tissues, I looked in the mirror, groaning inwardly at my puffy eyes, tearstained cheeks, and red nose. But this was me—the real, behind-the-curtains me. I bruised easily, felt things deeply, and cried when I was sad. I had no desire to hide that. If he wanted to let me in, he had to take all of me.

And give me all of him.

I found him in the living room, sitting on the couch, but he stood when he saw me. "You OK?"

"Yes." It surprised me how steady my voice was. How self-assured my stance. "Did you mean it when you said you wanted more?"

"Yes." He said it firmly, looking me right in the eye.

"That means opening up to me. Being honest. Showing

me who you really are—not just the charming Hottie-for-Hire Theo Woodcock, but *you*. Theo MacLeod."

"I will."

"And it means not bailing when things don't feel magical."

"I know."

"And it means you'll have to earn my trust back."

He nodded. "I know. I'm willing to work for it."

I almost broke down and hugged him, but I remained strong, folding my arms in front of me. "Good. Because this won't be easy. We're going to start with one night of truthful conversation about the real you, past and present."

He nodded, but I can't say he didn't look nervous. "OK."

"And we're not going to touch each other," I went on. "We already know we're very good communicating sexually, but I want more than that."

"I do too."

"Do you agree to the terms?"

"Yes." He paused. "I won't say I'm happy about not touching you, but if that's what it takes, then I'll agree."

"That's what it takes. I need to know exactly who it is that I'm giving this chance to, Theo. That's the only way I'll know whether you're someone I can trust with my whole heart. And if you want anything less than that, you should walk out the door right now." I pointed toward the front door.

He didn't even glance at it. "No," he said, his voice steady and sure. "I want to stay."

TWENTY-FIVE

Theo

FINALLY, I could breathe.

For a solid week I'd felt like I couldn't get enough oxygen, like a tank was parked on my chest, but now that I was here and she'd asked me to stay, I could breathe.

It hadn't been an easy decision, to come here and say those things, list all my faults, and ask for another chance. Part of me had thought she might say fuck you, no, and throw me out on my ass—it would certainly have been her right.

"But is she like that?" Aaron had asked on Christmas Day. I'd lain awake almost the entire night before, thinking about what to do, and I'd voiced my fears to him as we watched the kids open gifts. "From what you've told me, she sounds like a more forgiving person than that."

"She is," I'd said, frowning as I lifted my coffee cup to my lips. My head felt so cloudy this morning, probably because I'd slept so little.

A few minutes went by before he'd spoken again. "Can I ask you a question?"

"Sure."

"Have you forgiven yourself?"

I couldn't look at him. "For what?"

"For anything." When I didn't answer—couldn't answer—he'd gone on. "I think you should start there. With yourself. It's where I have to start, too."

"God. That's really fucking hard."

He'd put a hand on my shoulder. "Sure as hell is, brother. Nothing like a mirror to force you to see truth when you'd much rather see a lie."

His words had stuck with me throughout the following week. He was right—I had to stop avoiding self-reflection and start asking myself some hard questions. I continued to go to the gym and hang out at Aaron's house, watching the kids while Aaron hunted for jobs and Josie worked, but I spent a lot of time at my apartment alone trying to figure out who I was and, more importantly, who I wanted to be.

Now, I confessed it all to Claire.

"Aaron was right—I blamed myself for a lot of things, hated myself for them. And I hadn't forgiven myself at all. Not for hiding when our father abused him. Not for disappointing my coach by dropping out of school. Not for disappointing my grandmother. Not for being so ashamed I couldn't face her until she was already ill. Not for any of my crimes."

She looked up from the cutting board on the counter, where she was struggling to cut a squash in half. "But those aren't *crimes*, exactly. I mean, obviously stealing a car is a crime, but those other things are more like things you feel bad about doing."

My stomach turned over. "There were some other crimes."

"Crimes?" She blinked. "Like, plural?" She waved the butcher knife around.

"Uh, yeah." I slid off the stool I was sitting on and went around the counter to help her. "But it's all in the past. I promise you." I took the knife from her hand and halved the tough-skinned vegetable for her.

She pinned me with a stare. "Have you hurt people, Theo?"

"Never. It only involved money. More like unsavory business deals between—"

"But you're not involved with them any longer?"

I held up my palms. "No. I am clean as can be and plan to stay that way." I'd already called John Salinger and told him I was out of the game. "Aaron and I are going to try the carpentry business again, but I'll probably work at the stoneworks for a while too. Until we build up a good reputation and regular clientele."

"Good. Then I don't want to hear anything unsavory." She grabbed a big spoon from a drawer. "But thank you for telling me the truth."

"You're welcome." There. Another ugly piece of my life was behind me. I inhaled and exhaled, feeling as if my lungs could expand ten times bigger now.

"So go on." Claire picked up a squash half and began to scoop it out. "You were telling me about forgiving yourself?"

"Right." I sat down again, refocusing on what I'd been saying. "The funny thing was, when I wrote down all the things I felt bad about and stared at them, forcing myself to take a hard look at what I'd done, I realized the ones that mattered the most to me, the things that would be hardest to forgive, were the ones that meant I'd let other people down.

People I cared about—my brother, my grandmother, my coach."

She nodded, setting one half down and picking up the second. "What did that tell you?"

"I guess that I carry around a lot of guilt, which I've done my best to ignore." I scratched my head. "I'm good at burying painful stuff so I don't have to deal with it."

"You just move on instead?"

I nodded. "Yes. Much easier to pack up and go somewhere else, do something else, *be* someone else, than to stay in one place and face myself. Although honestly, I don't think I realized what I was doing. I'd just get that restless feeling, like I was cooped up and had to get out, and I'd take off."

"It's funny that you're so perceptive of other people, but not of yourself. Don't you think?" She looked up at me as she put a little water on the bottom of a baking tray.

"Yeah. But there was a reason, you know?"

"Self-preservation?"

I frowned. "I guess. When you put it like that, I'm an even bigger asshole, aren't I?"

She set the squash halves on the tray, cut side down. "I don't think you're an asshole at heart. I think you were probably dealt a shitty hand from the start and you never really worked through it. Instead, you acted out. Drifted. Pretended to be someone else. It all kept you from having to turn the focus inward."

Nodding slowly, I watched her stick the tray in the oven and set the timer. She looked so cute in her pajamas. I wanted to hold her again so badly, but I'd promised not to touch and I intended to keep my word. "I think you're right."

"Know what else I think?"

"What?"

Finally she stopped moving and stood opposite me, her hands on the counter between us. "I'm really sorry about what you and your brother went through as kids." Her eyes were wet. "Every time I think of it, I want to cry."

My instinct was to change the subject, but instead I took another deep breath. "Thanks. It was rough."

She bit her bottom lip, and I stared at it, the memory of her mouth on mine assailing all my senses. "Do you want to talk about it at all?" she asked gingerly.

"Fuck no. But I will."

She smiled ruefully as a tear leaked from each eye. Quickly wiping them away as if she was embarrassed, she came around the counter. "I know I said no touching. But I really need to give you a hug."

I stood up and she came into my arms, rising up on her toes to loop her arms around my neck. I wrapped my arms around her and buried my face in her sweet-smelling hair, choking up when I realized she was still struggling not to cry.

I wanted to tell her it was OK, I was fine, I'd survived, and I was going to do better. But I couldn't speak—my throat was too tight.

Instead we just held each other. And it was enough.

AFTER DINNER, when I finally got to taste the sweet, spicy chili that had been tantalizing me for hours, I helped Claire do the dishes. "I really need to learn how to cook," I told her as I scrubbed out the pot. "That was amazing. I would never have thought to use a squash like a bowl."

"I'm happy to give you the recipe." She loaded some

silverware into the dishwasher. "It's very easy, just involves a lot of chopping and simmering time."

"I need to get a big pot like this too." It was thick and heavy and made of enamel.

"A Dutch oven," she said. "Yes, you definitely need one of those."

I smiled. "I'll have to learn all the fancy names for everything too. And speaking of fancy, this is *not* a cabin."

"It's made of logs, isn't it?" But she was laughing.

"Yeah, about fifty thousand of them." I rolled my eyes. "Cabins do not have two-story cathedral ceilings, big screen televisions, or decks."

"Well, that's what we've always called it." She shut the dishwasher and turned it on. "It's a family tradition and my mother takes those very seriously, so it's not about to change."

Family traditions. I had zero of those, unless you counted skipping out on people. Failing them. "You came up here a lot when you were growing up?"

She leaned back against the counter next to me. "Yes. Tomorrow I'll show you my favorite trails for kissing."

I burst out laughing. "For what?"

"Hiking," she said, her cheeks turning scarlet. "I meant hiking."

"Too bad." I looked down at her, nearly nose to nose. "I like kissing."

A hushed moment of tension.

"Uh, I'll show you where you can sleep." She hurried away from me, moving around the counter and into the great room. "There's a nice bedroom downstairs with a view of the lake."

The only view I wanted was one with her in it, but I nodded politely. "Perfect. Thank you."

"Did you bring a bag?" she asked, looking around.

"It's still in the car. I'll grab it." I grabbed my keys from my coat pocket. "I wasn't sure you were going to let me stay."

"I wasn't even going to let you *in*," she said, crossing her arms over her chest and stepping back as I passed her. "But you wore me down."

"Wasn't that hard," I teased, walking backward toward the door. "Softie."

"I am a softie." She stood up taller. "I can admit it. And I believe in second chances."

"Lucky for me."

Her face lit up, her cheeks flushing pink. She was so fucking pretty. I felt like I'd never get tired of looking at her. Talking to her. Being with her.

And as I hurried through the howling, icy wind and snow to my car, I realized she'd made *me* believe in second chances, too.

"THEO."

I thought I was dreaming when I heard her whisper my name, but a moment later, I heard it again. Felt the mattress shift as she crawled beneath the covers.

"Theo."

I opened my eyes and looked toward her voice in the dark, my heart beating fast. "Claire? Are you OK?"

"Yes." She moved closer to me and I immediately put my arms around her. "I just missed you."

"I missed you too."

"Can I sleep with you?"

"Of course." I wasn't sure if she meant actual sleep or

something else, but I wasn't going to push it. If all she wanted to do was close her eyes and let me hold her all night long, I'd do it.

"I was lying in bed up there, and I couldn't stop thinking about everything you told me." Her left hand rested on my bare chest, one fingertip brushing back and forth over my skin. "Everything you've been through."

I swallowed hard, and tried not to think about my dick. "Yeah?"

"Yeah. I felt so sad. I keep imagining how hard it must have been for you guys to grow up without a mother, with a father who abused you. The two people who are supposed to love you the most and take care of you." She sniffed and snuggled closer, wrapping her arm around me. "I want to go back in time and hug you. Protect you. Rescue you. Change your life so that none of the bad stuff would happen."

I kissed her head. "Thank you. But you know what? I made it out OK. And I'm here now."

"Yes." She kissed my chest. Then she did it again. The third time, she left her lips on my skin. Rubbed them back and forth.

My cock stirred between us.

"Uh, are we still observing the no-touching rule tonight?" I asked as she kissed her way up my chest. "Asking for a friend."

"It's after midnight," she whispered, her breath tickling my ear. "Tomorrow is here."

"Oh, thank fuck." I flipped her beneath me.

She pulled her pajama top over her head and shimmied out of her bottoms while I shoved off my boxer briefs. As soon as I could get my mouth on hers, I kissed her hungrily, passionately, frantically, as if she might be a dream and I was afraid of waking up too soon. My hands sought all the places on her body they'd missed and longed to touch. My tongue stroked along all her curves and hollows. My cock grew hard and thick, aching with the need to be inside her.

She wrapped her hand around it, rubbed the tip over her clit, moaned with pleasure and impatient desire. When she slipped it down, I pulled back. If I didn't stop and get a condom now, I never would. "Hold on," I whispered. "Let me get—"

"Do you have to?" She reached for me again. "I want to feel you—just you—inside me."

I groaned. "You're killing me."

"If you're worried about being safe, I'm on the pill. Come on," she cajoled. "Let me feel you with nothing between us. Even if it's just for a minute."

A minute. Right. As if I was going to last a minute once I got inside her. And if I did, I knew there was no way in hell I was stopping to put on a condom.

"Please," she said softly, feathering my neck with kisses. "I need it. I need to feel that close to you."

God, I wanted to. I wanted to share something with her I'd never shared with anybody. I wanted her to have more of me than anyone else had ever had. But this was an ironclad rule! I'd never broken it—ever. This was more than my real name or my criminal record or my family history. This was *me*. Unprotected. Inside *her*. It was personal. It was intimate. It meant climbing levels of trust I'd never shared with anyone before.

And it scared me.

She moaned, slipping just the tip inside. "Mmmmm, see? Doesn't that feel amazing?"

Fuck fuck fuck, what was the right thing to do? This felt like a critical moment—like the decision I made would change everything. My last defenses breeched. My final wall torn down.

"Come on," she whispered. "Jump."

I gave up the fight, sliding all the way inside her with slow, sweet ease. When I couldn't go any deeper, she looked up at me, and even though it was dark, I knew what her eyes said.

I trust you.

I trust you not to hurt me.

I trust you not to lie to me.

I trust you not to break my heart.

As I moved deep within her, I vowed to myself that I would honor that trust. That I would keep my promises. That somehow I would become the man *she* saw when she looked at me, rather than the one I saw when I looked at myself.

I just had to figure out who he was.

And how to make him stay.

TWENTY-SIX

Claire

"COME HERE, I want to show you something." I grabbed Theo's gloved hand in my mitten-covered one and tugged him through the snow toward the tree with the tire swing. It was late afternoon, but we'd only just gotten out of bed a little bit ago. It was still snowing and the temperature was only about twenty-eight degrees, but the wind had died down a bit, and I felt plenty warm.

"Aha, there it is." Theo grinned when he saw it. His smile was so different today—*he* was so different. Still the same guy who loved to tease me and laugh (he was endlessly amused by all the accoutrements of the "cabin" as he was fond of calling it, complete with air quotes), but gone were his guarded responses and wary expressions. No shadow fell across his face when I asked about his past, his family, or his feelings. I can't say that he appeared to enjoy talking about himself, but he was doing what he'd said he'd would—letting me in.

"*That's* the swing you were scared of falling off?" he taunted.

"Yes." I giggled. "In my defense, it seemed higher up when I was little."

He shook his head, laughing. "Get on it. I'll push you."

I put my legs through the tire and held on to the sides. He grabbed me by the waist, pulled me back, and let me go. I laughed, stretching my legs out in front of me and my head back as I swung through the air, snow flurries drifting down around me. When I slowed down, he gave my legs a shove so I spun around in dizzying circles.

"Stop!" I shrieked, breathless with laughter. "I won't be able to walk when I get off."

He held it still and I waited a moment before getting off, hoping the world would stop spinning. But when Theo leaned down and kissed me, I felt even more light-headed.

"Was it fun?"

"Yes," I said.

"Not afraid of falling anymore?"

"Nope. I'm getting braver by the day, aren't I?"

"You are. I'm very impressed. Next I'm going to work on getting you to submit some artwork."

I narrowed my eyes at him and got off the swing. "Next you're going to work on building that business of yours. I don't want you supplementing your income by hiring your-self out as a Hottie anymore." I thumped him on the chest. "You're my hottie. And I don't like to share my toys."

He smiled and wrapped his arms around me. "I promise you, I'm all yours."

I'd never get tired of hearing that.

We spent another hour out in the snow—making snow angels, throwing handfuls of snow at each other, trying to catch snowflakes on our tongues. We attempted a snowman, but the snow was too soft for packing. Eventually the wind picked up and our fingers and toes grew numb, so we went inside to warm up.

Theo built a fire in the fireplace while I hunted for the ingredients to make real hot chocolate for us. Then he stood rapt at my side as I warmed milk, sugar, a cinnamon stick and a vanilla bean in one pan and melted good dark chocolate in the double boiler.

"What is that thing?" he asked, his face scrunching up. His hair was a damp, tousled mess, but he looked so adorable, I had to smile.

"It's a double boiler. Don't worry, you don't need one." After removing the stick and bean from the milk, I carefully poured in the melted chocolate.

"What if I want to make fancy ass hot chocolate for my girlfriend one day?"

My heart knocked crazily against my ribs. "Then you can use mine." I whisked the chocolate into the milk, and threw him a suspicious look over one shoulder. "Assuming the girlfriend is me."

"Um, your ass is phenomenal, your cooking makes my mouth water, and you give the best blowjobs known to man. It's totally you."

"I knew it. You just drove up here for the food and the sex."

"I'd be lying if I said those things weren't tempting." Moving behind me, he wrapped his arms around my waist and buried his face in my neck. "But you know that's not why I'm here."

"I know." Smiling like a lovestruck teenager, I added a tiny pinch of salt and chili powder, then shook him loose. "Shoo. I have to get this off the heat." He let me go, and I poured the fragrant chocolate into two hug mugs. "Let's drink it over here by the fire. I'm still freezing." I set the mugs on a tray along with a bag of marshmallows.

"Oh my God. Marshmallows?"

"Marshmallows. Your favorite thing."

He tugged a strand of my hair. "You're my favorite thing." A pause. "But now I have an idea that involves marshmallows too..."

WE SPENT all afternoon drinking and talking and sharing chocolate-flavored kisses in front of the fire. Snow continued to fall, blanketing the woods and the house, and huge drifts pressed at the windows. It made me feel like we were the only two people alive, tucked away from everything, hidden inside our own little fairy tale world.

"It's New Year's Eve." Lying on my side, I propped my head on one hand. "Doesn't that seem weird?"

"You're right." Theo's long legs were stretched out in front of him, and he leaned back on his elbows. "It does, kind of."

"Do you usually go out?"

"Depends. I did before I stopped drinking. What about you?"

"Yeah. I usually do something with my friends. Oh, shoot." I sat up.

"What?"

"I just realized I'm going to owe my friend Margot a hundred bucks."

His brow furrowed. "Why?"

"She bet me you'd apologize for walking out like you did by January first."

He feigned outrage, sitting up tall. "You bet against me?

How dare you!" Lunging for me, he pinned my body beneath his, shackling my wrists next to my head.

"I'm sorry!" I squealed, crushed by the weight of his chest. "I didn't know!"

"How *could* you?" He shook his head. "You faithless, heartless woman."

"Let me go!" Laughing, I tried kicking my legs, but he pinned them with his own.

"Never." He moved down so his hips rested between my thighs and brought his lips close to mine. "Never."

I wrapped my arms and legs around him as his tongue swept into my mouth, and slid my fingers into his hair. The fire crackled and sparked as we lay tangled together on the floor, but our passion burned even hotter. We never stopped kissing as we rolled and shifted to shed pants and shirts and socks and underwear. I ended up on top, straddling his hips, his cock sliding between my legs as I rocked my body over his. He moaned, taking my breasts in his hands, teasing the tingling peaks with his thumbs.

"I need you inside me," I whispered, reaching between us. "Right now."

"Should I go get—"

"No." Sitting up, I slowly eased myself onto his cock, watching his jaw fall open and his eyes roll back in his head. This morning, we'd used a condom—twice—and even though the sex was still incredible, there had been something there the night before that I missed. It wasn't a physical feeling—it was something else. I wasn't even sure what to call it.

"Fuuuuck," he moaned. "I cannot believe how good that feels."

When he was buried inside me, I held still just for a moment, letting my body adjust. "You're so deep," I whispered as I braced my hands on his chest. "How is it possible you feel even deeper? I can barely breathe." I started to move my hips in tiny circles, leaning forward so my hair brushed against his chest.

"God, I love your hair." He wove his fingers through it, wrapping his hands around my head and pulling me into a kiss.

"I love that there's nothing between us." As I set a sensuous rhythm above him, I realized that's what made this so different—there was no longer anything in the way. He felt deeper because he *was*. Because he'd bared himself to me. Because he'd let down his guard and showed me his true self. Sex without a condom was just a physical symbol of an emotional barricade destroyed.

I felt fearless—and I couldn't get enough.

I rocked my hips a little faster, the heat and friction between us growing feverish and frantic. I stayed tight to his body, rubbing my clit against the base of his cock, crying out as he pinched my nipples and sent me over the edge. Over and over again, my body throbbed around his bare cock, and I was delirious with the joy of it—he was here and he was mine and it was real.

Theo sat up and turned me beneath him, our bodies still connected. "You're so fucking hot," he growled, driving into me again and again. The tension inside me that had just unwound began to coil again.

"Yes," I breathed, bringing my knees up alongside his ribs. "Don't stop. Don't stop."

"Not until you come again for me."

I raked my nails down his back, grabbed his ass, and pulled him close. "Fuck yes, right there." It was insane how fast the second orgasm hit me, and I bucked up beneath him, my body a live wire. "Now you come for me," I panted. "Anywhere you want."

He groaned, getting to his knees and moving in and out of me with slow, deep strokes. He looked down at me. "Are you sure?"

"Yes." I paused, pushing myself to be brave and say what I wanted. "I liked it that one time, but I couldn't see you. I want to watch." The idea had sort of come out of nowhere, but it made sense—I wanted him to let me see him like that, masculine and virile and unashamed, but vulnerable too. And I wanted to offer my body that way. It was sexual, but also intimate.

It meant we trusted each other.

I ran my hands over my stomach, my chest, my throat. "Anywhere you want. You can cover me with it."

"Jesus," he whispered, pulling out of me and taking his cock in his hand.

"No one's ever done this to me before," I whispered, eyes wide as I watched his flesh slipping through his fingers. "You're the first."

"Good." Knees slightly apart, he squared his shoulders and straightened his spine. He looked like a god. The firelight burnished his skin to copper and made his dark hair glint with gold. The sculpted muscles of his arms and chest and abs flexed as he worked his fist up and down, faster and faster. His breath came hard and heavy.

"I love it. I love watching you." I kept my hands on my breasts, playing with them just like he had. His jaw was set, his eyes hooded, his chest rising and falling with an increasing rhythm.

"Oh fuck, oh fuck, oh God, you're gonna make me come so hard." His hand became a blur, his breathing even more strangled.

"Yes," I told him, over and over again, my body tingling with anticipation.

He widened his knees, his hips thrusting his cock through his hand. I watched, riveted, as he brought himself to the edge of climax and pushed himself over, unashamed and unguarded. Finally he leaned forward slightly, angling his cock toward my chest and came all over my breasts and stomach in hot, pulsing bursts.

It was the hottest thing I'd ever seen, but even better, it made me feel closer to him than ever before.

Still breathing hard, he sat back on his heels and looked down at me. "I'm trying for words, but I think my brain is broken."

I smiled. "It's OK." I started to get up, but he stopped me.

"Don't move." He stood up, pulled on his jeans, and disappeared for a minute. When he came back, he knelt next to me with paper towels in his hand. "Let me." He did his best to clean me up, but my skin was still pretty sticky.

"I think I should probably just shower," I said.

"Probably. Sorry." He stood up and reached down for me.

"I'm not." I put my hand in his and let him help me to my feet. "I loved every second of that. Didn't you?"

He laughed. "Um, *yes*."

"Want to get in the shower with me?"

"Again, *yes*. Got any more crazy questions?"

"Are you hungry?"

"*Yes*."

"Good." I started gathering up my clothes, and he did the same. "Let's take a shower, and then we'll eat, and then we can snuggle up on the couch and watch an old movie that will probably make me cry and you can poke fun at me."

"Poke what at you?"

"Ha. That too."

We went upstairs and I ran a hot shower in the bathroom across the hall from my bedroom. As we slipped beneath the spray, Theo asked if he could wash my hair.

"Sure," I said, surprised. "My shampoo is right there." I got my hair wet and turned my back to him, smiling blissfully as he lathered my head and massaged my scalp.

Afterward, I applied the conditioner and let Theo soap me up, laughing at how serious he was taking the job, and the way he claimed every new part of my body he touched was his favorite part. When I was all rinsed off, we switched places and I lathered him up from head to toe, running my hands along all his limbs, sliding my palms over rippling abs, rising on tiptoe to wash his hair.

Once he was rinsed, he pulled me under the water with him and wrapped his arms around me. I rested my head on his chest and twined my arms around his waist. His heart beat steadily against my cheek.

For a minute, neither of us said anything. Steam rose up around us, and water cascaded down our bodies, but we were still. I felt warm and safe in his arms.

"Thank you," he said.

"For what?"

"For trusting me. It means everything."

I hugged him tighter. Kissed his chest. "I know."

"I THINK we missed New Year's." We were finally worn

out, cuddled up beneath the covers in the same bed we'd slept in last night.

"Hold on, I'm trying to think of a joke about balls dropping."

I laughed, pressing as much of my skin to his as possible. "I can imagine."

We were silent for a moment, his fingertips brushing idly back and forth on my shoulder. "Home tomorrow?"

"Yeah." I sighed. "As long as the roads permit it. I wish we didn't have to go. I love it up here, just the two of us, no noise. But I would like you to meet my friends, eventually. And introduce you to my dad."

His body tensed. "The judge?"

"Yes. But stop worrying. My father is not a fire and brimstone kind of guy. He's very kind and has always believed in rehabilitation. And we don't even have to tell him about your past. It's not his business."

"The record is easily found."

"It's not important anymore. And it doesn't matter to me."

He breathed easier. "OK."

"And we already know my mother adores you."

"I don't know about that."

"I do. Trust me, she'll be cooking meals for you in no time. Baking cookies for you. Picking out sweaters for you."

He laughed a little. "She sounds like a great mom."

"A little overbearing, but yes. She loves to mother people."

We were silent again for a while, and I thought he'd fallen asleep, but he spoke again. "I don't even remember my mother."

A chill ran up my spine. "No?"

"No. She left when I was only one."

"I don't know how any mother could do that," I said.

"She left a note. It said, 'Tell the boys I love them.'"

The chill turned to goosebumps that blanketed my arms. "I'm...I'm sure she did, in her own way."

"But not enough."

I didn't know what to say.

A moment later, he said, "Doesn't matter anyway."

"It doesn't?"

"Nah. Like I said. I don't even remember her."

He didn't say anything more, but I didn't believe him that it didn't matter. What did that do to someone, to be abandoned by a mother who'd said she loved him?

I thought about how different my family was than his, how opposite our childhoods had been. The more I learned about Theo's past, the more amazed I was that he'd grown into such a warm, easygoing person. In many ways, he was much more at ease with himself than I was. But how much of that was an act, a mask he wore so he could keep the painful stuff buried?

No wonder he didn't like getting close to people. On some subconscious level, he was probably always worried they were going to leave.

I've fucked up every good thing in my life by giving up on it. Running away from it.

Because he was scared to stay.

And the reason I don't let anyone get close to me is because I know I'll disappoint them.

No, it was because he didn't think he was enough to make them stay. If she hadn't...why would anyone else?

A lump built in my throat, but I fought off the tears by concentrating on the warmth of Theo's body, the smell of his skin, the beat of his heart. He fell asleep first, and I kept still, wrapped in his arms and lulled by the deep, slow rhythm of his breathing.

But I was awake for a long time.

TWENTY-SEVEN

Theo

THE SNOW HAD CEASED during the night, and reports said the highways were fine, so we decided to take off. Claire had things she needed to get done before school started again, and I had a ton of shit to figure out, too. We drove home separately, and even though I missed her two minutes after I hit the road, I was glad for the time to think.

Things had gone pretty damn near perfectly.

I'd told her exactly who I was, admitted all the shit I'd done, and warned her it wasn't easy to get close to me. But actually...it had been kind of easy. Or maybe she just made it feel easy. She didn't judge me, didn't tell me I was damaged, didn't insist I fix X,Y, and Z about myself before she'd consider giving me another chance. I'd known from the start she had a heart big enough to let me in, but I hadn't realized how much I wanted to be there. Or how quickly I'd want her in mine.

I loved hearing about her family, her students, her

memories at "the cabin." Laughing, I shook my head. Calling that log palace a cabin was like calling Mount Everest "the anthill." But even though she'd grown up privileged, she wasn't spoiled. The things she enjoyed most in life were not luxuries. She wanted to inspire and be inspired—that mattered more to her than anything. She wanted to take care of people and things. She wanted to feel good about herself.

She was pure gold, and no way in hell was I good enough for her. But if she was willing to put up with me, I'd do everything I could to make her happy, things I'd never done for anyone before.

Work hard and work honestly. Meet her friends and family. Introduce her to Aaron and Josie and the girls. Stay.

For her, I'd stay.

TWENTY-EIGHT

Claire

ON THE DRIVE HOME, I called Margot.

"Hello?"

"I owe you a hundred bucks." I couldn't keep the grin off my face.

She gasped. "Seriously?"

"Seriously. I went up to the cabin for some time away, and he showed up."

"Oh my God. And?"

"And apologized, just like you said. Told me he'd panicked. Asked for another chance."

"It's like I wrote the script!" she said happily.

I laughed. "It is."

"So things are good?"

"So far." I hesitated. "He's kind of...a complicated guy. One of those guys who has a lot of baggage and doesn't like to talk about it."

"Oh. Believe me, I get that. That's Jack to a tee."

"He was really open with me over the last couple days, but that was sort of my condition. I told him if he wanted another chance, he had to let me in."

"Good for you," she said firmly.

"And he did," I said. "It's crazy, Margot. For the first time, I feel really good about someone. Hopeful, but not in a rush. I'm just excited to see where it takes us, you know?"

"Perfect. Enjoy this stage of it—that newness is such a thrill. I will even let you keep your hundred bucks."

I grinned. "I'll buy you a nice wedding present."

"So when do we get to meet him? Before the wedding, I hope?"

"That would be fun. I'll get in touch with Jaime, and maybe we can find a date sometime this month."

"Sounds good. I'm really happy for you, Claire."

"Thanks." My stomach fluttered. "I'm happy, too."

TWENTY-NINE

Claire

GOOD THINGS HAPPENED IN JANUARY.

Theo and I finished my kitchen restoration—he even got me a discount on the gorgeous granite countertop I chose since he'd started working at the stoneworks again. We pulled up the old floor, laid the new travertine tiles, refinished the table, and above it we hung a fantastic vintage light fixture Theo found at a salvage shop.

We had dinner downtown with Jaime, Quinn, Jack, and Margot, and Theo charmed them just like he'd charmed me the first time we met.

"Oh my God, he's adorable." Margot grabbed my elbow the moment we got into the ladies room after dinner. "And you guys look so cute together—he's so tall!"

"He is." I giggled. "Sometimes it's a challenge."

"So how are things?" Jaime asked, taking her lipstick from her purse.

"Good." I shrugged. "I mean, it's only officially been a couple weeks, but it feels really good."

Jaime nodded, her eyes narrowing. "I've got the vibe about you guys. I don't know what it is, but it seems right."

"It's chemistry," said Margot. "Did you see the way he looks at her? I thought he was going to eat her for dessert."

Jaime smirked. "The night is young, Margot. Give him time."

Later, we got in the car and Theo exhaled. "Fuck. I was nervous."

"You were?" That surprised me. "It didn't show."

"Good." He turned the key in the ignition. "I like your friends. I can tell they're protective of you."

I smiled, patting him on the shoulder. "They are, so watch your step. Margot throws a mean scone." We'd laughed over that story at the table, and Jaime and had I exchanged a wink.

The following weekend was Margot's surprise shower, and it went off without a hitch. She cried (no one cries more elegantly than Margot Thurber Lewiston, with her delicate sniffles and monogrammed handkerchiefs to dab at tears), she laughed, she opened an endless number of china settings, and we all got a little tipsy on champagne.

Theo took me over to his brother's house and introduced me to his family—his brother Aaron, an older, stockier version of Theo with a warm handshake and quiet demeanor. Theo's sister-in-law Josie was a petite brunette with a lovely, welcoming smile and obvious devotion to her family. And three adorable little girls, who attacked Theo as soon as he walked in the door, hanging on him like little monkeys. Honestly, it had kind of surprised me. I hadn't imagined he was so good with kids.

"Your nieces are adorable," I told him on the ride home.

He smiled. "Thanks."

"They're crazy about you."

"Isn't everybody?"

I punched him on the arm. "You're so good with them. How did that happen?"

He shrugged. "I don't know. They're immature. I'm immature. It works."

"It's more than that, silly. You're genuinely good with them. Do you like kids?"

"I like *those* kids."

"Do you want your own someday?"

He gave me a frightened glance. "You're not trying to tell me something, are you?"

"No, no. I'm not pregnant."

He exhaled a huge sigh of relief. "Thank God. I don't think I'd make a very good father."

"I think you're wrong," I said, "but I promise the question was purely out of curiosity and not necessity."

"What about you? Let me guess—you want a whole dozen of them."

"Maybe not a *dozen*, but yes. I do." I sighed. "You'll probably think this is stupid and boring, but I love the idea of a house full of kids, a swing on the front porch, bikes in the yard, finger paintings on the refrigerator, lemonade stand on the sidewalk..."

"Wow, that's really specific."

"I know. It's just how my brain works—I picture all the details in the background."

"But it's not stupid or boring, Claire. And I happen to love lemonade." He reached over and took my hand, giving it a quick squeeze. "Hey, Peyton's birthday is coming up. Want to help me shop for a gift?"

I wasn't sure if he'd intentionally changed the subject or

not, but I let it go. It didn't really matter. We'd only been seeing each other for a month, after all, and I was enjoying myself. For once, my present was as enticing as my dream about the future.

But I warned my mother not to ask Theo a bunch of questions about the future when we met my parents for dinner. She seemed offended that I'd even make such a request, and I will admit that she behaved herself very well at the restaurant. Only once did I have to kick her under the table, when she sighed dramatically and lamented her lack of grandchildren: "It's like my daughters want to punish me or something."

Theo had been a good sport, although unlike when we were at dinner with my friends, he was visibly anxious—at least to me. My parents might not have noticed the jittering leg or the sheen on his forehead, but I did. Several times during the evening, I took his hand and held it beneath the table. Each time, he sent me a grateful smile.

The night went well. Although my dad was slightly disappointed Theo hadn't gone to Yale or Ohio State, they were able to talk a lot about football. And my mother was charmed by his manners, his smile, and his conversation skills. "You can just tell he was raised right," she said to me in the ladies room. "Even if he didn't go to Yale."

We spent most of our time at my house, but I did get to see his apartment one Saturday, a sparsely furnished one-bedroom with nothing on the walls, only the barest essentials in the kitchen, and a view of the parking lot from all the windows.

"Think you'll stay here?" I asked him, opening a kitchen drawer. "My God, Theo. You have plastic utensils. And they're not even in trays, they're still in the bags."

"Yeah, I meant to get some silverware; I just never got

around to it." He went into the bedroom to grab clean clothes for work the next day.

"Please let me help you outfit this kitchen," I called out. "And maybe put some pictures up. Or I'll give you a painting. But all these white walls are so sterile. It's creepy."

"I'd love a painting." He came out of his bedroom with a bag over his shoulder. "And speaking of that, did you send the application today for the July art fair?"

I blushed as I shook my head, my gaze dropping to the floor.

"Why not?"

"Because I'm scared."

"We talked about this. And the deadline is in two days."

I met his disapproving glare. "I know."

He grabbed me by the hand. "Come on."

Tugging me along like an obstinate child, he stuck me in the car, drove to my house, pulled me out again, and hustled me inside. "Get your laptop."

I dragged my feet, but I went into the spare bedroom I used as an office and unplugged it, bringing it to the living room where he stood waiting.

He pointed at the couch. "Sit. Open it."

I did as he asked, biting my lip when I saw the online application still up on the screen. The Submit button taunted me.

"Do it." Theo stood over me. His height and broad chest were intimidating.

My stomach churned. This was it. Once I hit that button, my artwork in the form of five attached images— would be out there for people to judge. I would be out there for people to judge. What if I wasn't good enough? "I don't think I'm ready."

"You are."

"No, really. I'm a good teacher, but—"

"Claire."

I looked up at him helplessly, searching for sympathy in his brown eyes, but finding only defiance. "You don't understand. You're asking me to send my naked heart and soul, my*self*, out there in the cold, dark woods where wolves will be prowling."

"*Claire.*"

"Maybe bears. And I'm naked."

"Oh, Jesus. Listen to me." He sat down next to me on the couch. "You are good enough. Say it."

"I'm good enough." But I didn't believe it.

"This is what I want."

"This is what I want," I repeated, and it was. "I just wish it wasn't so scary."

"I understand. I've felt naked and scared before too—like when I drove eight hours through a blizzard to ask you for another chance."

I swallowed. My throat was so dry.

"But I did it. And it felt good. Even if you'd said no, at least I would have known that I'd tried. Walking away would have been the easier thing to do, but I didn't want to wonder *what if* for the rest of my life. And you don't either."

"No," I admitted. My finger hovered over the mousepad.

"Do it," he urged. "Jump."

I held my breath. Counted to three. And hit the button.

Success! said the screen.

We'll see.

Theo wrapped his arms around me and squeezed. "I'm proud of you."

My heart was beating furiously, and my belly still

hadn't settled down, but I smiled. "Thanks. I needed the push."

"Feel good?"

I took a deep breath, grateful for him. I tipped my head onto his shoulder. "Yes. I do."

Things with us had only gotten better. The magic grew stronger. The more time we spent together, the deeper I fell for him. I'd never fallen in love before, but I was positive this was it. There were times I looked at him that I felt like my heart was going to explode. I wanted to be with him all the time—he was the first thing I thought of in the morning, and the last thing I thought about before I fell asleep at night. He was all I wanted.

Theo wasn't the type to offer up his feelings in words, but everything he did for me told me he cared, from the restoration work to building my confidence about my art to tolerating my sappy movies to meeting my friends and family to printing a picture of us and sticking it to his fridge (held there by a magnet his nieces had given him for Christmas that said Best Uncle Ever). And I knew that he hadn't grown up in a household like mine, where we expressed our feelings and said I love you and never worried that the people who loved us would leave us. I thought about what he'd told me about his mother's note a lot—to him, words like *I love you* were probably empty and meaningless. What you did mattered more than what you said.

Yet there were moments when I would have liked the words. It wasn't that I needed those *specific* words, exactly, just...some reassurance that I wasn't alone. That I mattered to him as much as he mattered to me. That we were meant to be together. I tried hard to make sure he knew he was enough for me, despite his initial misgivings that he wouldn't be.

But he remained silent on the subject of his feelings, and I didn't push.

When it came to sex, on the other hand, he was anything but silent. The things he said to me were shocking, but I loved every filthy word out of his mouth. And there was nothing he liked more than when I talked to him that way, telling him what I wanted him to do to me. Somehow our chemistry had gotten even hotter since New Year's, and often I found myself fantasizing about him at odd times—during teacher meetings, in line at the grocery store, when stopped at a red light. People would have to honk to get my attention. "Sorry, sorry," I'd mumble, giving an apologetic wave. But I wasn't sorry. It was the best sex I'd ever had—the dirtiest, the daringest and the most intense.

I felt like a different person. And I liked it.

By the time Margot's wedding day arrived, we'd been seeing each other for six weeks, spending almost every night together at my house. He was there when I received the notice in the mail that I'd been accepted at the July art fair, and didn't even tease me about how much I cried with relief and joy. He just held me and said over and over again how proud he was. How this was only the beginning.

I believed him.

THIRTY

Theo

SHE WAS ALWAYS BEAUTIFUL.

Especially first thing in the morning. I have no idea if sleep somehow erased the memory of just how lovely she was, but every time I woke up to find her sleeping next to me, I was amazed all over again.

Or maybe I was just amazed she was still there.

Frankly, I was amazed *I* was still there sometimes. I kept waiting for that restless feeling to kick in, that twitchy feeling in my bones that meant I was feeling trapped, it was time to pack up and move on, or at least change the routine. But it never did. For the first time, I found comfort in the routine. It didn't feel like monotony, it felt like ease. It didn't feel like a cage, it felt like heaven.

Aaron and I had put out some ads for Two Brothers Carpentry with a discount for new customers. We were getting calls, slowly but steadily, and Zack was very accommodating with my schedule at the stoneworks. He'd even given Aaron a job as well.

I'd survived meeting Claire's friends and family—actually, I'd even enjoyed it. Claire's mom was slightly overbearing, but she was kind and inquisitive, and it was easy to see where Claire had gotten her beauty. Her father, as promised, was easygoing and friendly, and I'd enjoyed talking about football with him. It was no trouble at all to pretend I'd been born in Connecticut (I was more than happy to forget about my early life in Kansas City), and even though I hadn't gone to Ohio State (Claire took the blame for that one, feigning confusion), I was able to talk college football with him. It was a little nerve-wracking when her father asked about my degree, but he didn't seem shocked or disapproving when I said I'd left school before it was completed. I probably felt worse about it than he did.

Meeting her friends was a lot of fun. I got a kick out of hearing stories about shy, awkward high-school Claire with braces, and the way they teased each other made it easy to see how well they knew each other. I had the feeling I was there under inspection, so I tried my best to be the kind of guy they'd choose for Claire while still being myself. If I felt less confident than I acted, I hoped it didn't show.

Aaron and Josie loved her, and my nieces kept asking me if she was my girlfriend. "I guess she is," I told them one day when I was there alone. "Is that OK?"

"Yes," said Ava. "Should we call her Aunt Claire?"

"I don't think just yet." Josie jumped in to rescue me. "Let's give Uncle Theo some time to get to know her better before we start calling her 'Aunt.'" But she'd winked at me. And later my brother had said, "That girl is the real deal. Don't fuck this up."

I was doing my best. But this was a new world to me, and I wasn't always sure I belonged in it.

Most of the time, the magic between us was enough to allay the whispers in the back of my brain, the ones that said things like, *Don't kid yourself, asshole. You're not what she wants and sooner or later she's going to realize it.* After I met her friends, the voice would add things like, *You'll never be able to give her the things a successful guy like Quinn would. Jack owns forty-four acres, a house, and six horses. What do you own?*

Um. A six-year-old SUV? Some tools? A Best Uncle Ever magnet?

The list was embarrassingly paltry.

But I did my best to ignore those voices and bury the worry they produced because Claire made me feel better than anyone ever had. I didn't have to be anybody else when I was with her, and she didn't care who I wasn't. She didn't care who I'd been in the past. She was happy with me—it was so fucking crazy. *I* made her happy.

I was starting to think I'd finally bested my demons, finally broken the MacLeod curse, finally reached a time and place in my life I never wanted to leave.

THIRTY-ONE

Claire

MARGOT WAS the calmest bride I'd ever seen.

And the most beautiful.

"How many minutes?" she asked, standing in front of a three-way mirror in the bride's room at the church. She was the epitome of elegance in an off-the-shoulder ballgown with three-quarter sleeves. Her long blond hair was coiled at her nape into a classic bun from which not one strand escaped. A cathedral-length veil flowed from the top of her bun to beyond the train of her dress, and the diamonds at her ears twinkled in the lights. Jaime and I, her only female attendants, wore long, navy strapless mermaid gowns, diamond earrings (a gift from Margot), and carried white roses.

"About five," said the coordinator from the doorway. "The grandparents are being seated now."

"OK. Thank you." She beamed at her reflection, her perfect white teeth sparkling. "I'm ready."

I caught her eyes in the mirror. "You look so beautiful, Margot. I should stop looking at you because I keep crying, but I can't look away."

She laughed. "No crying. I'm the bride. If I don't cry, you don't." She turned around and looked at me. "But you have the hankie I gave you just in case, right?"

I nodded, showing her where I had it tucked into my palm, hiding by the thick stems of my bouquet. It had been one of her gifts to Jaime and me, delicate lace-trimmed white handkerchiefs monogrammed with our initials. "Got it."

"Even I might cry," admitted Jaime. "I've held off so far, but I'm a little nervous about the ceremony."

"No tears," Margot insisted.

"No promises," Jaime replied. "God, Margot. I can't believe this is really it."

"Me neither." She shook her head gently, closing her eyes. "OK, I might have spoken too soon about not crying." Inhaling and exhaling slowly, she took a few deep, calming breaths.

"You OK?" I asked sympathetically.

"Yes. Just emotional. I never thought we'd get here." She reached for our hands, and Jaime and I each took one. "I love you guys. You're the best friends I could ever ask for. Thank you for everything you've done, and for always being there for me."

"Oh, God," Jaime moaned, blinking frantically. "That's it. My mascara is doomed."

Margot smiled. "Sorry. I'm almost done being sappy. I just wanted to take a moment and tell you both how happy I am to share today with you."

"We love you." I squeezed her hand. "And I could not be happier today if I were the bride."

"Me either." Jaime sniffed, composing herself. "You and Jack are perfect together. I'm so happy for you both."

"OK, ladies. Let's make our way down." The coordinator and an assistant helped Margot with her long train, and Jaime and I led the way out of the room, down the stairs, and quietly snuck into the back of the church. It was packed with guests, mostly on Margot's side, but a fair amount on Jack's side too. The organ music echoed throughout the beautiful old cathedral, and the pews and altar were decked in flowers.

Margot stayed hidden at the bottom of the stairs. Muffy came over and gave her two air kisses before smiling at Jaime and me. I couldn't believe how calm she was—my mother would have been a mess—but I supposed that's where Margot inherited her composure. Senator Lewiston appeared, bestowing a kiss on the bride's cheek before offering her his arm.

The coordinator lined everyone up. Jack's mother would be seated first, escorted by a family friend; then Margot's mother, escorted by Margot's brother, Buck. Once they were seated, Jack and his two brothers appeared at the front of the church, and Jaime and I immediately grabbed hands. They were all handsome, but Jack was breathtaking in his black custom suit. Margot's perfect match.

I was next.

When I got the nod, I took a deep breath and walked slowly down the aisle, smiling at people I recognized and struggling not to cry. I saw Theo sitting with my parents and my grin got wider. He looked gorgeous in his suit and tie—the same ones he'd worn the night of Elyse's wedding. I hadn't seen it since then, and I almost laughed out loud at the memory of it strewn all over my living room.

We'd come a long way since then.

When I reached the end of the aisle, I met Jack's eyes and gave him a smile. He looked nervous, way more nervous than Margot had seemed.

Jaime joined me at the front of the church, and we held hands as we watched the flower girl, Jack's niece, come up the aisle, followed by his adorable little curly-haired nephew, serving as ring bearer. When Jack saw the kids, he lit up, but it was nothing compared to the way his face changed when Margot appeared at the foot of the aisle on the arm of her father.

He was transformed, watching his radiant bride come toward him. And when she met his eyes, even Margot's composure seemed to slip, her bottom lip trembling. Jaime and I lost it, both of us frantically trying to save our eye makeup with our hankies as tears leaked from our eyes.

We managed to sniffle only once or twice during the vows, but fell apart again when everyone was asked to rise and the officiant presented us with "Mr. and Mrs. Jack Valentini!"

It's real, I thought as the entire church burst into applause and cheers. *Love is real and it's powerful enough to conquer any odds.* I caught Theo's eye one last time, as I walked back down the aisle on Jack's brother Brad's arm. He winked and smiled as he applauded, and my heart threatened to burst wide open.

I love him, I thought, tearing up all over again. *I love him and I'm going to say the words.* Why should I hold back? What was there to be afraid of? Embracing Margot and Jack at the back of the church, I felt even more certain. Love was a beautiful thing, and today was all about celebrating it. I wouldn't care if he didn't say it back. I loved him, and I wanted him to know it.

Tonight.

THIRTY-TWO

Theo

"HAVE YOU BEEN OK?" Claire looked up at me, concern in her eyes. She'd been busy all day and most of the night with bridesmaid duties, but I finally had her to myself on the dance floor, wrapped in my arms as we swayed to an old standard.

"I've been fine," I promised her. "Your dad and I have been discussing the Super Bowl."

"Still?" She wrinkled her nose.

"Yes. For football fans, it's kind of a big deal. But I'm much happier now that I have you to talk to."

She smiled radiantly, stars in her eyes. "Me too."

I wasn't much for public affection, but I couldn't resist dropping a quick kiss on her lips. "I love when you wear the red lipstick. It reminds me of the first night."

Her scarlet smile widened. "Oh yeah. God, that night seems so long ago, doesn't it? I was thinking earlier when I saw you were wearing that suit, we've come a long way."

"We have," I agreed. The memory of wanting to be with her and telling myself I couldn't was sharp.

"Are you happy?"

"Of course I am."

"Good. Because I am too." Her cheeks were pink, and her voice went a little breathless. "I've never been this happy. I've never felt this way about anyone."

God, she was so beautiful. I was so lucky. Pulling her in a little tighter to my chest, I pressed my lips to her temple.

"I'm in love with you," she said softly. "I know we haven't been together that long, and maybe it's crazy, but it's what I feel."

I'd stopped moving, and she leaned back at the waist to look at me. "Are you OK? Was it too soon to say that?"

"No," I managed. My body had gone completely still, like a rabbit under the shadow of a hawk. But I wasn't scared. I didn't know what I was. I felt strange in my skin.

"Then what is it?"

"No one's ever said that to me before." I don't know if I'd even realized it. "I'm just feeling a little...off balance."

"But not upset?" She looked worried, as if she might have insulted me with her love.

"No. *No*," I repeated, my feet suddenly remembering to move. I kissed her trembling lips. "I promise you, I'm not upset. Maybe a little surprised, but not upset."

"Whew. OK good," she breathed, tucking herself against me, laying her head on my shoulder. "I wanted you to know how I felt."

We stayed on the dance floor for another song, but I wasn't listening to the music. I don't even know how I managed to keep a rhythm. I felt like two different people— someone who loved hearing those words and wanted to hear them again, and someone who was trying not to panic that the words came with certain expectations and I was in over my head.

In a way it was like tasting something unfamiliar, something you'd never even seen before, that turns out to be delicious. You take a bite, let the flavor and texture roll around on your tongue, chew it up, swallow, and your body sends a message to your brain—*we like this! Give us more!* But the brain might caution restraint—*hold on there, we don't even know what this is yet, it could be poisonous.*

My body was happy, flushed with heat and tingling. My heart was beating quickly, and I even felt a little out of breath. *I like this feeling. I like that she loves me. Tell me again, Claire. Let me hear the words again.*

But some stubborn part of my brain couldn't let go and enjoy it. Couldn't quite believe it was true. Couldn't say the words back.

Why? Didn't I love her? Didn't she make me happier than anyone ever had? Didn't I hate the thought of losing her?

Questions started to worm their way inside my brain, and I did my best to keep them out and stay in the moment, focus on the physical—my hand on her back, the scent of her perfume, the whisper of her breath on my neck.

But concentrating on the physical aspects of Claire had consequences, and I started to get hard. *Yes*, I thought. Sex was something I understood. Something I was good at. Something I could offer her. My body could succeed where my words would fail.

I spoke low in her ear. "I'm dying to taste you. Think anyone will notice if I put my head up your dress?"

She laughed. "It is a long dress, but yes."

"Then when can I get you alone so I can bury my face in your thighs?"

"Mmm, that's tempting."

"I'm so hard right now."

She gasped. "Are you?"

"Of course I am. I can't think about my tongue in your pussy and not get hard."

"Oh, God."

"That's what I want to hear—over and over again. I wonder how many times I can make you come tonight. Is three realistic? I like to aim high—I'll go for four."

"Theo." She'd stopped moving.

"Yes?"

"I'm ready to go."

We didn't even wait for the song to finish, just grabbed our coats, said goodnight, and raced for the door.

I DIDN'T EVEN WAIT until we got home.

"Pull up your dress," I told her, my eyes on the highway, my hand on her leg.

She hesitated, glancing out the passenger window at the other cars on the highway. But she did as I asked.

"Good girl," I said, sliding my hand up her inner thigh. "Now open your legs for me."

Less than five minutes later, she was writhing in her seat, one palm flattened against the window, the other on the ceiling. I kept my eyes on the road and tried not to come in my pants.

"One," I said when she was quiet again. Then I touched my fingertip to my tongue and pressed harder on the accelerator.

I gave her the second orgasm on the stairs going up to her bedroom. Her dress around her waist. Her legs slung over my shoulders. Her pussy squeezing my fingers while her clit throbbed under my tongue.

"Two," I said, loosening the knot in my tie.

Then I unzipped my pants and delivered number three before she could even catch her breath.

I gave us both a little break before number four, just enough time for us to take off our clothes and get ready for bed. While she was still in the bathroom, I went up to the bedroom, got in bed, leaned back against the headboard, and took my cock in my fist. I watched her come up the stairs, hair down, makeup off, and nothing but a t-shirt on, which she whipped over her head and tossed aside as she moved toward me.

"I love when you do that in front of me," she said, crawling up the bed, feline and seductive, her hair brushing my legs. "It makes me so hot. Can I watch?"

"Not tonight." When she was straddling my hips, I positioned my cock between her legs. "Tonight I want to be inside you."

With her hands on my shoulders, she lowered herself until I was buried deep. "Yes," she whispered, her eyes closing, head dropping back.

Ten minutes later, I was nearly out of my mind with the need to come, but I was three quarters of the way to my goal. I couldn't stop now. I tipped her onto her back and slipped my hands beneath her ass, tilting her hips up.

"Oh, God," she gasped against my shoulder. "I can't, I can't."

"Yes, you can." I knew the best chance of getting that final victory lay in keeping her aroused and not letting up. "And you will." Fighting off my own orgasm, I thought only of hers, fucking her deep and tight to her body, grinding against her. I needed her to know how I felt about her, how much I cherished her, how nothing in my life had ever been this good.

I love her.

"Fuck," I said, feeling control slip through my fingers. "It's too good. I can't stop."

I love her.

"Oh God, I'm gonna come again," she said frantically, like she was afraid of it. Her nails dug into my ass and her teeth sank into my shoulder.

I love her.

Silvery lights exploded in front of my eyes, all the tension inside me releasing in white hot bursts as my body emptied itself inside her and hers contracted around me in simultaneous ecstasy. It was the most amazing thing I'd ever felt—and it wasn't just giving her four orgasms or coming inside her without a condom or the wordless language our bodies had taught each other.

It was acceptance. It was trust. It was love.

I felt it.

But I still couldn't say it.

OVER THE NEXT SEVERAL DAYS, Claire told me she loved me at least once a day, usually at night as she was falling asleep. Every single time, it made my heart beat a little faster, my breath feel short—an adrenaline rush. I always held her a little tighter after she said it, but even though I wanted to say the words back, they refused to budge from my heart to my lips.

It bothered me. Why couldn't I tell her how I felt? I knew it would make her happy, I knew it was the truth, and I knew that I should. I'd promised her I'd let her in. People in relationships trusted each other with their deepest feelings.

But I just couldn't get there.

I started to think my head knew something my heart didn't. I started to feel like maybe I was giving my heart too much sway and I needed to take a step back. The same words that had made me feel so good the night of the wedding started to eat away at me just five days later. Questions nagged me.

What did it mean to love someone? What kind of power did that give someone over you? What kinds of ways could loving someone come back to haunt you? What kinds of ways could the beloved hurt you? By confessing your love, weren't you essentially telling someone *I need you? I don't want to lose you? I'm vulnerable to you?* It was like laying down all your weapons and asking for them to be used against you, wasn't it?

I started to wonder.

THIRTY-THREE

Claire

ON THE WEDNESDAY night after Margot's wedding, I met Jaime for weekly GNO. I hadn't seen or talked to her since the wedding, so we spent the first half hour looking at pictures on our phones and talking about how beautiful Margot had looked, how perfect everything had gone, and how happy we were for her.

"You disappeared awfully quickly after the cake was cut." Jaime raised her eyebrows and picked up her drink.

"I said goodbye, didn't I?"

"Yes, but you were already halfway out the door." She smiled knowingly. "How was the rest of your night?"

"Good." My breath caught at the memory of that night —the drive home, the stairs, my bedroom.

And what I'd said.

He hadn't said it back yet, and I was OK with that. I understood it would probably take some time for him to be comfortable with the words, especially since I was the first person to say them to him. I knew I had to be patient. But something had felt a little off with him ever since that night. It was nothing I could put my finger on—he just felt a little distant. Maybe Jaime would have some advice.

"I told Theo I loved him that night."

Her eyes widened. "You did?"

I nodded, focusing on the wine in my glass. "But I'm thinking it may have been a mistake."

"Why? He didn't say it back?"

"No. He didn't. But it's not that so much. I sort of knew he might not be ready to say it back. I was prepared for that."

"Did he say *any*thing?"

"Yes. He told me I was the first person to say those words to him."

"Whoa. That's fucked up." She narrowed her eyes. "How's that even possible?"

I sighed. "I haven't gone into Theo's background much, but he had a really tough childhood. Mom left when he was one. Dad was abusive. He took off too eventually, about the time Theo was eight."

She blinked. "Holy shit. That's a lot of baggage. He seems so well-adjusted and happy-go-lucky."

"He's a good actor," I said sadly. "Anyway, I don't think emotional attachment comes easily for him."

"How could it?" She shook her head. "Poor guy."

"So I get that saying 'I love you' might not come naturally to him."

"*Love* might not come naturally to him," Jaime pointed out. "He might not even recognize it in himself. But Claire, the guy is crazy about you."

My lips turned up a little. "You think so?"

"Yes. It's totally obvious. You should see the way he

looks at you." She imitated a cartoonish lovestruck stare, sighing heavily and propping her chin in her hand.

I laughed. "He does not look like that."

She sat up again. "Yes, he does. So don't let it bother you that he's not all verbal about it." She shrugged. "Some people aren't."

I toyed with the stem of my wine glass. "He just seems quieter than usual this week. A little removed. It's giving me a weird vibe."

"I bet you're imagining it because of what you said. You're worried you're not on the same page, so you're looking for things to confirm your fear."

"Am I?" I bit my lip. It was possible she was right.

"I think so. Are you still having sex?"

"Yes," I admitted.

"And he still stays over?"

"Yes."

"Then I really wouldn't worry about it," she said confidently, picking up her martini glass. "Give him time."

I exhaled and sat up a little taller. "You're right. I'm being silly, looking for trouble where there isn't any. Things are great with us."

EXCEPT THE VERY NEXT night was Valentine's Day, and he didn't stay.

"Where are you going?" I asked when he got out of bed and started putting his clothes on. We'd gone out for dinner and had come back to my house.

"Some furniture is being delivered to my apartment tomorrow morning, and the time window they gave me starts early." He didn't even look at me.

"You bought new furniture?"

"Just a new couch. The old one was pretty bad."

I nodded, pulling the covers up to my chest. It was a small, stupid thing, maybe, but I was sort of hurt he hadn't mentioned the purchase. "Oh."

He sat on the bed to tie the laces of his boots but said nothing.

"I wish you didn't have to go." I rubbed a hand up and down his back. "It's Valentine's Day."

"Sorry," he said shortly.

I took my hand back, biting my lip. "See you tomorrow?"

"Yeah." He stood, turning to kiss me quickly. "Night."

He was gone before I could even tell him I loved him.

But maybe that was the idea.

THIRTY-FOUR

Theo

I WAS *SUCH* AN ASSHOLE.

I'd done some shitty things in my life, but I'd never felt worse than when I left Claire alone in bed on Valentine's Day, confused and hurt, naked beneath the covers because I'd just fucked her.

Yeah, you did.

Grimacing, I shut the door behind me and hurried through the dark to my car. The snow had melted, but the wind was still biting cold. I thought of her, warm and soft under the blankets, and wanted to put my fist through my car window.

But I had to leave. I had to get away.

Inside my car, I growled a string of curse words at myself, but none of them made me feel better. I peeled out of her driveway and sped down the street, tires squealing.

"Fuck!" I yelled. I was so mad at myself. And I was mad at Claire too. As irrational as it was, I'd started to get angry with her for telling me she loved me. Maybe even for loving me in the first place.

For making me love her.

Because I did. I loved her so much I couldn't see straight. I *needed* her. And I was powerless because of it.

Fuck it all, she didn't understand what that did to me! How terrified I was that any minute now, she'd come to her senses and realize what I'd told her was true—I was no good for her. I'd never be the man she deserved. When had I ever been anything but a disappointment to anyone?

I felt like I was on an elevator whose cables were about to snap—heading for the inevitable crash that would happen when she discovered the truth. I had to get the fuck off.

What had I been thinking to let myself love her? To let myself need her? Why had I thought for even one second that I was capable of this—of surviving the loss of her?

Because I knew in my bones that no matter what you did or said or tried, love wasn't enough to make anyone stay.

The realization that one day this would all be over and she'd be gone sliced right through my heart. It stopped beating. My throat closed up. I couldn't breathe. I couldn't breathe. I couldn't breathe.

Pulling over to the side of the road, I put the car in park and tried to get control of myself as I gasped for air. *You are not a child. You are a man. You can fight this. You still have control. You can get out of danger. You can leave first.*

By the time my breathing returned to normal, and I could feel my heart beating again in my chest, I'd made up my mind.

It had been a mistake to let her break down my walls. It would hurt her, but in the long run, I'd be doing her a favor. The sooner she realized love was a losing game, the better. Or maybe loving *me* was the losing game, and she'd have a better chance at happiness with someone else. Someone who believed in her fairy tale life with the porch swing and the bikes and the lemonade stand. Someone who could give it to her. Share it with her. Someone who could love her without disappointing her.

But it wasn't me.

It had never been me.

———

I COULDN'T FALL asleep that night. Instead I lay awake trying to think of how to leave her. She was going to be furious no matter how I did it. She'd call me names. She'd say I'd lied to her. She'd accuse me of breaking all my promises.

I could take it. Hell, I deserved it.

What I knew I couldn't take were her tears. Her pleas to stay. Her vulnerable sweetness. If she fell apart, it would kill me. So why force myself to watch it? Why make this any harder than it had to be? But I couldn't just leave without saying *anything*. I owed her a reason, at least.

A text was too insulting, even for me. But a letter could work. I'd write her a letter and leave it at her house—I had a key. If I got it done tonight, I could take it there tomorrow after she left for school. She'd find it in the afternoon when she got home.

I got out of bed and went into the kitchen, where I grabbed a pen and a notebook. Sitting down at the counter, I stared at the blank page in front of me. *This will crush her. She doesn't deserve it. It's all your fault.*

"Fuck off," I growled at myself. Then I put the pen to paper.

Dear Claire,

I'm sorry. I thought I could do this, but I can't be what you want. You are better off without me.

Theo

My stomach churned. Burying my face in my hands, I sat there in agony for a few more seconds, unable to even look at the letter in front of me. For the first time in years, I wanted a drink. Wanted to numb myself to the pain of facing my true self.

Fuck-up. Liar. Coward.

I was. I was all those things and worse.

But at least no one would have the power to hurt me again.

I ripped the page from the notebook, folded it into thirds and dug an envelope from a drawer. When the letter was safely sealed inside, I left it by my keys on the counter and went back to bed.

I tried not to think about her. I turned on the television. Opened a book. Buried my head beneath the pillows as if they could keep a thought from getting in. But nothing worked. I was awake all night long, imagining her face when she read that letter. It made me sick.

At least I wouldn't have to see it.

THIRTY-FIVE

Claire

THE HOURS PASSED SLOWLY.

I couldn't sleep, and I had a pounding headache. At one A.M., I went down and took two ibuprofen. At two, I drank another glass of water. At three, I gave up on sleep and reached for my phone, tempted to text Theo and ask him if everything was OK. I couldn't stop thinking about him—something was off, I just knew it. Even the sex had seemed less intimate tonight. He was closing himself off for some reason. Was he losing interest already? Or was he upset about something? Maybe I'd made a mistake telling him how I felt. I'd thought it would make him feel good, but maybe it had put too much pressure on him. Maybe it was too much, too soon.

I sighed and set my phone down again. Texting him at three in the morning wasn't the answer if he was feeling pressured. We'd just have to have an honest conversation so I could tell him he didn't have to worry—I wasn't expecting anything different or more than what we had. I just wanted to share my feelings for him because it felt good to do it. And I wanted him to know how happy he made me.

I'd known that being with Theo wasn't going to be a piece of cake. He carried a lot of pain around with him that he refused to confront, and that meant trust was tough for him. *Maybe I can try to talk to him about it again. Get him to open up more about the past and what love means to him. Why it's scary for him. What I can do to help.*

I picked up the phone again and called the substitute teacher line for the district, requesting a sub for the next day. It had been months since I'd taken a day off, and I knew I wasn't going to feel like getting up and going to work in three hours. I hadn't even slept yet, and this headache was brutal. After making the request, I hung up and went downstairs again for some melatonin and a couple more ibuprofen. Then I went back to bed, hugging the pillow Theo normally used and breathing in his scent.

It calmed me, and I fell asleep knowing that tomorrow, everything would be better. I could fix this.

A NOISE WOKE ME.

I lifted my head from the pillow. Had I imagined it? I'd been sleeping so hard, my head was a bit muddled. Maybe the noise had been part of a dream.

A moment later I heard footsteps downstairs. My pulse rocketed. Who the hell was here? I jumped out of bed and threw my robe on over the t-shirt I'd slept in. With my phone in my hand in case I had to call 911, I tiptoed down the stairs.

The front door was open, and through the clear storm

door, I saw Theo's SUV in the drive. *Oh, thank God.* Smiling, I started to walk through the living room just as he came into it from the dining room.

"Hey, I almost called the cops on you. You scared me." But it was Theo who looked scared. No, terrified. He was white as a ghost. "Everything OK?"

He appeared to be trying to swallow a tennis ball. "I—I didn't think you'd be here."

I smiled. "I took the day off. I didn't sleep well at all last night. Come on, let's have some coffee and talk."

I walked past him, heading for the kitchen.

"I have to go," he blurted.

"Just one cup," I pleaded. "Give me five minutes. I want to—what's this?" On my kitchen table was an envelope that said Claire in Theo's neat, square lettering. My heart started to pound, and not in a good way. I grabbed it and raced back into the living room, where Theo was nearly out the door. "Hey, wait!"

He paused, his back to me. "Read it after I go. Please."

"No." My hands shook—my entire body shook—as I ripped it open and unfolded the page.

No. Oh no, he fucking didn't.

But he had. The words were right there on the page.

Dear Claire,

I'm sorry. I thought I could do this, but I can't be what you want. You are better off without me.

Theo

"What is this?" I asked, my voice quavering. "What the hell is this?"

He stood still, but his body radiated nervous energy, his hands curling into fists at his sides.

"Turn around and look at me, Theo. You want to break my heart, you do it to my face."

Slowly, he turned around, his chest expanding like he was taking a deep breath. But he said nothing.

"You're *sorry*?" I read the letter again. "You can't be what I want? What the hell is going on here? Tell me!"

He opened his mouth. Shook his head. "I can't do this anymore."

"Can't do what?" The tears began to fall, and I swiped at them with the sleeve of my robe. "I don't understand."

"I can't—be with you." His voice shook.

"Why?"

"I told you from the start. I'm no good for you." He was delivering his lines, but his acting wasn't good enough. As I stared at the man in front of me with the bloodshot eyes, face drained of color, hands flexing, I saw someone who hadn't slept all night. I saw someone who hated what he was saying. I saw someone scared.

"Bullshit."

His jaw clenched. "It's the truth."

"You're running away." It was as if a bell had pinged, and everything was crystal clear. "Like you always do. You're giving up on us because you're scared of what you feel. You're worried you let me get too close."

Color returned to his face as his anger spiked, but I wasn't about to give him a chance to argue with me.

"And you're scared of what *I* feel. This all started when I told you I love you." The pieces were falling into place one by one. "*That's* the real truth, and you know it."

"Maybe it did start then," he admitted. "But it only confirmed what I already knew—this has to end."

"No, it doesn't. Don't go, Theo," I changed tactics, pleading with him. *Be gentle.* "What we have is good. It's scary because it's powerful. And it makes you feel vulnerable. I know it's hard for you to trust me, Theo. But you have to. I won't leave you."

"Don't say that!" he exploded. "Don't make promises like that. You won't be able to keep them."

"Yes, I will! That's what it means to love someone this way. You stick around even when it's difficult. You stay when it would be easier to go. You don't give up."

"It's not enough. Love's not enough to make someone stay. You think it will be, but it's not." His eyes shone, and in them I saw the hurt of a child who felt that *he* hadn't been enough.

My heart was breaking. "I'm not her, Theo."

"I have to go." He turned for the door and I rushed straight at him, grabbing his shoulders and forcing him to meet my eyes.

"Look at me. Look at me and tell me you don't love me."

"I can't," he said, his voice cracking.

"Tell me!" I cried, wishing I could shake him. "Tell me you don't love me enough to stay!"

A sound of frustration ripped from his throat and he grabbed my head, crushing his lips to mine. I clung to him desperately, begging him with my lips and tongue and hands not to leave me, relieved when his arms came around me too. *He loves me, he loves me, he loves me...* I was drunk with it.

Five seconds later, he tore himself from my embrace and stormed out the front door.

I was alone. I was in shock. I was crushed.

But I had my answer.

He might love me...but not enough to stay.

THIRTY-SIX

Theo

GODDAMMIT!

I slammed the door to my apartment and threw my keys at the wall, where they left an angry black mark. But it didn't relieve any tension, so I backhanded a lamp, knocking it off an end table.

"Fuck!" I yelled, breathing hard and heavy.

How had this gone so wrong? What did the universe have against me that my plan to avoid a fight had failed so miserably? I wanted to punch someone, mainly myself. It had been even worse than I'd imagined it—her shock, her anger, her tears, her accusations.

The way her hands trembled as she tore open the envelope—she must have known somehow what it contained. Those hands that had been everywhere on my body and brought me so much pleasure.

The way her voice shook when she asked me why, when she said my name, when she said she wouldn't leave me. That voice, which had whispered sweet words so many times in the dark, had spoken my name with something near reverence while I moved inside her.

The way her eyes challenged me to say I didn't love her, dared me to tell her that lie. In them I saw hurt and anger and fear. Those eyes that had looked at me with such devotion and trust only yesterday.

My heart ached. I'd never have any of it again. I'd given it all up when I walked out the door.

The loss of her cut me to the bone, and I dropped my head into my hands. Every heartbeat was a knife to the chest. Every second that ticked by was agony—*I lost her, I lost her, I lost her.*

No, I hadn't lost her. I'd *left* her.

And if I felt this aching for her with every breath for the rest of my life, then maybe I deserved it.

But at least I was safe.

And she was too.

THIRTY-SEVEN

Claire

AFTER CRYING my eyes out on my bed for an hour, I texted Jaime and asked if she could come over after work. She immediately called me.

"What's wrong?" she asked as soon as I picked up. It sounded like she was driving.

"Theo and I broke up." I didn't think I had tears left, but my eyes filled again.

She gasped. "*What?* Why? When?"

"This morning," I sobbed hoarsely. Was I coming down with something? My chest felt thick with something and I couldn't breathe right.

"Oh my God. Are you at work?"

"No. I took the day off." A coughing fit seized me.

"I'm coming over. I'll be there in ten."

"OK." I tossed my phone aside and reached for another tissue, but the box was empty. Wiping my nose with my sleeve for the time being, I went downstairs and grabbed another box from the bathroom closet. When I saw Theo's toothbrush by the sink, I felt like stabbing him with it. How could he do this to me?

I took the box of tissues with me and went back upstairs, yanking off the top and pulling a clean one out. I considered getting dressed but couldn't muster enough energy or the will to care what I looked like. I pulled on some flannel pants and thick socks, then tucked the tissue box under my arm again and went down to wait for Jaime.

Throwing myself down on the couch, I lay on my side and stared at the spot where he'd stood and given up on us. Where he'd kissed me for the last time. Where he'd broken my heart. How was I ever going to walk through this room and not remember that? Not feel the pain all over again?

Fresh sobs erupted, and I cried into tissue after tissue, letting them pile up on the floor in front of me.

When I heard the knock at the door, I sat up and stepped over them on my way to answer it. To my dismay, both Jaime and Quinn walked in.

"Sorry, he wouldn't let me take him home," Jaime said as she hugged me. "We were on our way to lunch."

"I want to help." Quinn shut the door behind him. "I think I'm good at this stuff."

"It's fine." I fussed with my hair a little and gave up. "Come on in, but I'm not sure anyone can help me."

"What happened?" Jaime asked, shrugging out of her coat. She was dressed for work in a black pencil skirt and jacket.

I stepped over the pile of soggy tissues again and flopped back onto the couch. "He left. Said he couldn't do this anymore. But he can—that's not it."

"What do you mean?" Quinn sat down on the chair by the window, crossed his arms over his chest and an ankle over his knee. He was tall like Theo, maybe a little thinner, with dark blond hair and the bluest eyes I'd ever seen on anyone, man or woman.

"He's scared," I said, sniffing. "This is what he does when he panics that he's let someone get too close to him. He runs away. He flat out told me as much when we were at the cabin."

"Did you tell him that?" Jaime sat next to me and pushed my hair back from my face.

"Yes." I pulled another tissue from the box. "I called him out on everything."

"What did he say?" she asked.

"Nothing," I said, dabbing at my sore nose. It had to be bright red by now. "He couldn't even bring himself to lie and say he didn't love me. That's what hurts so much. It would almost be better if he just dumped me because he didn't feel the same. But I know he does."

Jaime put her arm around me. "I'm sorry, Claire. This sucks."

Quinn cleared his throat. "Can I offer some insight?"

"Of course," I said.

"This could be a simple case of a guy freaking out when he realizes that he loves someone. Happens all the time. A lot of guys don't like feeling emotionally vulnerable that way. But I don't think that's the whole story." He uncrossed his legs and leaned forward, elbows on his knees. "Jaime told me a little bit about Theo's background on the way over here."

"I hope I wasn't betraying a confidence," Jaime said quickly. "I just wanted to bring him up to speed. And the more I think about it, the more I'm convinced that's what this stems from." Jaime had majored in psychology and was always good at analyzing people.

"It's OK." I tipped my head onto her shoulder for a second. "I know you want to help."

"I agree with Jaime," Quinn said. "And as someone who was really affected by the loss of his mom as an *adult*, I think if he never grieved the loss he experienced as a kid, never came to terms with it, he's never going to be able to connect emotionally." He paused. "I felt a lot of guilt after my mom died, and I had to work through it."

I nodded. "I'm positive he has unresolved feelings about his mother, and it's affecting his ability to trust me. But he won't admit that. He just buries anything he doesn't want to think about."

"Has he ever gone to therapy?" Jaime asked.

"No. He's too stubborn, I think." I closed my eyes, trying to fight back against tears. "I love him, but I think I just have to get over him. Because even if he came back tonight and said he was sorry, I'd be afraid he was going to do this to me again."

She sighed and squeezed me tighter. "And he would. You can't make him better, Claire. No matter how much you want to. Trust me when I say he has to want to fix himself before he can love you the way you deserve to be loved."

"She knows what she's talking about," said Quinn. "I wanted to love her way before she wanted to let me."

Jaime stuck her tongue out at him.

It made me laugh a little, but it made me sad too—Jaime and Quinn were so lucky they'd figured it out. "It just seems so unfair. After all this time looking for the perfect man, I fall for someone so broken."

"We're all a little broken, aren't we? And I'm not surprised at all." Jaime rubbed my arm. "You're a nurturer, Claire. It's what makes you such a good teacher and friend.

You see the good in people and draw it out. You see the hurt in people and want to help them heal. But it's not always possible. Some people don't want to get better."

I heard what she was saying, and I knew she was right. As much as it hurt to let Theo go when I knew I could make him happy, I couldn't force it on him. He had to want to be happy, and he had to want it enough to work for it.

But it hurt a lot. Because when it came down to it, I had to face the fact that even though he couldn't bring himself to say the words, the action spoke plenty loud.

He didn't love me enough to stay.

I DIDN'T CALL HIM. Didn't text. Didn't drive by his apartment. Over the next ten days, I did the best I could to put him out of my mind—deleted all his photos, threw out his toothbrush, told my friends and family it was over between us. (I think my mother was as upset as I was. "But we were doing so well," she said tearfully.)

I was furious with him. Sad for him. I missed him terribly. What was he doing? Had he stayed in town? Kept his job? Did he think about me? Did he miss me? What was he feeling? Every night I went to bed with a hollow ache inside me, and every morning it was a struggle to find the positive energy I needed to get through the day. But my students deserved a teacher who made class fun, especially art class, so I forced myself to be "on" when I had to be.

It was agony.

I spent a lot of time wondering what I could have done differently. Was this somehow my fault? Had I rushed it? Had the relationship been more one-sided than I realized? But no—he'd wanted to stay with me nearly every night.

He'd taken me to meet his family. He'd called me his girlfriend first. This couldn't be my fault.

But that didn't make the breakup any easier.

At home, I put the house projects on hold and channeled my emotions into creative passion. I went to the antique bookstore, found an old volume of mythology that included the tale of Cupid and Psyche, and felt immediately inspired. At home, I began sketching a design based on Canova's famous sculpture of Cupid and Psyche's kiss.

The work didn't heal the wound in my heart—Cupid's aim was never so good, nor his arrow so sharp—but it did bring some comfort, and at least I'd have another book to display at the art fair. I also made a list of local shops I thought might be interested in selling some pieces, and I gave myself a one-week deadline for approaching at least two of them. Then I surprised myself by going to all five stores on the list—and three of them said yes!

The other two said they weren't busy enough right now but might be interested in the future. They gave me business cards and asked me to approach closer to summer, when they'd get busy again. It was much less painful than I'd anticipated, and gave me the confidence to start up my own shop on Etsy. Jaime helped me set it up and then took me out for dinner over the weekend to celebrate my new ventures.

"So how does it feel?" she asked.

"Good." I smiled, grateful that I finally felt hopeful again. "Like I'm moving forward."

"I'm so glad to hear that." She raised her glass of wine. "Cheers, babe."

I touched my glass to hers, took a drink and set it down. "And guess what else I decided?"

"What?"

I took a deep breath and forced myself to say out loud what I'd been thinking about for the last week. "I'm going to book a trip to Paris."

Her eyes went wide. "But what about the flying thing?"

"I'm going to deal with it." I sat up taller, feeling even more grit and determination return. Being with Theo had taught me that I liked the way I felt about myself when I stepped outside my comfort zone. Faced my fears. Put on the red lipstick. And watching him let his fear ruin us had forced me to think about all the ways I still let fear hold me back. "I've wanted to visit the museums in Paris since I was a little girl. Yes, I'm scared of flying, but I'll be damned if I'm going to let anxiety keep me from making that dream a reality. I can't go through life being afraid and careful all the time. At some point, I have to go for what I really want and trust in fate. What's meant to be will be."

Jaime blinked at me. "I feel like I should applaud right now. This is the strongest you've sounded since the breakup for sure, maybe even ever." She grabbed my wine glass. "What's in here? I want some."

Laughing—God, that felt good—I took it back from her. "It's not the wine. It's just that I've had a lot of time to think recently. When I first met Theo, he said something to me I often repeat to myself. He said, 'You don't have to be anyone else. You just have to stop staring over the edge and jump.'"

"Good advice."

Talking about it brought even more clarity. "You know, I think for so long I felt like there was something innate about me that wasn't good enough, exciting enough, resilient enough, talented enough to put myself out there. I talked myself out of so many things because I looked at them as opportunities to fail, not as opportunities to succeed. I was so afraid to fall that I never let myself fly. Does that make sense?"

"Of course it does." Jaime reached out and put a hand over mine. "I agree one hundred percent, and I have known you a lot of years. As much as the breakup hurt, I think this relationship was good for you."

I nodded slowly. "I think so too. I just wish it hadn't ended like that. Or at all. I can't stop thinking about him."

"How long has it been?"

"Ten days." I met her eyes, feeling mine get misty. "I miss him. When will I stop missing him?"

She patted my hand. "I don't know, sweetie. Give your-self more time, and don't feel bad about missing him. You loved him—of course you miss him. I bet he's just as miserable."

"Maybe." Somehow that didn't help. I didn't wish him misery—I wanted him to be happy.

"In fact, I bet he's even more miserable since this is his fault. I was in his shoes once." She shook her head. "It's the pits."

"Yeah, but you weren't like Theo."

"I wasn't damaged like Theo, maybe, but I was stubborn as hell. It took me some time to come around. You never know."

Her tone carried a note of hope, but I wasn't too opti-mistic. I wished I could turn back time and return to our snowed-in days at the cabin. We'd been so happy there.

But I couldn't. I had to move forward, but at least I would do it having more courage, more confidence, and more self-awareness than I'd had before.

No matter what, I'd always have Theo to thank for that.

THIRTY-EIGHT

Theo

THE FIRST FEW days after I broke things off with Claire were the darkest in my recent memory. A huge weight sat on my shoulders. My limbs felt heavier. A constant ache throbbed in my chest. I went to the gym in the morning, worked during the day, and sat at home every night, wallowing in misery and loneliness. At work I played a role, burying my sadness in order to appear friendly, helpful, knowledgeable, and caring.

In truth, I didn't give a shit about anything or anyone.

Just Claire.

At night, I thought about nothing but her, my head was full of all the things I loved and missed. Her kindness. Her sense of humor. Her laugh. Her lips curving into a smile. Her eyes. The way she talked about her students. The way she loved working with her hands. The way she got excited over little things like hot chocolate and snow and old books.

The way she worried about being boring compared to her sister, as if there was anything boring about her.

I'd lie on my back, staring at the ceiling, and remember the way she'd looked at me and touched me and kissed me and taken me inside her. Pretty soon I'd get hard, and I'd close my eyes, take my dick in my hand, and get myself off to the memory of her. But it wasn't even a close second to being with her, and I never felt relief when it was over—just anger.

Why did this fucking hurt so much? Hadn't I done the right thing? Not only had I saved myself from a lot of heartbreak down the road, but I'd spared her, too. Now she was free to find the perfect guy she dreamed about all the time.

But if I ever saw them together, I'd fucking take his head off.

Everywhere I went and everything I saw seemed to remind me of her. Women with long hair. The granite slabs at the stoneworks. Anything flavored with sugar and cinnamon or chocolate. I couldn't even drink a fucking lemonade without missing her.

I didn't bother to hide my mood from my brother when it was just the two of us on a job. He asked me a few times if I was OK in those early days, but I brushed him off. I wasn't ready to talk about it.

A week after I'd walked out, he finally brought her up by name. "Did something happen with Claire?"

We were on a lunch break from an installation job, sitting across from each other at a small booth in a sub shop. "Yeah. It's done."

He paused. Took a bite of his sub. "Why?"

I shrugged and took a bite of mine without even tasting it. I was unable to meet his eye but figured I'd test out an impassive mask. Act like I didn't care. Maybe I'd convince myself too. "It was time."

"It was?" Aaron shrank back a little. "Didn't look like it to me."

"Yeah, well. Things aren't always what they seem."

He was silent for a minute or so, but I felt his knowing eyes on me. Sizing me up. *Seeing* me. "She break it off?"

"No. I did." I stuffed a few potato chips in my mouth.

Aaron set his sandwich down and leaned his elbows on the table. "You bailed on her."

"So?"

"And you did it not because it was time, or you don't care about her, but because you *do.*"

"Fuck off."

He shook his head. "No. You're fucking this up on purpose, Theo, and I don't want you to do it."

I finally met his eyes. "It's none of your business."

"The hell it isn't. Brothers look out for each other. And when they see each other making a big mistake, they speak up."

I threw my sandwich down on the wrapper and set my fists on either side of it. "Fine. You spoke up. Now let it go."

"No. I've watched you make too many bad decisions in your life to let this go. You want to tell me you don't care about her? Fine. I'll let it go. But I think you do, and I think you left her because you're scared."

"Fuck you, Aaron!" I was being too loud, and people were looking over at us, but I didn't care. "Who are you to talk to me about leaving? You're the one who left your wife and kids for two months—*this* time."

"Shh. Keep your voice down." Aaron glanced over his shoulder and back at me. "You're right. I *have* made mistakes. I *did* leave my wife and kids. And there isn't a goddamn day that goes by I don't regret it. I'd give anything to go back and do things differently, Theo, but I can't. I don't want to watch you make the same mistake."

"You know I told her she should leave?" I was being a spiteful dick, and I knew it, but I couldn't stop. I wanted someone to feel as bad as I did. "Every day I told her she should leave and take the kids away. I never understood why the hell she didn't."

Aaron didn't take the bait. "Because Josie's not like you, Theo. She believes when you love someone, you stay."

I tried again. "Then she's a fool. You're only going to leave her again."

"I'm not. I made a promise to myself that I intend to keep. I had to face down a lot of monsters to get here, Theo, but I'm here and I'm not going anywhere."

I'd run out of insults to throw at him, and it was only making me madder that my brother was so calm. That he'd figured out how to keep a promise. That he trusted Josie— and himself—to stay. That he'd finally faced his monsters and come away stronger for it.

Why was I the only one who couldn't get a grip on my fear? Was it my fate to be alone for the rest of my life? I shoved out of the booth, dumped my trash, and went out to my car. Aaron came out a few minutes later, but we didn't talk on the drive back to work or for the rest of the day. I knew I owed him an apology but I was too busy being pissed off and sorry for myself to offer one.

That night, I lay in bed and thought, *fuck it. I don't need this grief. And no one here needs me. I should just leave. Take off again. Hit the open road like I used to and see where it takes me.*

But the open road no longer held any appeal. I didn't

want an unfamiliar bed or a faceless fuck or lonely miles of highway stretching out endlessly in front of me.

I wanted to be in Claire's bed, holding on to her. Feeling her hold on to me. Hear her tell me she loves me. Say the words back. Make her a promise and keep it.

But how?

THE NEXT DAY, Aaron and I worked a job that Zack at the stoneworks had thrown our way. I nursed my self-pity for a couple hours that morning, but when noon came around, I swallowed my pride and asked my brother to come to lunch with me. Because he was a good guy, and because he could see I was suffering, he got in the car without a word.

"I'm sorry about yesterday," I said once we were on the road. "I was an asshole."

"Yeah, you were. But I get it."

We drove in silence for a few minutes, then I asked him a question that had been troubling me. "How do you know? How do you know you're not going anywhere? Or that she won't?"

"Because I trust her," he said simply. "And now I trust myself too."

Exhaling, I shook my head. "I can't. I don't know why I can't, but I can't. Every single time, I panic. I feel like I'm tied to the tracks of an oncoming freight train."

"You can't trust her? Or yourself?"

"Either of us."

"That's because you've never been shown how. You don't have any reason to trust anyone because all you've seen your entire life is people taking off, starting with Mom and Dad. You learned early on not to trust anyone who's supposed to care."

Something had started to twist in my gut, and I didn't like it. "You think..." I had to work hard to swallow. "You think this goes that far back?"

"Yeah. I do."

I stopped at a red light. In my mind I heard Claire telling me *I'm not her*. She knew. She'd seen right through me. "I love her."

"I know you do."

"I only left her because I was scared of being a disappointment to her. I was scared she'd leave me." I took a deep breath. "And I didn't think I could take it."

"I know."

I looked over at him. "I guess that makes me a coward."

"Nope. It makes you human. You're a coward if you don't confront that fear, though. Work through it. Put it behind you so you can be with Claire and neither of you are worried that any moment, one of you is going to walk out."

The light turned green, and I moved forward. "How?"

"I don't know if I can tell you exactly. For me, my worst fear was becoming Dad. Failing as a father. I thought it was inevitable."

"So how'd you get over it?"

"I don't know if I'll ever get over it completely, but I stared it down. I finally talked about it at meetings and with Josie, even a little bit with you."

I nodded, remembering our conversation on Christmas Eve.

"And I think by putting it out there, I took back some of its power over me. By admitting what I'd been scared of, I weakened its grip on my life. Does that make sense?"

"Yeah. It does." I thought about how much better I'd felt

after talking to Claire at the cabin. Maybe I just hadn't gone deep enough to see what fears were buried there. Maybe I'd been afraid of seeming weak.

"I realized I'm my own man," Aaron went on as I pulled into the deli parking lot. "I'm more than just the product of some shitty DNA. Yes, I've made mistakes, and I'll probably continue to make them, because I'm human, but not because I'm him. I'm *not* my father. The past doesn't have to repeat itself. I'm *choosing* not to let it—I have that power."

I turned off the engine. "I wish I felt that way," I said quietly.

"You can, Theo. All it takes is a hard look at yourself and some honest conversation. I'm here for you. And I bet Claire would be too, if you'd let her."

I frowned. "I really fucked that up."

"Hey, nobody understands fucking up better than I do. But guess what?" He was smiling when I looked over at him. "I'm sixty days sober today."

"Are you really? That's fucking awesome, Aaron. Congratulations." For the first time in a week, I felt good about something.

"Thanks. Josie has to work tonight, but I'm cooking a celebration dinner for the girls after my meeting. Want to come? We can talk a little more, if you want."

"Yeah. I'd like that." I'd been holed up in my apartment and hadn't seen the kids in a while. They always made me smile.

We ate lunch, although I wasn't all that hungry and ended up throwing half my sandwich out uneaten, and went back to the job. I spent the entire afternoon thinking about what Aaron had said. I'd always blamed the family genes for all my shortcomings, but maybe it was time to take a closer look. Maybe I was doing this to myself.

Maybe I hadn't been born to failure—maybe I was choosing it.

AT AARON'S house that night, I played with the kids, helped Aaron cook dinner (thanks to Claire, I was no longer totally clueless in the kitchen), and raised a cupcake to Aaron's milestone. I was proud of him, and I told him so after I helped him get the kids to bed and we were cleaning up.

"Thanks," he said, loading plates into the dishwasher.

"I mean it. You've come a long way, and this is the healthiest I've ever seen you." I brought the girls' princess cups over to the sink.

"It's the best I've ever felt."

I exhaled, turning one of the cups in my hand. "I'd like to feel better. I thought leaving Claire would give me some peace, but it hasn't. I feel worse."

Aaron nodded. "I know that feeling. When the choice you've made was the wrong one, and it just makes you hate yourself more."

"Exactly."

"It takes a strong man to admit when he's wrong and try to make things right. Especially when it means you've got to face a few monsters first."

I nodded slowly. "I've kept mine locked up a long time. They're mad as fuck."

He chuckled. "Let 'em out. Let 'em do their worst. Then tell them they don't scare you anymore. Beat the hell out of them." He glanced at me. "You're strong enough. I know you are. Look at the way you were able to quit drinking. That was hard, and you did it."

"Yeah. It was."

"And it was the right decision."

Exhaling, I set the cup on the counter. "I really fucking miss her. Everything about her. It *hurts*."

"I know. I've been there. But I promise you, if you can get past this, things will be even better than they were before. For both of you."

I WENT home that night and thought about the things he'd said.

I've watched you make too many bad decisions in your life.

When you love someone, you stay.

You learned early on not to trust.

The past doesn't have to repeat itself.

It just makes you hate yourself more.

It takes a strong man to admit when he's wrong and try to make things right.

I could be a stronger man. A better man. Maybe not perfect, but better.

I was dying to call Claire—or better, go see her and hold her and kiss her—but I couldn't do that just yet.

You've got to face a few monsters first.

Lying on my back in the dark, I put my hands behind my head. I stared at the ceiling, but what I saw was the bigger picture of my life. The patterns. The mistakes. The fear. The sabotage. The guilt. The self-inflicted punishment.

I saw a child who grew up wondering why he hadn't

been enough to make his mother stay. Who wondered if anyone loved him. Who wondered if love meant anything at all. Who never felt safe.

I saw a teenager who had everything going for him. Who panicked when things got too hard. Who figured he was destined to turn out a fucked-up failure anyway, and if his own parents hadn't cared, why should he?

I saw myself at twenty-two, getting out of prison and realizing I'd done more than just lose a year of my life. I'd lost rights, opportunities, and freedom. I'd lost respect, possibility, hope. But I didn't think I deserved those things, anyway, so I drank to numb the pain.

I saw myself at twenty-five, when Aaron's first child was born. He'd invited me to come see them, let me hold Ava —me, holding a *baby*. I'd never forget that day. He'd smiled and placed that red-faced, tiny-fisted, wailing little bird-boned creature in my arms. She was so frail, so small, so innocent. I'd stared at her, and at my brother, in complete amazement. He trusted me to hold her? It had meant everything to me.

I never took another drink.

But looking back, I saw how I'd continued to avoid facing my fears by pretending to be someone else wherever I was. I'd avoided having to commit to anyone by moving around all the time. And I'd convinced myself that I didn't want anything but temporary, superficial games and good times.

But now I wanted more. I wanted to stay, I wanted to trust, I wanted to love. I wanted to build something strong enough to last.

And I wanted to build it with Claire.

I hoped I wasn't too late.

OVER THE NEXT day and a half, I thought hard about what I could do to convince Claire to give me another chance. To see that I was willing to work on myself. To believe in me. It wouldn't be easy—for all she knew, I was just going to walk out again the next time I got scared. And there would be a next time. I wasn't going to pretend I'd never feel that fear of being abandoned ever again, but like my brother said, by admitting it, putting it out there and talking honestly about it with her, I could lessen its hold on me.

But how could I even convince her to have that honest conversation? If I were her, I probably wouldn't even want to let me in the door. I needed to think of a way to show her I was in this for real.

I was dying to tell her I loved her, but words wouldn't be enough.

What mattered to Claire? What would prove that I had listened to her well enough to know what it meant to say, *I love you and I can make you happy—will you let me?*

It came to me while I was watching my nieces, two nights after my conversation with Aaron and ten days after I'd last seen Claire. Josie was working, and Aaron had asked me if I'd mind coming over so he could attend a meeting. I was sitting on the floor trying to read them a story, but they were climbing all over me like a human jungle gym.

"Uncle Theo, Daddy says you build things. Will you build us a playscape in the backyard?" Ava asked, attempting to sit on my shoulders. "We don't even have a swing."

"I guess I could." I set the book down and took her by the hands to help her balance. "But it depends on how long you guys are going to live here." Recently Josie and Aaron had talked about moving to a bigger house as soon as they could afford it. "We don't want to build something if you're not staying."

And just like that, I knew what to do.

THANKFULLY, the next day was Sunday and I didn't have to work. I skipped the gym and bought the materials I'd need, then I brought them all over to Aaron and Josie's. After I explained what I was doing, Aaron was more than happy to back his truck out of the garage to give me the work space required, and Josie said she wouldn't mind the noise out there for a day. She even brought me a little heater so I wouldn't be too cold, and a thermos full of hot coffee.

"You're the best," I told her, taking a sip and setting the thermos on the bench. "Thank you."

"You sure you don't want help?" my brother asked. "It would get done faster."

"Nah." I picked up his sander. "I want to do this myself. But is there any way you could work for me tomorrow? I know Monday is usually your day off, but I'd like to get this up while she's at school."

"No problem." He clapped me on the back. "You're doing the right thing."

As soon as he was gone, I slipped on a dust mask and got to work.

THIRTY-NINE

Claire

AFTER WORK ON MONDAY, I stopped in at one of the gift shops that had offered to sell my work and dropped off a few pieces—three altered books and two small paintings of birds. It felt a little like leaving my children unattended, but I managed to get out the door without tears, at least. On the way home, I called Jaime.

"I did it," I said. "I now officially have art for sale."

"Yay!" she crowed. "I'm so proud of you. Any sales on the Etsy site yet?"

"No, but it's only been a few days. I'm going to put a few more photos up."

"Good idea. How are you feeling?"

"Pretty good." I turned onto my street. "At least about the art. And the sooner I—oh my God."

"What?"

I slowed my car as I approached my house, whispering as if I might be overheard. "He's here."

"Who? Theo?"

"Yes. His car is parked on the street. He's in the driver's seat. Oh, God, he saw me. He's getting out!" I pulled into the garage, my heart hammering. "Quick! What do I do?"

"I don't know!"

"What if he's sorry?" In my rearview mirror, I saw him walking up the driveway. "What if he wants another chance?"

"Fuck! I don't know, Claire! Just—just hear him out. Be strong, but be understanding. Listen to your heart."

"My heart is currently performing a twenty-one gun salute in my ears. It's not helping." Theo appeared at the driver's side window. "Oh God. I have to go."

Jaime let out a strangled cry. "OK, but call me as soon as you can! I'm dying!"

"I will." I stuck my phone in my purse and took a breath. My stomach was jumping all over the place. *Strong. Be strong. Put on your armor and don't let him get past it without a good goddamn fight.*

As I pulled on my gloves, he opened the door for me and offered his hand. I hesitated a moment, then I took it, letting him help me out. My legs felt like rubber.

He shut the door behind me. "Hi."

"Hi." My body reacted to his nearness as if nothing had gone wrong between us. My stomach fluttered. My breath caught. Goosebumps rippled down my arms. I pressed them to my sides so I wouldn't throw them around his neck. *God, I missed you. Say something—anything—to help me understand.*

He shook his head slowly, his eyes drinking me in. "I rehearsed this a thousand times. I had things to open with. Words of apology. Reasons why you should hear me out.

But looking at you, all I can think is, *She's so damn beautiful.*"

"Not a *terrible* start," I conceded stiffly, leaning back against my car for support. "But not good enough."

"I know. Give me a second." He exhaled, his breath a silvery puff in the cold, shadowy dusk of the garage. "You were right. The argument we had the morning I left, you were right—I *was* running away because I was scared. Because I don't know how to trust. Because I didn't have the guts to own up to any of it. And I'm sorry."

"You hurt me." My bottom lip trembled. "I gave you my heart, Theo, and you stomped all over it."

"I want it back." He took my head in his hands, and his eyes pleaded with mine. "I love you. I *love* you. I've never said those words to anyone in my entire life. And I've never said them to you before now because I was scared to give you that kind of power over me. I guarded them, because I felt like handing them over would give you weapons to use against me."

He loves me! He said it! His words were putting serious chinks in the armor, but still. Weapons? "Theo, I'd never hurt you like that. You should have talked to me."

"I didn't know how. So I panicked. Bolted. Tried to convince myself I was doing the right thing, but being apart from you didn't feel right at all. It just felt miserable."

He did look miserable. And sincere. And different— something about the way he was meeting my eyes. I saw no mask on his face, no studied indifference, no panic. Just clarity. Devotion. Truth. I felt myself swaying toward him. "I've been miserable too."

"I've done a lot of thinking, Claire. About all the things I've been through. The things I never talk about. The things that make me who I am." His thumbs brushed my cheekbones. "I was wrong to think that by burying them, they wouldn't affect me. In fact, it was the opposite."

"I could see it," I whispered, my throat tight. "But I didn't know how to help."

He shook his head. "I wasn't ready to let you, until now."

I bit my lip.

"Tell me it's not too late," he begged. "Tell me you still love me."

"I still love you, Theo, but—"

He crushed his lips to mine, and I nearly melted at his feet. Maybe I should have been angry, pushed him away, told him he didn't have the right. But I'd *missed* this. The tingle in my toes. The butterflies in my stomach. The shiver up my spine that said *yes kiss me yes hold me yes be mine completely because all I want to be is yours.*

He lifted his head, and it took me a moment to open my eyes and realize I was still on two feet.

"God, I missed hearing that." A little smile on his lips. "I missed everything about you. And if you still love me, Claire, please give me one more chance."

"I want to, Theo, but I'm scared. How do I know you won't hurt me like that again?"

"You don't." His brow furrowed. "Believe me, I tried my damnedest to think of a way to prove it to you. Words I could say. Things I could do. Promises I could make. But it all comes down to this." He took my hands in his. "I'm asking you to trust me. And I'm going to trust you, too."

"But what's different this time?"

"What's different is that I had to live without you in my life for the last ten days. And I hated it. With you, I'm stronger. Braver. Better." He spoke a little quieter. "With you, I know I'm safe. I can be who I am."

"Yes." I smiled up at him, tears in my eyes. "You can."

He kissed me again. "Come here." Taking me by one hand, he led me out of the garage, around the front of the house, and up the steps onto the porch, where a beautiful wooden porch swing hung from silver chains, swaying a little in the wind.

I gasped, bringing my gloved hands to my cheeks. "Oh my God!"

"I made it for you."

"You *made* this?" I moved closer, detecting the scent of fresh cedar. I took off my glove and ran a hand along its smooth, narrow boards. No one had ever made me anything like this before.

"I hope it's as nice as the one you dream about in your future."

"It's beautiful," I said tearfully. "Even better than the one I imagined."

"I know it's winter right now, and we won't use it for a while, but I'm going to be here come spring. And summer. And the summer after that." He took me by the shoulders and turned me toward him. No regret or sorrow in his voice now—it was strong and sure. "I was wrong, Claire. Love is enough. Let me stay."

I tried to speak but couldn't. My whole body had started to shiver, but it wasn't the cold.

He rested his forehead against mine, rubbed his hands up and down my arms as if to warm me. "I've made a thousand mistakes in my life, and I might make a thousand more, but walking away from you won't be one of them. I don't deserve you, but if you were mine, I'd spend every last damn day of my life trying."

"Theo." I finally found my voice. "Come inside with me."

———

IT WAS both a reunion and a new beginning.

A dream remembered and a story not yet told.

Our bodies moved together with familiar ease but each kiss, each caress, each breath shared between us felt like the first.

When he was deep inside me, my legs wrapped around his waist, our fingers locked together next to my head, his eyes on mine, I felt like I was falling for him all over again— and also like I'd loved him forever.

"Stay with me, Theo," I whispered softly, desperately, as he rolled his hips over mine in smooth, sinuous motions that had me writhing beneath him. I wanted to come and I wanted to hang on to this feeling forever, this dangling-over-the-edge feeling right before the euphoria of jumping off.

"Always." He moved a little faster, thrust a little deeper. "God, I missed this. Your skin. Being inside you. Feeling you come."

"Yes, yes..." I struggled to free my hands so I could touch him but he had them pinned to the mattress.

"Come for me. Now. *Now*..." His words fell away, becoming strangled breaths, and I matched his rhythm, rocking my hips beneath his, hearing the crescendo of our cries, watching the room beyond him turn to liquid gold, until there was nothing in the world but *this, this, this, this, this*.

This moment. This magic. This healing.

This feeling of belonging and acceptance.

This knowing *I am yours and you are mine.*

It was real. It was ours. It was love.

And it would always be enough.

EIGHT MONTHS LATER

Theo

"SEE YOU TONIGHT." I kissed her cheek like I did every day before leaving for work. This would be nothing like any other day, but she didn't know that.

"Bye, love. Have a good day." She smiled at me, and my heart stuttered a time or two.

She had no idea.

No idea how much I adored her, no idea how many times a day I thought of her, no idea how happy I'd been when she'd asked me to live with her over the summer.

And she *really* had no idea I was going to propose to her today.

It had taken some planning, but I'd had help—from her friends, from her principal, and especially from her students. I'd been trying to think of a clever way to ask her to marry me for two months. When she mentioned the fairy tale project, I knew it would be perfect.

As I walked out the door and down the porch steps, I laughed to myself. She didn't have a clue. It was so perfect.

I stuck my hand in my pocket, wrapping my fingers around the ring box. Talk about not having a clue—I'd gone to the jewelry store by myself at first, but had gotten overwhelmed immediately. A phone call to Jaime had fixed that. In exchange for promising to tell her exactly when and where I was planning to propose, she gave me some direction.

"Claire is traditional but artsy," she'd said. "Tell the jeweler you want something pretty and feminine but strong."

In the end, I'd chosen a princess cut diamond in a floating halo style, and sent Jaime a picture of it.

It's perfect, she'd texted back. **Claire is going to love it!**

That was all that mattered.

In the last eight months, she'd brought more joy to my life than I even realized was possible. She was patient and kind and forgiving, even when I struggled with episodes of doubt or anxiety. Those had grown less frequent, and in fact, I hadn't experienced one at all since the beginning of fall. She listened when I wanted to talk, pushed me to open up when I'd rather shut down, and helped me see the past with better perspective. She made me excited about the future, which for the first time I could see clearly. I knew exactly where I wanted to be when I looked ahead, and I wanted her right beside me.

Today was a giant step in that direction.

After glancing in the back of my car to make sure my clothes were there, I took off down the street as if I was heading for work. In reality, I was headed for Aaron's house, where I'd change out of my work jeans and boots and into something a little nicer. Then I'd head over to her school.

I couldn't stop smiling.

CLAIRE

"OK, places please! Boys and girls, did you hear me? Places!" I clapped my hands, trying to corral Elyse's fourth graders into a line near the mic I'd set up in front of the stage in the gym. They'd been studying folklore and had written their own fairy tale, and in art class, we'd painted scenery for it, complete with a tower for their princess. Tomorrow they'd act it out live for parents, and today was sort of the "dress rehearsal." But the kids were being unusually goofy, giggling and jumping around and whispering behind their hands into one another's ears. Elyse had no experience with staging a play, so I'd taken the lead.

At least, I was trying to.

I used my strict teacher voice. "You have until I count to three to get in line and be quiet or you're not performing. One." There was a mad dash for the line. "Two." The line straightened out. "Three." Finally, I could hear myself talk.

"OK. Characters, you need to go backstage with me. Narrators, you should be lined up according to speaking order. If you don't have your script memorized, you can use it to read." I turned the narrators over to Elyse, and took the kids playing the roles of characters backstage. "You all have your lines memorized?" I asked. None of them held scripts.

"Yes," they chorused before a few of them collapsed into

giggles. One girl hit a giggler next to her, shushing her loudly.

I shook my head. "Jeez, what is with you guys today? OK, I think we're ready to start. Princess, go on up." I gestured toward the step-ladder, which was hidden by a cardboard "tower" painted to look like it was made of stone and covered with vines. "Prince, you go to the other side of the stage and wait in the wings. Witches, wizards, and toads, you stay here." When everyone was in place, I called out to their teacher. "We're ready back here!"

"Ms. French! Ms. French!" The princess came down from the stepladder and hopped from one foot to the other. "I have to go to the bathroom really bad!"

I sighed and took her script. "OK go, I'll fill in for you. But hurry up."

She took off, I climbed the tower, and the curtain went up.

A female narrator began. "Once upon a time, there was a handsome prince named Prince Theo. He was the handsomest, bravest knight in the land."

I made a face. Prince Theo? Had they changed his name? That was a coincidence. I glanced at the script, which read Prince Verlander.

A male narrator continued. "Prince Theo had an older brother who stood to inherit their father's kingdom, so Prince Theo was free to roam the land, slaying dragons, defeating evil wizards, and searching for a princess to rescue."

What? Where were we? I looked at the second page of the script, but I couldn't find the lines the narrators were reading. Had they completely rewritten the tale? When I looked up again, I gasped.

Theo—*my* Theo—was standing onstage wearing the

crown the kids had made for the prince and carrying the prince's jeweled cardboard sword.

A few giggles could be heard in the gym. I blinked a few times and made eye contact with him—he winked.

My heart raced. What on earth was going on?

"Although the prince was the handsomest, cleverest, bravest knight in the land," a female narrator went on.

"Did you say handsome?" Theo interrupted loudly, striking a valiant pose. "Don't forget handsome."

The kids and grownups in the gym roared with laughter. I glanced at the crowd and noticed the principal, assistant principal, office staff, and several fellow teachers had gathered in the gym as well.

"Yes, I did," the girl said with a giggle. "Although the prince was the *handsomest*, cleverest, bravest knight in the land, he was not truly happy."

Theo spoke loudly and dramatically. "Alas, although I have every gift nature can bestow, I have never rescued a princess, therefore I am lonely and sad."

A new narrator stepped up. "The prince decided he would search far and wide until he found a princess who needed rescuing."

Theo pretended to ride a horse around the stage, peeking around corners and behind the scenery. "Hello? Any princesses in there? If anyone needs to be rescued, call 1-800-Handsome Prince." I laughed along with the kids, shaking my head in disbelief.

Another student continued. "One day, Prince Theo happened upon a castle in the woods, and it had a stone tower on one end. He'd heard the most beautiful princesses always reside in such towers, so he called out in greeting."

Theo approached my tower. "Excuse me! Is there a fair maid inside this castle?"

Before I could answer, the narrator went on. "The most beautiful lady the prince had ever seen came to the window. Her name was Princess Claire."

Theo dropped to his knees. "In all the heavens, I have never seen a star shine so brightly as you, fair maid. Should you fall from the sky, I shall gladly catch you." He held out his arms, and I covered my mouth as the narrator continued.

"To the prince's dismay, the princess he had discovered did not need to be rescued. But she said she would be glad to be his friend."

A new reader stepped up to the mic. "The Prince, being so clever—"

"And handsome," added Theo loudly.

"And handsome," the girl added with a grin, "knew that this was the princess for him, and if she would not consent to being rescued, he had to win her over another way."

"Aha!" Theo stuck a finger in the air and addressed the audience. "I will *make* her fall in love with me! I will give her a magic potion!" He turned back to me. "Come down from your tower, Princess Claire! I should like to share something with you!" Beckoning for me to come down, he gave me a smile that was real.

I backed down the ladder and took his hand, letting him lead me to center stage. "I can't believe this," I whispered.

"Just wait," he said under his breath. Then he pretended to present me with something. "Would you like a snack?"

"The prince always carried around magic marshmallow puffs in case he had to make anyone fall in love with him," a student read, "but he had never used them on anyone before."

"Eat one," whispered Theo, his eyes twinkling.

I pretended to take a bite. "Mmmmm. Delicious!"

Theo grinned widely, giving the audience a wink.

"As expected, Princess Claire fell madly in love with Prince Theo. He did not feel bad about tricking her because he loved her so much and knew he would make her happy."

I played along, resting my chin on the backs of my hands and batting my eyelashes at him. But when Theo got down on one knee, I dropped the act, my hands going to my cheeks.

"Princess Claire," he said loud enough for everyone to hear. "You are without a doubt the loveliest, kindest, dearest princess in the land. Alas, I have no kingdom to offer you. No subjects to rule. No castle of my own. But if you would do me the honor of becoming my wife, I should be very happy to stay here in your castle and stop roaming the land being so handsome and clever and brave all the time. I will devote myself to slaying dragons only for you. I will protect you and cherish you forever." He reached into his back pocket, pulled out a small black box, and opened it up.

My breath stopped. My heart boomed. My eyes blinked. It was the most beautiful ring I'd ever seen, and it sparkled as it caught the light.

"Princess Claire, will you marry me?"

The entire gym was hushed.

With tears in my eyes, I spoke softly. "Yes."

"Louder, princess. They can't hear you in the back," Theo said.

"Yes!" I cried, flapping my hands and jumping up and down. "Yes!"

The entire gym erupted with cheers and applause as Theo slipped the ring on my finger. When he got to his feet, I threw my arms around his neck, knocking off his cardboard crown. He lifted me right off the stage, wrapping his arms around me and swinging me from side to side as I cried with joy.

When he set me back on my feet and let go, he had tears in his eyes too.

"And as you can guess," said someone in the microphone, "they lived happily ever after!"

———

"YOUR FACE WAS THE BEST!" Jaime cried, clapping her hands. We were all at dinner that night to celebrate the engagement—Theo and I, Jaime and Quinn, and even Margot and Jack. Unbeknownst to me, Jaime and Quinn had been in the gym, too, along with Aaron and Josie.

Margot was sorry she'd missed it, but she was ten weeks pregnant and had terrible morning sickness these days. "Were you in total shock?" she asked.

"I was," I admitted. "I had no idea."

"I knew," Jaime said, "and oh my God, it was so hard not to let it slip."

"So who wrote the script?" Margot wondered. "The kids?"

"Nope, I did." Theo smiled. "And I gave it to the fourth grade teacher. She just told them about it this morning."

"Those poor kids." I shook my head. "No wonder they were so squirrelly. And I can't believe Elyse managed to keep that secret either!"

"Let me see the ring again." Jaime took my hand and sighed over it. "So beautiful. You did great, Theo."

He kissed my cheek. "Much better than I ever thought possible."

I smiled at him as my heart beat fast with love and pride and excitement. Theo was nothing like the prince I'd thought I wanted, but he was everything I needed, now and ever after.

THE END

ACKNOWLEDGMENTS

I am so grateful to the following people:

Becca Mysoor, book fairy and friend. This book is so much better because of you.

Kayti McGee, Laurelin Paige, and Sierra Simone, my sister snatches. Nobody gets past my INTJ RBF like you do.

To Jenn Watson, publicist and friend. Thanks for minding the nest again.

To Melissa Gaston, PA extraordinaire. You make my life so much easier.

To Candi, Nina, Sarah, and the entire Social Butterfly team, you're amazing. Thanks for all you do!

To Erin Remaley for answering my questions about art and generously letting me steal her "altered book" idea! Her work can be seen here: https://www.instagram.com/after_midnight_ink/

To Tamara Mataya for keeping my verb tenses consistent, my "wells" and "justs" under control, and all unintentional decapitations out of my books.

To Laura Foster Franks, for fast proofing. I never give anyone enough time!

To Rebecca Friedman, for always being a champion and soundboard for me.

To my fellow authors who were so generous with their advice and support while I wrote this book: Lauren Blakely, Helena Hunting, Staci Hart, Ilsa Madden-Mills, Nicola Rendell, Meghan March, and all the Shop Talkers. I'm learning so much from you.

To Margaret Provenzano, for being the kindest soul on earth.

To the PQs, for all your support and inspiration.

To my Harlots, for being the best fans around. I adore you!

To the bloggers and event organizers who work so tirelessly, all for the love of books. I appreciate every single one of you.

To my readers, you're always on my mind. I hope I made you smile today.

Finally, thank you to my husband, children, and parents, who understand why I'm not always there, even when I'm there. I love you.

ARE YOU A HARLOT YET?

To stay up to date on all things Harlow, get exclusive access to ARCs and giveaways, and be part of a fun, positive, sexy and drama-free zone, become a Harlot!

https://www.facebook.com/groups/351191341756563/

NEVER MISS A MELANIE HARLOW THING!

Sign up here to be included on Melanie Harlow's mailing list! You'll receive new release alerts, get access to bonus materials and exclusive giveaways, and hear about sales and freebies first!

http://www.melanieharlow.com/subscribe/

ABOUT THE AUTHOR

Melanie Harlow likes her heels high, her martini dry, and her history with the naughty bits left in. In addition to IF YOU WERE MINE, she's the author of MAN CANDY, AFTER WE FALL, the HAPPY CRAZY LOVE series, the FRENCHED series, and the SPEAK EASY duet (historical romance). She writes from her home outside of Detroit, where she lives with her husband and two daughters. She loves hearing from readers!

Connect with Melanie!

www.melanieharlow.com

melanieharlowwrites@gmail.com

13282359R00176